FIDELITY

JAN FEDARCYK

SIMON & SCHUSTER

New York   London   Toronto   Sydney   New Delhi

Simon & Schuster
1230 Avenue of the Americas
New York, NY 10020

First Simon & Schuster hardcover edition October 2016

SIMON & SCHUSTER and colophon are registered trademarks of
Simon & Schuster, Inc.

For information about special discounts for bulk purchases,
please contact Simon & Schuster Special Sales at 1-866-506-1949 or
business@simonandschuster.com.

The Simon & Schuster Speakers Bureau can bring authors to your live
event. For more information or to book an event, contact the Simon
& Schuster Speakers Bureau at 1-866-248-3049 or visit our website at
www.simonspeakers.com.

Manufactured in the United States of America

1 3 5 7 9 10 8 6 4 2

Library of Congress Cataloging-in-Publication Data is available.

ISBN 978-1-4767-3386-9
ISBN 978-1-4767-3389-0 (ebook)

Nothing contained in this novel reflects any endorsement by,
or opinion of, the FBI.

For my mom, who instilled a love of books, and
for my dad, a source of encouragement

For my husband, Mike,
for your love and support—
none of this would have happened without you by my side

PART 1

In a wilderness of mirrors. What will the spider do . . .

—T. S. ELIOT

PROLOGUE

S HE WOULD be waiting at the airport with a "go bag," Dmitri was certain—a false passport, a few thousand in U.S. currency, a change of clothes and dummy luggage. She had always come through for him in the past—never missed a meeting, never blown a drop. Responsible, prudent, cautious. If there was such a thing as an ideal handler, then she was it. For years now, the two had worked in perfect tandem, conveying his information back to the U.S. and the shadowy bureaucrats in the ranks above her. He was as valuable a double agent as the U.S. had ever enjoyed, at least so far as Dmitri, a man not given to undue humility, was concerned.

So of course she would be at the airport. The taxi made good time down Kashira Highway. Dmitri's watch read three fifteen. His flask of vodka was almost full.

What made a man spy on his country? Dmitri wondered idly. In his case it had been money: that was the sole reason; Dmitri was comfortable in admitting it. They had been right about that much, at least, the old gray-clad comrades with their five-year plans and their steely eyes, right that money corrupts, that capitalism reduces all relationships to mere greed, as his own behavior was evidence. They had simply underestimated the strength of it, the sheer rolling force, so much vastly more powerful than

Marxism that, looking back, it was hard to believe the contest had ever seemed even, like a man going twelve rounds with a child. But it had lost, utterly lost, as you could tell walking down Tverskaya Street, old women selling cheap geegaws, pretty girls from the interior winking from open windows, offering their own wares with an equal lack of decorum. The ruble was the Lenin of modern Russia, as the dollar was the Washington of America. Dmitri was confident that he would fit comfortably into his soon-to-be homeland.

Three twenty-three. His flask of vodka was less full than it had been. He put it back in his pocket, visions of vomiting at check-in swirling through his mind. He was the only one who could ruin it now; as long as he held it together he'd be home free. Hadn't he been careful, as careful as he always had been, and wasn't that careful enough to have spent the better part of twelve years selling the innermost secrets of the SVR, the KGB's successor, to their most hated enemies? Could an idiot spend twelve years selling Mother Russia's secrets to Uncle Sam? No, an idiot could not, and thus, by the process of induction, Dmitri was not an idiot. And therefore, as the final step in the equation, she would be waiting at the airport. There was simply no other way around the matter.

Especially with what he had. Six months prior, they had met in a crowded mall in downtown Moscow, walking and talking quietly, the same as usual except of course that it wasn't at all. A spy is to falsehood as a shark is to water, and a conversation between two of them is as dark as a spoon of beluga caviar. But the gist of it was clear enough. Dmitri's bosses had someone in the CIA, someone important, someone who had been rolling up the CIA's own network. She needed a name. She needed a name, and now he had one, and she knew it, and so she would be waiting at the airport.

Of course, if she was not there—*if she was not there*—then

he was dead and worse than dead. If there was one thing to be said about Mother Russia, beyond that she had the best writers, liquor and women, it was that she was not a nation that had ever been shy about killing its own citizens. And in his case, at least, such retribution would be far from unjustified. Even in less bloodthirsty countries, treason is a crime taken very seriously, very seriously indeed.

Dmitri's watch read three thirty, and his flask of vodka was not full, not full at all. He had not been certain until a few days earlier, when a stray folder came across his desk. It was pure good fortune—it was information he shouldn't have access to, a random mix-up, the sort of thing that might happen in any very large bureaucratic system, even a covert one. He had looked at it, put it back in its folder, eaten a long lunch at a nearby restaurant: cold borscht and a chewy pork cutlet, and enough alcohol to keep the thing from sprinting off once it was safely settled in his stomach. On the way back to the office he had stopped off at a pay phone and called a wrong number, the first step in the elaborate process that would let her know that he needed to see her immediately, as in *right now*, because the file he had looked at had lit a fuse underneath him, and he knew it didn't have long to run. At a parking garage in the Arbat district that evening he had told her simply, "I have the name you've been looking for," and "It will not come cheaply."

She had looked him over and told him that she'd need to talk to her people. He had known she would say that; written in bold lettering on the heart of every intelligence officer from MI6 to the Chinese MSS was "Don't make promises you can't keep," but still it infuriated him to see how cautious they were, here in the moment when celerity was called for.

But all he could do was go back home and then to work the next morning, to avoid anything that would arouse suspicion, to putter about his job with his usual middling competence, to sit with his back against the wall and keep one eye over his shoulder. Three days he had been doing this, each evening getting more desperate—feeling, with that easy paranoia of a professional spy, the web getting closer, ineffably and inescapably. When word came through that morning—a potted plant placed almost conspicuously in the front window of an apartment a few blocks from his house—the fear became almost overwhelming. It took everything he had to sit quietly at his desk for a few hours, to continue giving his impression of normalcy. But he was free now, or good as. She would be at the airport, and soon he would be out of the reach of the SVR, and all of this would seem nothing more than an unpleasant dream, albeit one that had gone on for the better part of his adult life.

The taxi pulled into Domodedovo International Airport. Dmitri reached into his pocket, took out a thousand rubles, thought it over a moment and took out a thousand more. Why not, right? He could afford it. She would be waiting for him inside, and she would have everything he needed to start a new life in New York. Swimming pools and palm trees and movie stars—wait, that was L.A., wasn't it? Dmitri laughed to himself. He'd have time to figure it out, plenty of time, because she would be there.

Except then the door opened, and a group of hard-looking men in bad suits stood on the sidewalk, none of them smiling, and behind them were several men in uniform carrying assault rifles, and they were not smiling, either, not even a tiny bit.

"Dmitri Ulyanov," one said evenly. "You will come with us, please."

Three thirty-eight. The flask of vodka was empty. Dmitri stepped out of the vehicle and into the waiting arms of his executioners.

1

K AY MALLOY sat hunched down in the driver's seat of her old Buick, back aching, eyes strained. Outside, the winter sun was shining and birds were chirping and little black boys in single digits waited sharp-eyed to erupt in Baltimore city's common call of warning—*"Po-lice, Po-lice"*—the word stretched out to fill a sentence. Kay had turned the engine off after rolling slowly into the back alley across from the subject's house, and February leaked in through the windows. She shivered but she didn't button up her coat, nor the suit jacket beneath it, and uncomfortable as it was to sit motionless with a .40-caliber Glock on her hip, she didn't move that, either.

"Your car can become your coffin," they had told her at the Academy. Better cold than dead.

On the seat next to her she had set the subject's picture, although she didn't need to look at it anymore. Months on the case had imprinted his face into her memory like an old lover— light-skinned and dead-eyed, a furrowed brow and lips that didn't smile. James Rashid Williams, age twenty-two. Where Kay had grown up, twenty-two was the cusp of adulthood, a college diploma beneath your belt and the world open and bright ahead of you. Here on the east side of Baltimore, twenty-two years was enough to make you a drug dealer, a corrupter of children, a parasite and a killer. Twenty-two years was enough to earn you an FBI file a half inch thick, enough to get a squad of federal Agents to hunt you down and stick you in a cell.

Kay had spent the last two weeks doing just that, following Williams across the city, trying to figure out his daily routine, who he met with and where he slept. Two weeks of lukewarm coffee and stale bagels; two weeks trailing one of Baltimore's most dangerous criminals across the length and breadth of the fading urban metropolis. They'd be moving on him soon, the end result of a case the Bureau had spent the better part of a year building.

Outside, the sun dimmed and the temperature dropped. Inside, Kay stayed motionless or nearly so, binoculars trained on the front door. It hadn't been easy to find a spot that offered her a decent view of the subject's house without marking her out to everyone else on the block. A white woman sitting alone in her car for hours on end, in this neighborhood? You didn't need to have graduated Quantico to figure out that she didn't belong there. Although it was only her training that helped her stay focused for long hours on surveillance, bleary-eyed and bored beyond reason. And still, when the door finally opened, she felt herself somehow unprepared; had an absurd moment of . . . well, not quite fright, exactly—Kay was an FBI Agent, trained not to feel those sorts of things—but perhaps some distant cousin to it.

There was something about Williams in person that didn't quite carry through in the picture, a sense of menace like a foul smell. Even in her few short years with the FBI, she had met hundreds of boys and young men overlaid with a facade of toughness, a lifetime of pop culture criminality to live up to. Most of them folded quickly enough once you got them alone in an interview room and set them to staring at a few dozen years in prison. But Williams was the real deal; she could have told that even if she hadn't had a thick dossier detailing the usual list of crimes: drug dealing and money laundering and the not-at-all-infrequent murder so as to continue on with the first two; could have told that from the way he sauntered out into the late-afternoon light like he owned the block and the neighborhood and the city out beyond that.

His gang of lurking children greeted him respectfully, even reverently, but he didn't answer, didn't seem even to acknowledge them, just trained his eyes slowly back and forth across the streetscape, searching for anything out of place. You didn't make it to where Williams was by being careless, not with half the city looking to put him in the ground, take his place as neighborhood kingpin. A man like Williams had spent years of his life dodging rival dealers and law enforcement; caution was second nature.

Kay found herself reaching instinctively down towards her service weapon, had to fight to bring her hand back up to the steering wheel. The rest of the Agents assigned to the case were all veterans, and going after Williams was just another day at the office. But Kay had only been in the Bureau two years, and as much as she tried to feign the casual hardness of her colleagues, the truth was that something about Williams had gotten to her. Watching the gang of children vie for his attention, eyes bright with hero worship, left a bitter taste in her mouth and her Glock weighing heavy on her hip. For weeks now she had been putting in extra time on the case, hoping her diligence would earn a spot on the entry team. The thought of coming through the door with a dozen other Agents, wiping that grim line off Williams's face, frog-marching him to a lifetime behind bars—it was something that Kay had seized on, the reward for a job that promised long hours and hard work and not a great deal in the way of pay.

But that would never happen if she slipped up at this last moment, gave Williams a hint they were on to him. Kay sank lower into her seat. There was no way he could see her from where he was, but all the same Kay found herself turning the engine on and removing the safety brake. Williams continued his slow, silent gaze, staring out over his domain. After a long moment he leaped down off his stoop and cantered down the block, ready to begin the night's ugly business.

She gave it a little while, then shifted into drive and nosed slowly back out onto the street. "You to yours," Kay found herself thinking grimly, "and me to mine."

2

THEY DID not have public tours of the FBI's Baltimore Field Office in Woodlawn, which was just as well, not only for basic notions of operational security but also because it was quite tremendously ugly, and all things considered it would likely kill off some of the Bureau's mystique if the citizens whom Kay had sworn to protect ever got a look at it. Functional, you might have called it. Utilitarian, if you were being very kind. Kay had been ready for the long hours, the work that alternated between deathly dull and eye-achingly sad, the strange looks she got when she told people what she did for a living. Ready for all of it. But at the very least she had imagined the most powerful law enforcement agency in the world would be capable of providing her with a decent computer.

Kay dropped her coat over the chair and herself down into it.

"Our boy in attendance?" Torres asked her from across the desk.

"He's still there," Kay confirmed.

Torres had been her partner for eighteen months now, and it had taken much of that period for them to get to liking each other. If he had seen, at first glance, a callow, overeducated greenhorn, she had taken one look at his never-polished shoes and his ill-fitting suit and written him off as past his expiration date. But first impressions aren't everything, and it spoke praise for both of them that they'd been able to get past theirs. Torres had been chasing criminals for nearly as long as Kay had been alive, and he was clever enough to have learned a few things along the way, which not everyone else could claim. He was utterly unflappable: the building next to him could explode while he was shaving and he'd come out of the bathroom without a nick. He knew everything there was to know about Baltimore—which Kay had taken several months to learn was pronounced *Bawl-moor*, swallowing the *t* and mangling the middle portion. He knew where to get the best crab cakes, and which bars you could still smoke at, and who Little Melvin's top lieutenant had been back when he had sold ninety percent of the heroin in the city.

Also, Torres was about as big as a Mack truck, and when you were a five-foot-seven woman with less than thirty years to your credit, it was an asset being able to walk up to a suspect with him standing behind you, a mountain of Pig Town gristle that hadn't taken shit from anyone in so long, he had trouble remembering the smell. "Not for very much longer," Torres said happily. "Cold enough for you out there, Ivy?"

In a bit of foolishness that she had spent a year and a half kicking herself over, Kay had come in the first day with a Princeton coffee mug and immediately caught a raft of mockery for it. In fact, it had been Kay's only coffee mug, and she had actually been using it to drink coffee, and she hadn't even liked Princeton particularly—certainly did not take any excessive pride in having matriculated from there; but of course none of these truths had been enough to stop the office from heaving "Ivy" on as her tag. This long into it she didn't even mind. Everyone got made fun of for something. Maybe the women got it a little worse, and certainly the newer Agents did; but to Kay's thinking, anyone who let that sort of thing bother her was no better than a child.

At least Torres meant it endearingly, which was more than could be said for some of her other colleagues.

"I'm an FBI Agent," Kay said, leaning back and stretching out her legs. You wouldn't think sitting in a car and staring at a stoop would be so damn exhausting, but then again you'd be wrong. "I'm trained not to feel cold."

"I must have missed that day in Quantico," Torres said, standing and gesturing for Kay to do the same. "We're getting the rundown in the conference room in about two minutes."

Kay sighed, stood, followed Torres into the conference room. Most of the rest of the team was already inside: fifteen or so Agents, all more experienced than Kay, some even more competent. The Williams bust would be one of the year's largest, a joint effort between the FBI, the DEA and local police, and in honor of which they were graced with the presence not only of the Assistant Special Agent in Charge but of the Special Agent in Charge as well, neither of whom generally had much involvement in the day-to-day running of the case. This was primarily handled by Supervisory Special Agent James Dickson, who, on any given morning, would be handing out assignments and coordinating tasks.

Dickson wasted little time in getting the meeting started, projecting a PowerPoint presentation onto the back wall. "This is James Rashid Williams," he said, nodding towards the picture that had long become ingrained in Kay's memory. "Born Baltimore City. Had a couple of busts as a juvenile, but nothing since. Which means?"

"That he's an altar boy?" Torres joked.

"That he's smart," Kay muttered.

"Indeed he is," Dickson continued, shooting Torres a nasty look. SSA Dickson did not find Torres amusing. It was Kay's sense that Dickson, generally speaking, found very little amusing.

He would have been a very bad audience member at a comedy club, but he was thoroughly competent to oversee a criminal investigation. "Two years ago he came up on our radar as an East Baltimore up-and-comer. Since then he's well and truly arrived. So far as we can tell, he's the man at the top of the pyramid for all the corners running from Patterson Park to Broadway. A man doesn't get that much real estate without dropping a few corpses," Dickson said, then clicked ahead to display a number of these: corpses on front stoops, corpses in bullet-ridden cars, corpses on the floors of crack houses, and finally the corpses of two adolescents lying prone on good old-fashioned Baltimore asphalt.

"Those last two were Deyron and Ai'don Thomas, two brothers with the audacity to try and visit the corner store when some of Mr. Williams's underlings were firing handguns at some men who *used to be* Mr. Williams's underlings."

The room got a little less friendly. It was hard to get worked up about murderers murdering each other; it wasn't the sort of thing you could just overlook. They were the FBI, after all, but neither did Kay find herself weeping into her pillow late at night at the thought of there being one less gun hand scuttling through the city's byways. Civilians were a different matter, and not just civilians but children, two little plots of land out in Mount Auburn Cemetery, grandmothers weeping over coffins. Kay realized that she was gritting her teeth, then stopped before she gave herself a headache.

"Yes, it's been a bloody run for Mr. Williams, one which we'll bring to an abrupt end tomorrow at five a.m. We'll be serving indictments against Williams and seven other individuals, lieutenants and top-ranking enforcers. We'll have the assigned Assistant United States Attorney standing by in case we need to write paper for additional warrants. If my little photo presentation did not convince you, then let me remind everyone outright that these are very dangerous men, and it would not at all be out of character for them to decide they'd prefer to see a pine box than a jail cell, and would be even happier if they had a few members of law enforcement as company. It's mandatory for everyone to wear body armor and raid jackets, and make sure your radio is coded before you head out today. We go in fast, we go in hard and we make sure everyone comes out safe." Dickson then began to go through each specific target, which Agents would be assigned to which location. Kay held her breath as he went through each suspect, lieutenants and minor members of Williams's crew, waiting to hear her name called. It was foolish to get emotionally invested in a case, Kay knew, and this personal antagonism she had been cultivating against Williams had no place in an investigation.

All the same, it stung to discover she wouldn't get to slap the cuffs on him. "Malloy," Dickson said, "you'll be assisting Torres, Marcus and Chapman when they make the bust on Williams."

Kay worked carefully to keep the frown off her face, listened as Dickson finished reading the assignments, then dismissed the room. She already had a reputation amongst some of the criminal squads as something of a prima donna, owing more to the fact that she was good at her job and came from a privileged background than to anything else, she thought privately. But still there was no good to come from displaying disappointment; the mission came first, after all. The mission always comes first.

Torres, of course, wasn't fooled. "Don't look so cross, Ivy," he said as they walked out of the meeting. "You think James Rashid Williams is going to be the last person ever who tries to get rich in Baltimore selling crack cocaine? Or just the last one the FBI is ever going to arrest? Believe me, the final shot in the War on Drugs will not be fired tomorrow morning. You'll get to take out James Rashid Williams 2.0 in another six months, or in six months after that. One upside to the whole thing: there's always more bad guys."

Torres made it sound simpler than it was. Williams was clever and Williams was careful, and it had taken the better part of a year for the FBI, with all the technology and resources at their disposal, to finally land themselves this shot at him. But Torres wasn't altogether wrong, either. In the street they talked a lot about "the game," epitaphs stolen from hip-hop songs, the usual distorted warrior-creed horseshit. They never seemed to realize that the game was stacked, that the best any corner kingpin could hope for was to slide under their radar awhile and avoid drawing down the wrath of law enforcement, which was belated, erratic and inevitable. Or one of their own people would put them in the ground, or—and this happened with astonishing frequency—they would find some way to ruin it themselves by getting drunk and wrapping their car around a telephone pole or finding themselves stabbed in a bar fight with a random stranger. There were upsides to being a drug dealer, Kay supposed: the money, the neighborhood fame or infamy, perhaps the excitement. But longevity was not generally one of its virtues.

A fact that they would be reminding James Rashid Williams of early the next morning.

3

KAY SLEPT three hours that night, woke with the moon still heavy against her curtains, jumped out of bed sharp as a stropped razor. She dressed in less time than it took her coffee machine to brew up a pot, dumped that in a thermos and moved swiftly to her car. As she drove out to meet the rest of the squad, she ran through in her mind the morning to come, savoring the anticipation. She would not get to go in through the door—fine, fine, that was disappointing but ultimately irrelevant. Tonight, this morning, they would take James Rashid Williams off the streets, put him in a cage where he would spend the rest of his life, or the vast majority of it. There was such a thing as right and wrong—there was such a thing as justice—and Williams would learn that soon. Learn that there were consequences to evil, that the righteous did not sit idly by and allow themselves to be poisoned, abused and dominated.

"You all right there, Ivy?" Torres asked, sipping from a mug of coffee the size of half her torso. "You know we're just here to arrest the man; you don't get to eat him."

"I just wish I got to haul him in," Kay said.

Torres put a hand on her shoulder. It was a rare moment of affection, and Kay did not miss it. "Forget about who gets to kick in the door," he said. "This is as much your collar as anybody's, and more than most. Dickson knows that, and so do I."

Kay tried not to blush. The only other time Torres had offered a compliment, it was regarding Kay's ability to down cans of Natty Boh without stumbling, and whatever his feelings on the matter, she felt that was not altogether a thing of which to be proud.

Torres winked and guzzled the rest of his coffee, then set the cup aside and forced himself into his armored vest. A standard precaution, although in this instance almost certainly unnecessary. This was a priority location, and so Torres and the rest of the squad would be following SWAT—special weapons and tactics—into the building. Being an FBI Agent very little resembled the popular perception of the job, but SWAT was part of that very little. There were many people in the world who thought of themselves as hard, who liked to walk with a swagger and brag about their gun collections. Some of them even were tough, so far as it goes, even frightening or dangerous. And all of them, every one, were rank amateurs when compared to SWAT. These were professionals in the field of human violence, and watching them take down a door was like watching an NFL team play pickup football against a group of schoolchildren.

No, this was it for James Rashid Williams. The wheels of justice grind slowly, but they grind . . .

"Ivy—look alive, for Christ's sake," Torres said. "Dickson is here."

Kay snapped to it. Kay didn't particularly like Dickson, but she had to admit he was an asset in this sort of situation. He seemed cool and collected as ever, unruffled by the moment ahead of them. A last-minute check to make sure everything was in place, and then Kay slid quietly through the side alleyway, stopping finally at the eastern exit to the alley that ran behind

Williams's stash house. "Malloy in position," she said quietly into her walkie-talkie.

She stood next to a broken-down fence: Was it really a fence if it was broken down? Wasn't the point of a fence that it marked a boundary between two spaces? What was a thing that did not deliver on its essential purpose? Idle questions to be asked as the morning began to creep out over the night as the first rays of sunlight broke slowly onto the city.

A flash of movement brought her back to her senses, reminding her of how foolish it was to be distracted, even for a moment. She might not be on the entry team, but nor was she browsing through a bookstore. "FBI," Kay said, firmly but not too loudly. "Keep your hands where I can see them."

The man coming down the back stoop from one of the houses a few blocks down from Williams's turned his coat up over his throat, looking tired and cold, like anyone would look very early on a freezing morning in February. There were a few naked inches of skin between the heavy ski cap he wore and his upturned collar. "I gotta get to work," he said dully, unimpressed with her announcement or with the FBI raid jacket she was wearing over her body armor. Kay supposed this was the kind of neighborhood where the occasional intervention of law enforcement was not a subject to get particularly thrilled over—one of the many scarred battlegrounds over which the cops and the crooks fought their nightly battles, like half the city.

"This is police business, sir," Kay said. "I'm going to have to ask you to return to your home."

The man sucked his teeth, pulled his cap farther down over his head, looked back warily at the way he'd come. "Boss gonna fire me if I don't get in on time," he said unhappily, like he already knew what Kay's answer would be. "Boss ain't gonna be interested in any police business."

"As I said, sir, we're in the middle of an operation. For your own safety, I'm going to have to ask you again to return to your home."

"You gonna sign me a note?" he joked bitterly. "I don't go to work, I can't pay my bills; I can't pay my bills, they gonna take the house. Come on, lady, I been late twice this month 'cause the bus never comes in on time. Third strike and—"

There was a sharp sudden noise from the stash house, Torres and the rest going in fast and hard, as they'd been trained, overwhelming anyone inside with speed, with numbers, with the sheer intimidating force of authority. Another twinge of regret that she wasn't amongst them.

"All right," Kay said, shrugging, "but hurry up and keep your head down."

He thanked her and brushed past, heavy eyes still on the day's labor. Kay's own were keenly trained on the back door of the stash house, the sound of the action from inside bringing her senses back in hyperawareness. If Williams or one of his peons tried to make a sprint for it, she promised herself, they'd better be going west down the alleyway. Kay felt like a set trap, a grinning wolf, a cat ready to pounce.

But when the back door finally opened, it was only Torres, looking puzzled and annoyed and waving for her to enter. Inside was a beat-to-heck couch facing a gigantic flat-screen television that had not been properly affixed to the wall, a rough hundred thousand dollars in heroin on the scarred wooden coffee table, three young black males cuffed and kneeling next to it, looking furious and a little bit scared. None of them, it did not take Kay long to note, was James Rashid Williams.

"Where is he?" Torres asked one of them.

Staring up at Torres and twenty years in prison, he shrugged and smiled nastily. "Who you talking about?"

"Dickson," an Agent shouted from the kitchen, "you need to come take a look at this!"

Which he did then, and rapidly, with Torres and Kay following in his train. The kitchen had not been used to cook anything but crack in years and years. Stacks of empty pizza boxes rivaled empty beer cans in height and depth. The door to the adjoining storage room was open. Inside was a hole and a ladder leading down below the building. Two Agents had already gone to take a look at where it led, and one of them had come back and poked his head up to spread the info. "It heads down to another house half a block away," he said.

"Motherfucker," Torres said.

Dickson looked hard at Kay. "Anyone slip past you, maybe from one of the adjoining buildings?"

"Motherfucker," Kay agreed.

4

K AY HAD not seen Christopher in nearly a year and had only spoken to him a handful of times in the interim, the phone buzzing while she was fast asleep, looking over at the alarm clock groggily and seeing the little red LED lights blinking 3:37 or 2:18 or 4:25, sighing miserably and picking up anyway. The voice at the other end of the line slurred or talking much too quickly, despondent or upbeat depending upon the moment's drug of choice, begging apology for past failures or full of enthusiasm over some new plan that would never come to fruition. He had not visited since she'd moved to Baltimore. Kay had no idea how he got her address.

And yet, when she saw Christopher sitting on the stoop of her house in Fells Point, a small, quaint, lively neighborhood a few blocks from the water, Kay felt no hint of surprise. Because that was the way it always was with Christopher. He had a strange way of showing up when you least expected him. He was wearing a beat-up pair of jeans and a gray hoodie. He stretched himself up from his seat, smiled and waved her forward with his fingertips. "Hey there, little sister."

And just like that, every other time was forgotten, because there is such a thing as family, thank God, and Kay didn't have enough left anymore to pick and choose. Embracing him, she was saddened but not quite shocked at how thin he had gotten—she could feel his shoulder blades through his T-shirt. "Brother."

"This is a nice place you got here," he said. "Got an extra bedroom?"

"There are three things to love about Baltimore," Kay told him. "Seafood, the Ravens, and for the cost of a one-bedroom in the East Village you can pay off the mortgage on a mansion."

"I hate the Ravens," Christopher said.

"There's probably a bridge somewhere you can sleep beneath," Kay said, but then she unlocked the door and waved him inside.

"You eat yet?" Christopher asked.

Kay had not given any thought to dinner. It had not been that kind of day. She had given a lot of thought to drinking, however; had planned on walking down to her neighborhood bar and seeing if the day's sorrows couldn't be drowned in a few cans of Natty Boh. But as a rule she did not drink with Christopher, not since they'd been kids cribbing beer from the local bodega with fake IDs, not since it had become clear that her brother was not a casual drinker any more than he was a social imbiber of cocaine. "Not yet," she said.

"Perfect: me neither. I'll whip something up."

"I don't have much," she was saying, but he had already dropped his faded duffel bag in the living room and found his way into the kitchen.

Kay couldn't really cook. Kay couldn't really draw, Kay couldn't really sing. Kay wasn't much good at making small talk or at winning over new friends, at flirting with her preferred sex, at living enthusiastically in the moment. Fate had given these qualities to Christopher in abundance, however, by that curious process by which two siblings, formed from the same strands of genetic material, arrive in the world separate and distinct and somehow seemingly entirely alien creatures. He buzzed about in her cabinets for a while, came out with a frozen chicken and a selection of condiments accumulating dust in her refrigerator and was well on his way towards whipping up a feast by the time Kay had finished changing her clothes.

She took the opportunity to inspect him silently for a moment and did not like what she saw. He'd been beautiful back in the day, dark and sharp and always smiling, the first person you looked at when you walked into the room. How many girlfriends of hers back in high school had blushed and giggled and asked if he ever asked about them, Kay doing her best to explain that her brother was a person best stayed away from as one stays away from a bonfire or a sharp knife or a pool of furious piranha. Fifteen years of hard living had worn half a lifetime into his face. He was thin all over, the skin hung loose off his face and his eyes weren't bright like they had been.

But, watching him cook, she could almost see the years slough off him. Kay remembered her eleventh birthday, the first without their parents, a fourteen-year-old Christopher trying his hand at a strawberry shortcake, nearly burning their house down in the process but still, so lively and jubilant that she had all but forgotten her troubles. He had always done his best to look out for her, Kay thought. At some point he had just stopped being very good at it.

They made a point of not talking about anything serious. Nothing about her work, nor whatever he was doing in lieu of it. Nothing about their family or their past. Just superficial non-sense: if she was seeing anyone (no), if he was seeing anyone (lots of people), if they'd seen any good movies lately, the usual pop culture nonsense. He put the finishing touches on the chicken, spread it on two plates and gave Kay one of them. Then he tore a corner off Kay's roll of paper towels, tore that corner into two halves, gave one to Kay. "The very lap of luxury," he said.

"Lots of white cloth napkins in your flat?"

"I'm between flats at the moment," Christopher explained, "though when last I had them Jeeves made sure the napkins were exclusively silk."

Kay laughed.

"I'm sorry I forgot your birthday," he said after a couple of bites.

Kay shrugged. It was something that she had long gotten used to. Christopher did not show up to things: dinners and graduations, court dates and appointments with parole officers. At a certain point you make a decision to keep loving a person in spite of themselves, regardless of what they do to you, or you remove them from your life completely. And Kay wasn't a cut-and-run type, not when it came to family. Not when it came to anything, really. "Don't worry about it."

"Can I hold your gun?" he asked, joking. Maybe joking: you could never tell entirely with Christopher.

"You're lucky I let you use my kitchen knife."

"You think I don't know how to fire a pistol, little sister?"

Kay did not like to think about everything that her brother knew how to do. Much of it was unsavory and most of it was unwise. "You can't hold my gun," Kay affirmed. "You been to see Uncle Luis lately?"

"It's been a while since I ran into the Don," he admitted, making a face and using their childhood name for Luis. They'd always had a difficult relationship, Christopher and Uncle Luis, at least since Luis and his wife had taken them both in as children. Mostly Kay chalked this up to the fact that Christopher had a difficult relationship with everyone he knew who wasn't a stone-cold junkie; that his erratic and often outright foul behavior was enough to isolate anyone who wasn't a blood relative. Mostly. "I bumped into Aunt Justyna last month. She seemed well." Then, switching topics abruptly: "How was your day?"

"I let the biggest drug dealer in East Baltimore escape a trap we'd built for him," Kay said bluntly. "Real scumbag. Killed two kids in a drive-by a few months back. He had a back exit rigged up in his stash house and I let him walk right past me. Even called me 'ma'am,'" she recalled. "In some dive bar near the office, at this very moment, a half dozen of my colleagues are talking trash about the Ivy League princess that's been foisted on them."

"So, run-of-the-mill, then?"

Kay chuckled. There was a lot to say against Christopher, but the fact that he could always make her laugh made up for a lot of it.

"Don't worry yourself too terribly, little sister," Christopher said. "Remember, I've got three whole years on you, and with those years has come wisdom. These little problems—work, men, money, credit scores, having allowed a modern-day Al Capone to escape the clutches of justice—in time, what do they all really amount to?"

"Your devil-may-care attitude was more amusing back when we were children."

"But I still act like a child in most ways, so I think it counts."

Kay laughed again.

"They'd be proud of you," Christopher said, turning serious all of a sudden and resting his hand on top of hers.

"They" were Paul and Anne Malloy, beloved father and mother of two, resting silently amidst a patch of grass in Green-Wood Cemetery, four hours north in Brooklyn.

"Thanks," Kay said.

"I'm proud of you too," Christopher said.

Kay smiled but didn't say anything, enjoying the moment, knowing it wouldn't last much longer.

"Kay," he said, tightening his grip, "I need to borrow some money."

She sighed but did not withdraw her hand. "How much?"

5

THE NEXT week was not one that Kay would remember with much fondness, with evil eyes rolled at her in the break room, hushed voices talking her down. All except Torres's. Torres did his talking to her face, which was a nice change and one of the things she liked about him.

"See, we're supposed to catch the bad guys," he'd explained to her the next morning. "Not let them get away."

"Thank you."

"Didn't they get around to teaching you that at Princeton?"

"I majored in psychology."

"I'd think they'd have at least mentioned it at Quantico."

"I may have skipped that day."

"Well," he said, laughing, "now you know."

If Kay had not been the hardest-working Agent in the Baltimore Field Office before the situation with Williams—and she probably had been—she sure as hell was now. That evening with Christopher was the last time she allowed herself to wallow. Williams had slipped the bait; that meant they needed to set another trap. Kay redoubled her efforts, spent early mornings drinking bad coffee alone in the office, early mornings and long afternoons and late evenings, going back through the records, trying to find a way to trace where Williams had holed himself up.

She came home after one of these long days and found the house dark and Christopher gone; spent a few minutes looking around for a note that she knew she wouldn't find. Then she ordered a pizza from down the block and sat in front of the stack of papers she had brought home with her. Things were how they were. It was cold in February, hot in August, her brother could not be relied upon. Made as much sense getting upset about the third as it did the first two.

One of the countless falsehoods imbibed by any consumer of modern media is that investigative work is exciting, that it consists of very handsome people in dim rooms yelling at one another, or even handsomer people in front of futuristic-looking computers saying "Enhance, enhance, enhance," and then magically they find the secret clue that blows a case wide open. Even after two years in the FBI, Kay still sometimes found herself thinking this way, especially midway through a long afternoon staring at old leads. Of course it was all nonsense: investigating was like building a brick wall—first a row of stone, then a slab of mortar, repeat, repeat, repeat. You pulled the pictures together, you identified the subjects. Then you went after them, and this was, somehow, even less pleasant than finding them. Endless hours in her car, drinking coffee that had been nasty when it was warm and outright vile after an hour sitting in the cup; coughing on Torres's endless chain of cigarettes, inhaling enough second-hand smoke to choke a camel.

Better than being on the other side of it, especially those last few weeks in February, which would go down as some of the bloodiest in Baltimore history. No small feat in a city that averaged well over three hundred homicides per year, ten times the murder rate of New York for a city a twentieth the size, comparable to Mosul in Iraq, though a few graves safer than South Africa's Johannesburg. Williams had gone to ground, disappeared amongst the endless blocks of boarded-up row houses, the all-purpose convenience stores selling rat-eaten cereal and loose cigarettes, the basketball courts with their busted rims, the project housing pointing towards a kinder or more naïve age. Disappeared so far as the FBI was concerned, although any number of corpses could attest to his continued existence: former lieutenants found rotting in Dumpsters or just left cold in the passenger seats of their Escalades. It had become a race against time for all of them: Would Williams manage to kill enough of his former organization to make any case against him untenable? Or could they find someone who would roll on him first?

On a bleak and unfriendly winter morning, with little else to do, Kay was once again searching through old files about Williams, everything that had ever been collected on the budding criminal mastermind since he was still a youth. There wasn't much to go on. Other than a few cases as a juvenile—all sealed—there was almost nothing about Williams in the years before he had come onto the FBI's radar.

Almost nothing, but not quite. "The last time Williams got picked up he had just turned eighteen, fighting outside a club, some kind of minor beef. Judge let him go in the custody of his grandmother. Might be worth checking on her."

"Might be, if we had any idea who she was," Torres remarked. "Come on, Ivy, you've been doing this long enough to know that 'grandma' doesn't mean grandma, it means any woman older than forty who's looking after kids rather than hanging out in clubs. Could have been an aunt, or a second cousin, or who the hell knows what. Both of Williams's biological grandmothers are dead, and whoever that woman was, we have no idea who she is, much less where she used to live."

Kay grumbled quietly and went back to her files: on Williams and on his organization and on all the other players within it, his top people and the many bottom-feeders subsisting beneath them. The silence dragged on. Outside, it had begun to rain.

"What about this guy: Ricky Thomas, two tiers down from Williams, not quite a lieutenant but he went to the same high school? And there's an outstanding warrant for failure to appear at his arraignment on local charges."

"Thomas?" Special Agent Chapman looked up from his desk and shrugged. It was obvious to Kay that he had no idea who Ricky Thomas was, equally so that he didn't want to admit it. "What about him?"

"Why hasn't anyone gone and knocked on his door since Williams slipped into the wind?" Kay asked.

"Since he *slipped*?" Chapman said, drawing attention to Kay's moment of incompetence in hopes of covering up his own. "I guess we've been pretty busy since Williams *slipped* into the wind, Ivy. I guess we haven't had time to take a shot at every Baltimore corner boy with two vials of crack in his pocket."

It was not the first insult Kay had ignored, and she very much doubted it would be the last. "I've got a few minutes," she said simply, taking her service weapon out of her desk and slipping it into its holster. "Torres? You coming?"

"What the hell," he said, standing and pulling on his coat. "But you're springing for a Reuben at Attman's on the way back."

6

I T TOOK them forty minutes to find Ricky Thomas's last known location, an apartment in the projects set uncomfortably close to the Inner Harbor, owned by Shawnee Terice, girlfriend or baby momma or some such. Torres did the honors, pounding on the thin wood with his ham-hock fists. "Federal Bureau of Investigation," he boomed. "Please come to the door."

The commotion inside was loud, and sustained enough to get Torres to give Kay a long, heavy look and for Kay to put her hand around the butt of her service weapon. The door opened to reveal a harpy in stretch pants. "What you want?"

Torres spread his best aw-shucks grin on his face, although Kay wasn't sure who he thought he was fooling. People in this part of Baltimore were not fond of the police, in the same sense that cats are not fond of dogs. "Good afternoon, ma'am. I was wondering if you had a few minutes to answer some questions for us?"

"Ricky ain't here," she said—yelled, really, the noise cutting through the aperture, along with a fair bit of Shawnee's spit. Shawnee was shaped like a pyramid, a pointed head leading out to a body squat as a radish. The skin of her face was wrinkled and strained from hard living and bad decisions. She looked at the two of them with eyes the color of rusted metal.

Torres smiled a little wider, his eyes flickering over to Kay, then back at the door. "Ricky who?" he asked.

She blinked twice. "I don't know no Ricky," Shawnee said, adjusting herself so that her fleshy bulk shielded the interior. "Who said anything about anyone named Ricky?"

"You know, ma'am, and I hope you don't mind me saying so, but I don't see much of a future for you as a professional poker player," Torres said before setting one hand on her shoulder and casually shunting her aside.

"You can't come in here! You ain't got no warrant! You can't come in here!"

"It's called exigent circumstances," Torres began to explain, though he didn't get the chance to finish, because as he pushed open the door there was a quick flash of movement, and Torres tore forward like a hound after a coursing hare. Half Torres's size and probably a third of his age, still the suspect—who Kay thought was Ricky but couldn't say for certain—seemed like he was moving in slow motion. Torres got one hand on the back of his hooded sweatshirt and then the sound of tearing fabric was followed, in close succession, by the sound of Ricky being slammed against the linoleum floor. Kay winced in unconscious sympathy.

"Christ, Ricky, you see what happens if you aren't careful?" Torres continued in his easy lilt, bending down to cuff the suspect. "You could have really hurt yourself. And you went ahead and you ruined your shirt! Now what kind of thinking is that," Torres continued, standing the still-stunned Ricky up and setting him on the sofa. "Gotta be more careful, man. Whatever would Shawnee here do without you?"

In answer, Shawnee began to enter into a prolonged monologue of intense, even impressive vulgarity. Notwithstanding which, Kay cuffed her and set her down beside her boyfriend.

"Keep an eye on the loving couple," Torres said. "I'm going to have a quick look around."

Kay nodded and took up a position midway between the exit and the door Torres headed through, making sure she could offer her partner backup should the situation require it while still keeping an eye on the two suspects. Being put in irons had done nothing to halt Shawnee's continued slew of high-pitched invective, a torrent at once unceasing and shockingly profane. Ricky kept quiet, although he looked up at Kay with unconcealed hate. It was a look Kay had long since grown used to from working law enforcement in Baltimore, and she no longer felt any particular way about it.

Especially with Shawnee still screaming madly in her ear. One thing that even a casual involvement in law enforcement will teach you—or life generally, for that matter—is that woman, whatever her deficiency in size or strength, is in no way inferior to man in viciousness. And since humanity, in its wisdom, had seen fit to create all sorts of tools by which a weaker person might defeat a stronger one—knives and spears and shining black 9-millimeter Berettas—it behooved a person not to treat a perp casually on account of their sex.

". . . and your mother was twice as bad," Shawnee finished.

"Keep talking about my parents," Kay said flatly, turning to face the shrieking woman. "You're apt to piss me off."

Probably it wasn't a plan, exactly; probably Shawnee was just cracked out and hated cops, and had enough practice being arrested not to be particularly frightened at the concept. But either way, in the instant when Kay's attention slipped from him, Ricky was up from the couch and hit her turned head with his shoulder hard enough to set her tumbling. Then he was off at a sprint, drugs forgotten, house forgotten, girl forgotten, nothing left but freedom, freedom, freedom.

He was two steps out of the house when Torres caught him with a blow to his temple that sent him flying off the stoop and into the surrounding bushes. One of the upsides to these little shotgun shacks was that they didn't take long to search and they had back exits. After finishing with the first, Torres had apparently used the second to cycle back around to the front. A fortuitous scenario, otherwise they'd have been left to chase Ricky down Pratt Street with his hands cuffed behind his back, a situation that wouldn't have done much credit to anyone.

Torres managed to stand Ricky upright, but you could see he was still dazed from the punch, blinking and trying to focus on anything besides the pain in his head and the buzz in his skull.

"Don't hit my partner," Torres said. "What the hell kind of gentleman are you? Didn't your momma teach you any manners?"

Ricky's girl was still screaming, an ongoing stream of profanity spewing forth like the blood from Kay's nose.

7

ARRIVING BACK at the office, they put Ricky and his ingenue into separate holding cells and turned to processing the narcotics they had taken from his house. At one point a few drops of blood from Kay's nose fell on the cellophane wrapping of a cube of heroin. Torres took one look at the eyes above the wounded nostrils, the rage not quite simmering, and decided not to make a joke about it.

Afterward, however, when it was time to have a chat with the man who had broken her nose, Torres decided to make what he knew would be an unsuccessful effort to get his partner to take a few hours off. "You sure you want a piece of this, Ivy? You got tagged pretty good there."

Kay threw the bit of bloody cotton into a nearby wastebasket. "I'm sure."

"We won't even get anything from him anyway. Whatever time he's looking at on the drugs won't be enough to convince him to rat on his boss, not with Williams cutting threads like he was a tailor."

Kay didn't respond, just turned her cold green eyes towards the room where Thomas sat shackled.

"Your problem, Kay," Torres said, shrugging and unlocking the door, "is you're too damn chatty."

Torres was widely considered to be one of the best interrogators within the Baltimore Field Office. Some combination of his size and good-old-boy manner had the effect of convincing casual criminals and half-hard corner boys to drop their guard, chat a little, get loose and talkative—sometimes, though of course not always, and Kay thought this was going to be one of the not-always days. Looking at Ricky Thomas, a veteran of the gangster culture since he was a youth, well versed in criminality and in the strategies law enforcement used to combat it, Kay did not see a particularly tractable opponent.

Especially when he saw Kay walk in behind her partner, a nasty smile sliding out over his stony facade. After two years working violent gangs in Baltimore, Kay had grown used to that sort of look: searching, sexual, aggressive. It meant nothing to her. It rolled off her like the winter rain off the Bureau car.

"How you doing there, Ricky?" Torres asked, lowering himself into a chair with an audible sigh. "How's the head? We can get you another ice pack if you want one."

The aforementioned ice pack sat on the table, lukewarm and untouched. Ricky had not seen fit to use it. "It don't hurt none," he said. "How about you, girl? How's that shiner I gave you? Looks like a beaut."

Kay did not respond except to take the seat next to Torres—next to and just a bit behind him. She pulled out a small leather journal and a pen, opened the first and held the second between thumb and forefinger.

"Now what kind of a way is that to act?" Torres asked, shaking his big bull head. "I thought we talked about this already, Ricky: you gotta show respect to women. Didn't your mother teach you anything?"

"You're wasting your time," Ricky said.

"You don't even know what we want yet," Torres answered

through a smile. "Maybe we want to send you on a free visit to Disneyland. Maybe we want to give you tomorrow's winning lotto numbers. Would you say no to that?"

"You think this is my first time in a box? I grew up in these rooms," he said, gesturing at the four walls surrounding him. "And I know how all this works."

"If you've got such depth of experience," Torres said, smile slightly less bright, "then you ought to understand what it means that we caught you holding two kilograms of heroin."

"I know what it means."

"I've seen your record, Ricky," Torres continued over him. "I mean, I've browsed it: the whole thing makes for heavy reading, like carrying around a dictionary. And unlike Agent Malloy over there, I've never been much on studying. But still, I got enough of it to figure, what with you on parole till, hell, the year 2100 or some such, that whatever judge we pull might not prove so sympathetic to your being slapped with possession with intent to distribute. And what was that one other thing . . ." Torres snapped his fingers loudly, the sound echoing like a shot in the tight confines of the room. "Assaulting a federal officer. Let me ask you a question, Ricky: How you feel about Christmas?"

"It's fine."

"New Year's?"

Ricky shrugged.

"Halloween? Easter? Cinco de Mayo? Do they celebrate Cinco de Mayo in prison, Ricky?"

"I don't know. I don't think so."

"No? That's too bad, I'm all sorry to hear that, I truly am—because without your cooperation, it's going to be a long time before you get to kiss a girl beneath the mistletoe, or eat turkey with your family, or go on an Easter egg hunt. Something like . . ." Torres spent a moment in deliberate consideration.

". . . twenty years?" he asked, turning back as if asking Kay for her input. When she didn't respond, even to look up from her book, Torres turned back to Ricky. "Maybe a few less, if you get some lefty judge to hoodwink." Torres had a big, boozy sort of voice, like an carnival pitchman, and it echoed in the small confines of the room for a second or two after he spoke. Then there was silence, just the breathing of the three inmates, barely audible. It went on awhile.

"Let me tell you how this is going to go," Ricky said finally. "You gonna dick me around here for a while, because it makes you feel like a big man, and then I'm gonna tell you where to go with it and demand to see whatever shit-for-brains public defender gets assigned my case, and then I'm going to spend the next couple of years in a box. Ain't no thing. Ain't no thing to me, not a bit. Going inside, it's like going back home. Hell, they probably been keeping my cot warm for me." He leered as wide as a man in handcuffs could leer. "But one thing that's not gonna happen—one thing I'm not gonna do; one thing I wouldn't never do—is talk to any damn five-oh."

Kay sat mostly forgotten in the corner of the room. Her book was open but she wasn't looking at it, and the pen in her hands sat uncapped and unused. Kay kept meticulous notes, because it was important when building a case to create a clear paper trail, but for herself she barely needed them. In truth her exceptional memory was a mixed blessing at the very best: memories she would have preferred to forget kept shiny and new by the undiminished force of her own recollection. But professionally it was a valuable asset, one that had already gained her some renown within the Baltimore Field Office.

"You're that tight with Rashid Williams?" Kay asked quietly.

It was the first thing she'd said since entering the room, and that alone seemed to give it a certain weight, even for Ricky, who turned to look at her full on. "First, I ain't got no idea where Ra is hiding out at. That's what you're after, you're wasting your time. Second, if I did, I wouldn't tell you anything."

"Because you're so close?"

"It don't matter how I feel about Rashid. If I hated Rashid like the devil, you still wouldn't get nothing out of me."

"But the two of you are friendly."

"Brothers to blood," Ricky said, smirking.

"Interesting," Kay said. "Interesting."

Now it was Ricky's turn to be interested. "Why you say that?"

Kay shrugged, as if she weren't really paying attention. "Family interests me. The connections we build with people, the relationships. The things we owe one another, or the things we decide we owe one another."

"Family's all there is," Ricky said, nodding his big head in agreement.

"You're no kin to Williams, though."

"Close as."

"Came up together?"

"Shit, I known Ra since before anybody be foolish enough to let us hold weight. Playing pickup ball on the mini-baskets and drinking quarter waters," Ricky said, growing expansive with nostalgia.

"Just two young boys with dreams of becoming corner kingpins, dropping bodies and selling grams?"

"Fuck else we gonna do? Become bankers? Where we was from, it was sling crack or work at McDonald's. And I wasn't never about wearing one of those hats."

Kay had heard it before, and it wasn't altogether false, but she didn't think it was entirely true, either. Circumstances limit one's course of action, but they didn't define one's character, one's identity. Ricky had made the choices that would lead him to a jail cell, and Rashid had made the same. Of course, she allowed no hint of this disapprobation to show on her face. "Yeah, yeah, you and every other two-bit corner boy south of Penn Station want to drop Rashid's name like you were twin sucklings. I've read your sheet: you're at the bottom of the pole, Ricky, and just cause you once walked past Williams at a party when you were in high school doesn't make you friends."

"You ain't know what you talking about," Ricky said, getting heated. "Ra and I go back to when we was seeds. Used to bust into Rite Aid and walk out with all the candy we could carry, sell it the next day at school for a dollar a pop. Shit, only time we ever bothered to show."

"Where'd you hide the stash?"

"His grandmomma's house. Only place to. Down in the basement. Perfect till the rats got to it." Ricky smiled at the thought of malfeasance gone by. "Came down one day and found the wrappers torn up, all our work ruined. Must have eaten through four pounds of chocolate in one night."

Kay closed her book with a loud snap, turned her attention, or at least her eyes, to Torres. "Why are we wasting our time with this zero?" she said. "Says he won't tell nothing but that's just 'cause he's got nothing to tell. This guy knows Rashid Williams like I know the pope."

"You calling me a liar?" Ricky asked, simmering.

"Nice to see you're following along."

"Fuck you."

"Let me tell you something, Ricky: I know everything there is to know about Rashid Williams. I eat Williams every morning with my oatmeal. I know Williams better than any friend ever knew him, any lover. Ricky doesn't have a grandmother; both of his grandmothers are dead. We check that kind of thing."

"She was his mom's cousin or some shit," Ricky said. "Miss

Dee, we used to call her. I practically grew up in that woman's house; don't be telling me I don't know what I'm talking about."

"Yeah? You and Williams, the uncrowned kings of West Baltimore."

"West Baltimore?" Ricky looked like he was going to spit, then went ahead and decided to actually do so, a thick wad of phlegm going against the wall. "Potomac and Lombard—born there, come up there, gonna die there," he said.

"More likely the inside of a cell," Kay said, standing abruptly. "Let's go," she told Torres.

Torres looked up questioningly, trying to figure out his partner's ploy, what he was supposed to do to help her out with it.

But Kay didn't seem to be playing a game. "We got what we need," she said.

"Bullshit," Thomas said, but there was a damp spot on his forehead. "I didn't tell you nothing."

"You told us everything," Kay said flatly and with no excess of emotion, like she was explaining something simple to someone stupid. "You just didn't realize it."

But outside the interview room Torres seemed as skeptical as Ricky. "If this is a ploy to get him to open up," he said, shrugging, "I applaud the effort, but it won't work. We can let him stew awhile but he's not going to break."

"It wasn't a gambit," Kay said, showing some sign of excitement for the first time. "Name of Dee, lives near Potomac and Lombard. What do you think, Torres: Worth making another stop?"

8

I T DIDN'T take long to find the address of Dee Abbot, fifty-nine, owner of a two-bedroom house near Patterson Park. Had owned it since 1959, and driving down there Kay found herself wondering what the neighborhood had been like then, if it once held some fragment of the middle-class promise, as much of Baltimore had in the years before the cargo ships had stopped coming into the harbor, and Bethlehem Steel closed, and innumerable other blue-collar businesses had similarly disappeared. If so, it had been a long time since those dreams had rotted. The neighborhood looked like much of the rest of Baltimore: crumbling, vacant houses pushed against occupied domiciles in comparable states of disrepair; liquor stores alternating with the occasional small market, youths and children lounging, looking unfriendly in the late afternoon.

Torres spent most of the ride grumbling about the weather and about never having gotten his promised Reuben, but he was at least as excited as Kay. Most likely this would be another one of the innumerable leads they had been following that would not pan out, time wasted, but it was better than sitting on their hands, the only other option. They parked their car on the street and crossed over a small front yard of weeds and scattered detritus, Torres in the lead.

Kay was raising her hand to the front door when a hole appeared in the wood, and then another, and then she heard that half-familiar *budda-budda-budda*, the sound of a bullet leaving the muzzle of an assault rifle. Then she was flying sideways, courtesy of Torres, who had grabbed her from behind and launched the both of them off the stoop and into the comparative safety of the bushes.

They crashed down through them, branches clawing at Kay's face. It took a while to get free of each other, but finally Kay managed to right herself. Torres was saying something, but between the echo of gunfire and the rush of adrenaline Kay couldn't make out what it was at first. "I'm hit!" he insisted. "I'm hit!" And indeed, when Kay looked down, she saw they were both covered in blood and had a sudden flash of fear, thinking that she might have caught a round as well. But no, it was just Torres, a hole in his leg leaking scarlet over her.

Not for long, though. The assault rifle went silent for a moment and Kay was on her feet. A quick glance at Torres suggested he wouldn't die—not just then, at least, although of course everyone has that debt to pay the reaper, and Kay was thinking if she didn't do something quick, then their numbers might both be coming up soon. "Call for backup," she hissed, drawing her weapon, "and tag him if he tries to come out the front!"

Torres very clearly did not think this was a good idea. "Kay! Kay!"

But Kay wasn't listening; Kay was moving swiftly around to the back of the house. She kept her head down and made sure not to show any trace of herself through the windows, and what she was thinking as she did so—to the degree that she was thinking anything and not simply acting on instinct and training—was that there was no way in hell that James Rashid Williams was going to get away from her twice; no, sir, there was not. They would be putting one of them into the ground at the end of this, Kay felt with a grim sense of certainty.

Kay had not heard the sounds of an assault rifle since she had been at Quantico. It was the sort of ordnance that even your average Baltimore corner boy—not a species broadly renowned for caution or good sense—recognized. Williams had nothing to lose at this point; it was life in a cell or hold court on his stoop, and the deep-bass explosions echoing from the house made it clear which one he had chosen.

Kay kept her shoulder against the brick, down as low as she could get and still be able to move, maneuvering sideways until she was at the back end of the row house. The assault rifle had gone silent again, although it had left Kay's ears ringing, like she had strayed too close to the front of a rock concert.

"You out there, pigs?" a voice yelled, although before there could be any answer the cannon fired off again. "I got enough for all of you!"

Kay was directly below Williams now; she could almost feel the reverberation of his rifle and tensed her shoulders. Consciously, she could feel nothing but terror—would have told you, if you had asked, that she was too scared to do anything but shiver, certainly too scared to make and execute a tactical maneuver. But that wouldn't have been right: hundreds of hours at Quantico had done their grim work of turning her body into a machine that operated without assistance, a fighter jet on autopilot.

The rifle cut off in mid-burst, the familiar *snick* of a weapon jamming, and Kay was upright an instant later, almost unaware of her decision to move on the shooter. She could see Williams through the window—that same furrowed brow, those same dead eyes. He saw her in the same instant, having fixed the jam, and turned the muzzle of his weapon towards her.

Two bangs that were louder than the other bangs—bangs that Kay somehow did not realize for a long moment had come out of her gun; did not realize it until she saw Williams drop his gun and stumble backward, slapping one hand against his chest, then sliding down the wall, leaving a slick of red.

Success had robbed her of forward momentum, confused the instinct on which she had been operating. It took her longer than it should have to break the rest of the glass before climbing in through the back window, covering what she at that point was certain was Williams's corpse with the weapon she'd used to make him into that.

"All clear!" Kay yelled, as if the SWAT team was waiting for her command. "All clear!"

9

K AY'S GOING-AWAY party was a raucous affair, even
by the standards of the Baltimore Field Office.
Monaghan's, the dive bar where the FBI did some but
not all of its drinking, had not been closed for the event, although
anyone who had happened to wander in aimlessly would have
left quickly or found himself pulled into the cheering morass,
forced to raise a Natty Boh in a toast to Kay's future in New York.

Whatever ill feeling Kay had produced amongst some of
her squadmates—for letting Williams go the first time, or for
being a bit *too* gung ho about the mission, a bit *too* willing to
stay late and come in early, or just because she had the sort of
personality that not everyone enjoyed having contact with—
had been essentially erased with the body of Williams. Even
Chapman and some of the others who had never seemed to
have a good word to say to her had rallied around Kay after the
shooting, as much to show general support as because they were
legitimately proud of her.

Indeed, Kay sometimes felt she was the only one in the office
who had any doubts about her actions that grim winter day. It was
four months since they had shut down the Williams case, which
was a happy euphemism for a closed coffin. There had been an
immediate review of the shooting by the Bureau's Inspection

Division, and Kay had given up the weapon she had used and been issued a replacement. But she was quickly cleared of all wrongdoing—indeed, it was hard to imagine a more obvious case in which lethal force had been required. They had offered her counseling with one of the Bureau's resident headshrinkers, but Kay, despite her academic experience with cognitive psychology, preferred to keep her feelings to herself.

But sometimes, late at night, she wondered if maybe she wouldn't have done better to spend a few hours talking it through with someone. Admittedly Williams had been a very bad person, a very bad person indeed, and the world was, so far as Kay was concerned, unequivocally a better place without him in it. Still, she felt that perhaps it was a dangerous thing to feel too good about the facility with which she had ended a man's life. It was part of the job, she would remind herself in the early mornings that followed, watching the sun's rays crawl up her window. Part of the mission, and as always, the mission came first.

She was rather more excited about her transfer. Rotational protocols dictated that an Agent spend two-plus years in a small- or medium-sized office before being transferred to a larger one, unless they had been assigned to a large field office after graduating New Agent Training at Quantico. She had liked Baltimore, liked the city: low-key and livable, the people friendly when they weren't shooting at each other. Liked the food and the waterfront, liked the hipster kids up in Hampden, liked getting five-dollar tickets for Orioles games. And she'd liked the office; at least, she liked Torres. More than liked him: respected him, and was glad that she'd had the opportunity to learn from him, and felt confident that she was better for the experience. But New York was home. Christopher was there, and her adopted mother and father, her surrogate family. Not to mention her high school friends, although it seemed a long time since she'd talked to any of them.

The evening dragged on happily till towards midnight it was just Kay and Torres, neither of whom were what could be called strictly sober. Torres had taken to being shot in the leg with impressive fortitude, using it to coax drinks out of everyone long after he was on the mend. Another month or so and he wouldn't even need the cane. Was it good luck that the bullet had not found itself six inches upward, in his knee, or was it bad luck that the bullet hadn't found itself six inches to the right or left and missed him altogether? These were the sorts of questions Kay found herself asking several hours into her farewell party.

"Moving on from us, Ivy?" Torres asked. Slurred.

"Only in body and spirit," Kay said.

Torres laughed. "And what do we get to hold on to?"

"A fair portion of my liver."

"We'll take it," Torres said, "we'll take it. Who you going to be working for up in the big city?"

"Susan Jeffries, in counterintelligence."

Torres laughed. "You're working for Frowny?" He shook his head as if Kay had just told him she was planning on jumping off something high onto something hard. Then he beckoned the barman for two shots of Jameson. "Good luck."

" 'Frowny'?"

"You never read John le Carré? What the hell kind of spy are you, Kay? Frowny, like Smiley from the old novels."

"I did read John le Carré," Kay said, "although none of you apparently did with any clarity, because the joke with Smiley was of course that he never smiled. And besides, his name was George Smiley, it wasn't a nickname."

"Oh," Torres said, shrugging. "I guess we're not as clever in the FBI as they are at MI6."

"A bunch of loose-tongued intellectuals, the lot of them."

"God bless America," Torres said.

Two shots of Jameson disappeared down two gullets.

"So it's counterintelligence work for you, then? Going to make sure the Russians don't invade North Dakota? I saw that in a movie once."

"That sounds like a stupid movie."

"It was, but I think they remade it."

"Sounds like the kind of thing they would do."

Torres laughed. "You're all right in my book, Ivy," Torres said. From Torres it represented a ringing endorsement. "Not everyone has what it takes to do this job, but I think you do. If you can keep your head down and manage not to piss anyone off."

"God willing," Kay said happily, calling for the check.

PART 2

Nothing is more common on earth than to deceive and be deceived.

—JOHANN GOTTFRIED SEUME

10

GROUP CHIEF Mike Anthony cupped his hands in the basin, filled them half with water, dumped it and brought his damp fingers up against his hairless scalp. Balding since his twenty-third birthday, homely long before that. Anthony looked at the reflection in the mirror with the sort of unflinching honesty that he had always prized as the foremost asset of the intelligence professional: the ability to see reality as it is, rather than as one might wish it to be. How many otherwise excellent case officers, women of sharp mind, men of firm character, had come to ruin because of this simple inability to identify and adhere to the hard, unpleasant, sharp-edged facts of existence? Insisting all was well when this was clearly not the case, maintaining absolute certainty in their sense of direction even as it led them off a cliff? A truth was a truth was a truth, however unpalatable one found it.

He dried his fingers on a paper towel, threw it into the bin and fixed his tie. No, never a handsome man, not the one you first noticed on walking into a bar, but then again Anthony's was not a trade that prized good looks particularly. Indeed, his sheer unobtrusiveness had proved a virtue on more than one occasion. Once, many years earlier, before he had become firmly ensconced in the bosom of CIA headquarters in Langley, Virginia, when his cover had been blown on some or other ploy in some or other country, the local security services had put out an all-points bulletin for a "bald man in a suit," a sobriquet that Anthony still looked back on with some pride. Was this not the ultimate compliment for a CIA Case Officer? Faceless and unnoticeable, pulling strings without anyone ever being the wiser?

The ideal, though—like most ideals—was rarely reached. Anthony looked at himself one last time in the mirror, studying the laugh lines around his eyes, deeply etched as a delineation of his character, although he could not have been accused of any excess of jocularity. Not so many more years at this, he told himself, a promise often repeated that would someday need to be followed through on. But not yet. He grabbed his briefcase and went to start the meeting he had been dreading for the better part of a month.

The Associate Deputy Director of Operations was ten years older than Anthony, bumping close up against retirement and doing everything he could to hide it. His hair was the jet-black of a twenty-year-old, but if you were perceptive—and Mike Anthony was very perceptive—you could make out some gray amongst the roots. He wore a suit that was expensive, old-fashioned, out of style but still handsome. He sat at the boss end of a big wooden desk, and he had an unlit cigar in his mouth. Anthony wondered, as he did whenever he had to meet with the ADDO, if it was the same cigar or if he had a box of them in some drawer of the giant bureau, a dozen Churchills well chewed.

"Mike," he said, gregarious and expansive as ever. "Have a seat, let's talk through this thing."

"Director," Anthony said, nodding and accepting the seat.

The meeting was an informal formality. Informal because the ADDO liked it that way: loose ties and first names. A formality because they had only the one option set before them, and no conversation could get around that fact.

"Sounds like we got a little bit of a mess out there old Moscow way."

"I think that's exactly what we have, sir," Anthony answered.

"Tell me about it."

Which Anthony did then: a retread of what was in the report, all things that the ADDO already knew. Unhappy to do what needed doing, the ADDO would require an hour of cajoling, of pushing and prodding, although in the end he would follow the only course available to them. Resentfully, with some annoyance at the man doing the shoving.

The ADDO did not particularly like Anthony and had made that clear over the years in any number of ways big and small. Anthony had never been quite sure why—some long-forgotten insult, or a simple clash of styles, perhaps. He did his best not to hold the ADDO's antipathy against him. The two things that a lifetime working as a spy had taught Anthony—there were many things but the two main things—were an eye for human weakness, and sympathy towards it. People were not black or white, not good or evil, not one thing or another. They were many things; they were vices and virtues overlapping, sometimes so close that it was difficult to see where one left off and the other began. The ADDO had been a great man once—never an easy man, perhaps never a friendly one, but by the standards of their trade he had been a giant. Coming up through the ranks, Anthony had been weaned on the stories of the ADDO's victories, snatched from the cold hands of his grim-eyed Soviet counterparts.

Time passes. More and more the ADDO seemed out of sync with the development of the intelligence community, which, after the failures of 9/11, had increasingly stressed coordination and the shared communication of information through the various government agencies tasked with defending the country.

"I don't like it," he said, after Anthony finished running through what had happened to Dmitri—what had happened and what Anthony wanted to do about it.

"I'm not thrilled about it, either."

"You're sure there's no other way? Maybe Dmitri got foolish, started whispering secrets in public places after a few shots of vodka."

Anthony shrugged. Another thing that a full career as a spy had taught him: you could never be entirely sure what a person might do under any given circumstances. "It seems to me un-likely. Dmitri was, if nothing else, a professional. I can't imagine he'd be so sloppy. And all three of them?" Anthony shook his head. "We've got a mole."

The ADDO let loose a string of profanity that would have been noteworthy for its length and eloquence if Anthony hadn't heard so many variations of it before. "And there's no way we can handle this in-house?"

"If I thought that was a legitimate option, I'd have taken it." The CIA mandate was to gather and analyze intelligence on foreign entities. Legally it was not allowed to operate within the United States proper. That was exclusively within the purview of the FBI, responsible for counterintelligence gathering inside the nation. In practice, of course, the CIA had not always been known to play entirely according to the strictest rules of conduct, but neither was it set up to coordinate the sort of manhunt that was the FBI's core mission.

"Damn feds," the ADDO said, which by his standards was actually not even particularly profane.

"They're professionals," Anthony said. "They've got the resources to handle it, and the personnel. I'm not crazy about having Agency business spread any wider than it needs to be, but under the circumstances I don't see an alternative." Of course the ADDO knew all of these things—knew that the situation, for legal as well as practical reasons, required coordination with the FBI. But some people needed to be talked into things they had already decided on, and the ADDO was one of these people.

"And who were you thinking would be best equipped to help us sweep up this mess?"

Anthony made like he was thinking this over, although it was all for show. "Jeffries would be an ideal choice."

"Frowny?" the ADDO said, like it was the first time anyone had made the joke. Finished being pleased with himself, he mulled it over for a moment. "I guess there isn't anyone better suited."

There was not, which was why Anthony had suggested her. "She's earned her reputation for competence," though "genius" would really more accurately describe the common wisdom relating to Jeffries. "And she's not the loose-lips sort, either."

The ADDO snorted. "No, she certainly isn't." He thought it over for a while, or made like he was thinking it over. "If we've got to do it, we've got to do it," the ADDO said finally, in the sort of tone that suggested he held Anthony responsible for the situation. "But I want one of ours up in New York coordinating the effort. Let's just make sure that our . . . *associates* don't take this as an opportunity to go on a witch hunt through the Agency."

"Who were you thinking?"

"Andrew did good work in Kiev."

"He did," Anthony agreed. "It's a different sort of skill set, however."

"I think he's got the chops to handle it. Besides, it's time he learned something about cooperating with our sister agency. It's not all adventures in foreign lands. Internal politics is as important as external."

Which was as good as an order—and would have become one if Anthony had pressed, and so of course he didn't. Another thing he had learned as a spy was not to push a rock uphill if you could possibly avoid it. "I'll put him on it," Anthony said.

"Good." The tip of the ADDO's cigar dipped as he nodded his head. "And tell him to keep a close eye on the suits. The last thing we need is strangers going through our dirty laundry."

Lord knew there was enough of it to find, Anthony thought, nodding and excusing himself out of the office.

11

I T DID not take long for Kay to understand how Susan Jeffries had acquired her nickname. She was a dowdy, bespectacled woman of forty-five or fifty, but she was the sort of person who, Kay suspected, had looked forty-five at twenty, had given the impression of late middle age while still in adolescence. She had beady little eyes that were made too large by her out-of-fashion glasses; she had a quivering little contralto; she had not bothered to dye her hair in a long time. If you had passed her on the street, you would have thought her to be that breed of librarian who leaves the back stacks only to yell at rambunctious children, who sees every book under her care as a treasure on par with the *Mona Lisa*, who secretly dislikes it when people check them out and read them, getting their grubby little fingerprints on the covers, bending back the spines.

Well—there was no point in looking like a spy if you actually were one, and Kay suspected that Jeffries's charmless ubiquity had served her successfully in the long years she'd spent working counterintelligence operations. Suspected but didn't know, because—for all the rumors that flew around about her new boss—there was very little hard information to be found, even for those members of the squad who had worked with her for years and years.

Kay was a half hour early her first day, as she wanted to make a good impression, wanted also to make sure she didn't accidentally get lost en route; but Jeffries was there all the same, working quietly at the desk in her office. Kay got the sense that one needed to wake up awfully early in the morning to get the jump on Assistant Special Agent in Charge Susan Jeffries.

She called Kay into her office a few minutes later, introduced herself in a brisk but not unpleasant fashion, asked a few questions—how Kay was handling the transition, where her new apartment was—then promptly got down to brass tacks. "So they had you on gangs down in Baltimore?"

"Yes, ma'am."

"I think you'll find that your new slate of duties will require a rather different mind-set. You're going to spend your time doing a lot of what you might think is mundane work, reading FISA take and CI reports and doing surveillance." FISA was the Foreign Intelligence Surveillance Act, which prescribed procedures for electronic surveillance of foreign powers engaged in espionage or international terrorism against the United States. What was gathered from all of this was called "take." "It can be slow work, but it's the FBI's second-highest priority after terrorism, and we take it very seriously."

It was clear that Jeffries was not big on melodrama. "Yes, ma'am," Kay said again.

"If you have any questions about your new role, feel free to take them up with me."

"Absolutely," Kay said.

Jeffries handed Kay a list of manuals on counterintelligence that she suggested Kay familiarize herself with. Kay scanned the list quickly: *Venona: Soviet Espionage and American Response, 1939–1957* by Robert Louis Benson, *Soviet Espionage* by David J. Dallin and four more titles that sounded like heavy, ponderous, difficult tomes. Kay had anticipated a somewhat lengthier introduction to her new position, but she could also recognize a dismissal when she heard one. She thanked Jeffries and went quietly back to her desk.

The rest of the squad had arrived by the time Kay had finished her meeting. The FBI was not the sort of work environment where one slunk in in mid-morning hoping the boss wouldn't notice, and anyway it seemed clear that Jeffries noticed everything. Introductions were brief and not overwhelmingly enthusiastic as there was little common ground between working criminal and counterintelligence investigations. Kay knew it would take time to learn the new vernacular let alone be accepted by her new squad. That was fine: She'd done it in Baltimore, hadn't she? She'd do it again in New York.

Kay spent the better part of the morning engaged in the usual administrative tasks one gets embroiled in whenever one enters a new office. There was a grim efficiency to the squad that contrasted somewhat with what she was used to—less freewheeling, more formal. Part of that, probably, was the nature of the work itself. As Jeffries had intimated, counterintelligence was about as far from gang work as you could get. But part of it, Kay assumed, was Jeffries herself. An office begins to take on the characteristics of the person who runs it, and Jeffries was the epitome of the counterintelligence professional: cool and competent if not particularly gregarious. Midway through the morning Kay found herself missing Torres's attempts at humor, the easy back-and-forth she had acquired with much of the Baltimore Field Office.

Five o'clock rolled around and the rest of the squad began to fade out slowly, although Kay remained where she was—indeed, found that her work moved more quickly with the rest of the cubicles empty, computers shut down and silent, with just her in the bullpen—although of course Jeffries hadn't left but remained in her office as she had throughout the day. Admittedly, it was possible that the ASAC was playing FarmVille or updating her Facebook status, but somehow Kay did not really believe it.

When Kay finally left, she crossed paths with the janitorial staff, and the light in Jeffries's office was still on. Late enough already, she was made later still by the elaborate security procedures—understandable, given the nature of the work, but still not an ideal addition to what had already been a very long day. In the plus column, she had missed rush hour, and she was able to get a seat on the R train up to Fourteenth Street. The L, unfortunately, was busy and crowded and smelled strongly of unwashed flesh, and by the time Kay had made it back to Greenpoint she was in a mood not so shy of foul.

But stepping up out of the subway, she felt better. Early summer, and New York was a place to be—was *the* place, with handsome couples walking down the street, arm in arm; a thousand different restaurants, every cuisine and culture imaginable; a multitude of loud, laughing bars. Uncle Luis and Aunt Justyna had offered to let her stay in the spare room in their Upper West Side apartment—just for a little while, until she got her feet down—but Kay wanted none of it. She had seen enough of her old friends and classmates give in to that mid-twenties malaise that saw them move back in with the 'rents. And she had fallen in love with this part of the city almost as soon as she had seen it. It reminded her a bit of Baltimore: the unaffected locals brushing past overcute hipsters, old-fashioned Polish bakeries abutting fifteen-dollar-a-drink cocktail bars . . .

Kay hadn't yet eaten a real meal that day: she had been too antsy for breakfast, too focused once work had started, and she was feeling it now. With nothing to cook at home, she dropped into a little falafel spot, laid a few dollars down on the table, devoured the sandwich they brought her. Afterward she thought about going somewhere for a beer, but a quick check of the clock revealed that morning was not so far away—not so far away at all—and she found herself back in her apartment.

It was small, and the paint was faded and the brick was crumbling, and it had one window that looked directly into a window across the way, close enough that she could identify the spices on her neighbor's rack, cardamom and ginger and saffron. But at least it was hers; after two years alone in Baltimore there was no way Kay could have brought herself to live with a roommate.

Kay brushed her teeth and changed into her nightclothes. She had planned on reading awhile before going to bed, a text on cognitive psychology; Kay liked to keep abreast of current developments as best as her time allowed, which wasn't very much. Or perhaps she would do a few chapters in her Russian language textbook: since Kay had found out months ago that she would be transferred to Russian counterintelligence, she'd gone back to try to improve her speaking ability, her tongue having grown slack with disuse. Then of course there was the homework that Jeffries had assigned her; she'd need to start on that as soon as possible.

But the instant Kay felt the bed against her back, she knew she was too exhausted to get any more work done. She set her book down beside the two pictures that rested on her night table. The first was a photo of her parents taken a few years before their deaths, staring into the camera and smiling, looking happy and wholesome. The second was from outside the gym in Quantico, a tree that Kay had run past hundreds of times during her time there. Nailed into the wood were boards reading HURT, AGONY, PAIN, LOVE-IT and, beneath them, FAMILY, PRIDE, ATTITUDE, RESPECT, LOYALTY. Kay stared at both photos for a few moments, then hit the light and passed swiftly into slumber.

12

J USTYNA DĄBROWSKA Alvaro-Nuñez was one of those
woman who seemed, infuriatingly for the rest of the
world, destined to spend the entirety of her time above
the ground beautiful. When Kay was a child Justyna was a stag-
geringly attractive forty; when Kay was an adolescent she was
a stylish and handsome fifty; and now that Kay was a woman,
Justyna was a dignified sixty. Perhaps in the dim years before
her birth Justyna had experienced some period of awkwardness
when she was gawky and big-boned, but Kay could not imagine
it. Blond-haired, blue-eyed, the slightest Eastern European trem-
olo when she spoke, just enough to give her an air of mystery. Her
sense of fashion had always been unerringly keen, and her birthday presents were inevitably the best thing in Kay's wardrobe.

Today Justyna was in a smiling sundress from one of the
downtown boutiques that Kay liked to walk past but could
never really imagine buying anything from, shoes smart and
sensible, her earrings stylish but not overdone. The gloves were
the only off touch: they were too thick for a warm day in June,
not quite seamless with the rest of the costume. Beneath them,
Kay knew, although virtually no one else alive did, were seven
fingers, three on the left and four on the right, a souvenir of
a week spent beneath the less-than-tender ministrations of the

government back in Poland, now almost forty years in the past. Justyna had never spoken of it, retaining that ineffable sense of class that seemed to have died off with Grace Kelly, allowing her to remain just above the world's unpleasantness, never quite getting stained by it. What Kay had gleaned of Justyna's years before she came to America she had gotten from Luis, and he had been very nearly as closemouthed, referring simply to some "political unpleasantness" and leaving the matter at that. It was not until after the death of her parents that Kay learned more about the half-century-long nightmare that was the Soviet Union, the humiliations and outright brutalities inflicted by the secret police upon members of a recalcitrant intelligentsia. What exactly Justyna had done to draw their attention, and how she had managed to escape, was a mystery to this day, and one that Kay knew better than to attempt to plumb.

This was not at all on Kay's mind when they met for brunch at a very cute place on the Upper West Side that Kay would not normally visit.

"Kay, darling," Justyna said, leaning in for an air-kiss, which Kay, for all her practice, had never quite learned to manage as adroitly. "Sit down and tell me everything!"

It was the Saturday afternoon of Kay's first weekend since starting work in counterintelligence, and since she had spent the morning reviewing one of the texts Jeffries had recommended to her, it was also essentially the first time in six days that Kay was not actively working. She had to make a conscious effort to enjoy the moment, the sunny weather and her aunt's good humor. "Everything would take a while," she said.

It had been Justyna who had kept them together, Kay knew, kept them together that long first summer after her parents had both died. Luis was all but broken by it, wandering about the house, staring out the windows aimlessly, drinking probably more than he should. Christopher had just begun that stage of adolescence when nothing anyone tells you makes any sense at all, when you don't need an excuse for rebellion. Kay, three years younger, still a child, had been sad and scared and lonely and desperately confused.

It had been Justyna's quiet strength that had stopped them from collapsing completely. Christopher had determined—for reasons that to this day remained unclear to Kay, probably in large part because they remained unclear to Christopher as well—that he and Luis would be enemies; that nothing their surrogate father could do would gain favor in his eyes. But even Christopher's impressive sense of youthful rebellion, one that he had sustained far beyond adolescence, could not extend towards disliking Justyna. Perhaps somewhere in the world there was a person capable of such meanness, but Kay had trouble imagining who it was.

"How is the new position?" Justyna asked.

"Tiring," Kay replied. "Like the old one."

"I don't remember anyone forcing you into it."

"I'm not complaining," Kay said, and indeed she wasn't. "It's interesting. It's very different than what I was doing in Baltimore. There's a ton to learn," and even as she said it Kay could find her mind shifting back to the text on counterintelligence she had been reading earlier that morning. She would get back to it this afternoon, and of course there remained the two chapters of Russian she had assigned herself to finish that night before she went to bed. "Asking Directions in a Museum" was the title of tonight's first lesson, although Kay wasn't exactly sure how often that sort of dialogue would come up in her counterintelligence work.

She shook herself back into the moment. "Anyway, I'm still feeling things out. They haven't given me much to do yet."

"I'm sure that will change," Justyna said. "Have you spoken to your brother lately?"

"Not since he came to visit me in Baltimore. He's been dodging my calls since. You?"

"He sends me notes, sometimes. Postcards from little spots in the city that I've never heard of."

"Nothing more than that?"

"Your brother is . . . a free spirit," Justyna said lamely.

That was one way to put it. A slow moment of unhappiness, but Justyna turned the page quickly. She had a rare talent for seeing the happy side of anything. "You know, Kay, we're all so proud of you. Christopher too. We know what it took to get where you are, how few applicants are accepted into the FBI, how many wash out of Quantico. And you seem to have done so well in Baltimore, even the New York newspapers ran articles about your . . . about what . . . about the shooting."

"I'd rather not talk about that," Kay said abruptly. She did not regret what had happened to Williams on that long winter afternoon months earlier. It was part of the job, part of the mission, and Williams had forced her hand. But she didn't like talking about it, especially not with anyone from outside the Bureau, a civilian, even if that civilian was family. It sounded too much like bragging to Kay, however casually she discussed it; and there was something in her mind irredeemably foul about crowing over the death, however unavoidable, of a fellow human being.

"Of course, of course," Justyna said, graceful as ever. "I'm just trying to let you know: we're proud of you. Paul and Anne, if they were here, they'd be twice as proud."

Paul and Anne Malloy had met during their residencies at Johns Hopkins in Baltimore, two young ideologues meeting and bonding over shared passions. They married just before graduation and dedicated the better part of their careers to trying to bring the benefits of modern medicine to remote and impoverished parts of the third world, fighting leishmaniasis in the Congo, tuberculosis in India.

And then they had been killed. A robbery gone wrong in Colombia late one summer. Kay thought about it frequently but almost never discussed it. Not with her friends or acquaintances, not even very much with Luis and Justyna. If Christopher had ever been around, perhaps she might have discussed it with him, but given his habits and lifestyle this was rarely an option. It bothered Kay some—actually it bothered her quite a bit—that she could not remember much of her mother or father, or more accurately that all she could remember were the bits and bobs that a child could piece together: that they were kind, that they had loved her, that she missed them.

"You know, after their death was the first time I ever had any experience with anyone from the FBI. Coming from where I did, one did not have a very high opinion of state security." This was as close as Aunt Justyna would ever get to directly discussing having been arrested, jailed and tortured. "But they were very professional—friendly, even. I'd never have thought at the time that my little Kay would end up in their ranks."

Kay hadn't really been paying attention to the last few sentences, lost as she was in memories of her parents and her early childhood. It took a few seconds for her to seize on her aunt's comment. "FBI? What are you talking about?"

"You don't remember? Well, you were very young at the time. And I suppose there was a lot else going on. We had a visit from the FBI a few days after . . ." *your parents' death* was how that sentence ended, although Justyna had let it trail off. "Anyway, they wanted to ask us a few questions."

This was the first Kay had heard of this, and it didn't make any sense. "Why would the FBI have gotten involved?"

Justyna shrugged. "They said it was standard practice, a U.S. citizen dying abroad in such circumstances."

Except that it wasn't standard practice at all, as Kay well knew. "What did they ask about?" she asked, taking a sip from her drink to feign indifference.

"It was twenty years ago, dear, and to be honest I had other things on my mind." Justyna thought for a moment. "They said they wanted background information on your father. They had a few questions about his new job, though I didn't know much about that and couldn't really help them. They talked to your uncle awhile also, though not for very long."

If the FBI in the mid-nineties in any way resembled the Bureau that she was currently dedicating her life to, they would not have had the manpower to run about investigating every unfortunate accident that befell an American in a foreign country. There was something strange here, something off, and for a long moment Kay found herself worrying at it like a loose tooth.

"Kay? Kay dear? What's wrong?"

"Nothing, Auntie," Kay said, returning to the conversation but filing the information neatly away for later. "Shall we have another mimosa?"

13

A FTER A few weeks in the New York Office, Kay had
started to fall into the grind. Some days she almost felt
like being an FBI Agent didn't seem all that different
from working in any other high-pressure office, except that this
high-pressure office was inside a SCIF, a sensitive compartmented
information facility, where access was controlled by a keypad and
cell phones were prohibited to preclude electronic eavesdrop-
ping. Which admittedly was probably not something that the
bankers and public relations flacks and Wall Street wolves who
occupied the other buildings in Midtown had to deal with.

To the general public there were few things more exciting
than counterintelligence work. A firm century of misinforma-
tion, of legend, of Rudyard Kipling stories and Ian Fleming novels, had inculcated an almost comprehensive misconception of
what the job actually entailed. Within the Bureau itself, however,
counterintelligence was far from a plum assignment—indeed,
quite the opposite. Gone was any hope of street work, gone was
the thrill of the arrest, gone was the joy of wrapping up a case,
of taking a legitimate villain off the streets. A counterintelligence
operation could last years—decades, even—and involve endless
hours sifting through paperwork and engaging in other subtle
and obscure maneuvering.

It was a life for which Kay was not overly prepared. Perhaps more than any other law enforcement agency in the world, the Bureau's mission was extraordinarily varied. With fifty-six field offices in every state of the Union and more than sixty legal attaché offices scattered throughout the rest of the world, responsible for a portfolio of tasks ranging from counterintelligence to counterterrorism to white-collar crime to public corruption, the Academy could only equip an Agent with the essential skills that would be required of them upon being assigned to a field office: a background in the legal system, self-defense and firearms training; information on the Bureau itself and on law enforcement generally. Much of what was required of any given Agent would be determined by whatever their placement was: Kay had known little about the drug subculture of Baltimore before being sent there, but after two years she had left with no small level of expertise. No doubt if she had been placed in some other office, in some other part of the country or the world, she would have developed a different skill set, one tailored to the needs of that assignment.

But still, Kay felt certain, there could be few positions within the Bureau as taxing as counterintelligence. An Agent might be focused on a specific country, in which case they needed to become familiar not only with the current political and clandestine service structure of the nation in question but also its history, culture and language if possible.

It was a far cry from what Kay had been doing in Baltimore, her nose to the concrete most days, cleaning up the streets one savage at a time. "The needs of the Bureau come first," she would remind herself when the days started to drag long. "You didn't get into this job for the thrill of it" was another one she liked to use. "It beats mining coal" was her final card to play, although some afternoons, looking through reports or decade-old State

Department I-94 forms, she began to wonder if this was actually true or if she wouldn't be better off trading in her service weapon and badge for a hard hat and a pickax.

But most of the time Kay felt like she was settling into the New York Office well enough. Being the newbie on the squad always carried with it a certain amount of rising, but at least they had dropped the Ivy bit. Here in the New York Office she was far from the only Agent who'd attended an elite college. The Bureau prided itself on evolving to deal with the threats of the moment, and in the twenty-first century that meant the need for foreign languages, computer programming, and special skill sets mandated going after the best-educated and most driven young men and women. The Baltimore Field Office had been "old-school," with hard-bitten field Agents who knew the streets and the people on them, and for gang work there was nobody better. But it was clear that counterintelligence required a different sort of mentality. After two years swilling Natty Boh with Torres and the rest of the office, it was something of a culture shock for Kay.

The other Agents in the squad were sympathetic. Sitting in the break room early one afternoon, working their way through deli sandwiches and diet soda, the chatter drifted to her background in Baltimore.

"Bit of a comedown from putting murderers into the ground, huh, Malloy?" Marshall asked. Marshall was a short African American whose career had been confined to the New York Office. Despite that, he was comfortable with the work and the city, smiling often, and free of the "sharp elbows" that so often characterized hardened New Yorkers. Kay had come to like him almost as soon as she met him, a feeling he seemed to inspire in most of the people he came in contact with.

"Put who where?" Wilson asked. Wilson was tall and thin,

serious and, to Kay's mind, at least, a bit standoffish. In the time since she had transferred to New York, this was practically their first conversation that wasn't directly work related. He was also reputed to be very good at all of the elaborate stages of cultivating an asset, and had worked hand in glove with Jeffries over the years to help build the reputation for excellence that her squad enjoyed.

"You didn't hear?" Marshall paused to wipe a bit of ranch dressing off his chin, and to build anticipation. "Agent Malloy here is a straight gunslinger. Tracked down the biggest drug kingpin in Baltimore, challenged him to a duel at high noon, shot him down in the street like a dog."

"High noon, huh?" Wilson repeated drily. "Man, things really are different in Baltimore."

"Very little of that is true," Kay said flatly. She didn't like discussing the Williams shooting and would have been happier if it weren't public knowledge, although of course that was impossible. The FBI was like any other tightly knit organization, and the gossip flew pretty quickly, especially gossip as good as hers. There might not be an Agent on the East Coast who hadn't heard the story of her going at it with Williams; certainly she had figured it was common knowledge amongst her new squad. Being one of those rare few involved in a firefight had clearly given Kay a certain amount of status within the organization, but it wasn't one she relished. If it were up to her, that horrible afternoon with Williams would be the last time she ever had to draw her service weapon off the range, and she didn't quite appreciate the flippant way in which it was being discussed.

"You and Jeffries should start a club," Marshall said sardonically.

"What do you mean?"

"You don't know? Back before they put her behind a desk,

Jeffries was a stone-cold brick Agent," Marshall said, meaning an investigator who preferred not to enter into management. "Spent most of her time working the Iron Curtain countries."

"Lot of stories seem to be circulating about our Jeffries," Kay said.

"All of them true," Wilson responded. "She can drink three pots of coffee without peeing."

"She doesn't need to pee," Marshall corrected. "She has absolute control over all her biological functions. Haven't you ever noticed that she never sweats?"

"So she's a robot?" Kay asked.

"I don't think so," Wilson said, "though it's hard to say for sure. I think it's more like the way they say Buddhist monks can lower their heart rate through sheer strength of will."

"So she's the Dalai Lama?"

"I'm pretty sure the Dalai Lama doesn't carry a gun," Wilson observed.

"I've never heard of the Dalai Lama carrying a gun," Marshall agreed.

"What did she do before working counterintelligence against the Russians?"

Marshall shrugged. "Sucked on a pacifier, I suppose. Professionally she's been doing it since before I came into the Bureau. You know she speaks all those Iron Curtain languages."

"Which ones? Polish? Czech? Ukrainian? Russian? Hungarian?"

"All of them," Marshall said, probably joking. "She speaks all of them."

"No one speaks Hungarian," Wilson insisted. "Even the Hungarians don't really speak it; it's just an elaborate con they're playing on the rest of us."

"I'll make sure to mention that next time I'm in Budapest," Marshall said. "You know she can still make possible on the gun range."

"Possible" was the highest score that one could achieve on the FBI gun range, the name itself almost a challenge, as if to say, *It's possible, but you sure as hell won't be able to do it.* Kay, who had been one of the better shots in the Baltimore Field Office, had never gotten close.

"Bullshit. Everyone knows that when they promote you from a brick Agent, they take away your service weapon and replace it with a pen."

"I came in on my lunch break and watched her put two straight clips into some unfortunate theoretical subject's septum," Wilson insisted. "So that cap gun has quite a punch. You know they've been trying to send her up the chain for years now, but she keeps rejecting it. Won't take anything that might take her out of the day-to-day running of counterintelligence. It's all she lives for," he said, which Kay thought was a pretty strong statement to be making about someone as reticent about opening up as Jeffries.

"Never been married?" Kay asked. "No significant other?"

Wilson laughed, shook his head. "Sure, she's got a significant other: Pyotr Andreev, her Russian counterpart. It's a star-crossed-lover kind of thing, *Romeo and Juliet*–style. Pulled apart by politics, only able to demonstrate affection through elaborate attempts to entrap and defeat the other."

If counterintelligence was a game, then success meant knowing your opponent. The FBI kept files on their counterparts throughout the world: personal history, education, professional background, likes and dislikes—anything that might potentially be useful, that might offer some insight into the opposition's thinking. Pyotr Andreev was another part of counterintelligence lore, an ice-cold ex-Soviet who had done more damage in his long career to the U.S. security apparatus than Hanssen and Ames combined. Unlike some of his colleagues, there was very little on file about him, hearsay and rumor more than anything else, operations he might have been involved in. The only thing that could be said of him with any certainty was that he was as good at his job as anyone on the planet, and he had a strong affection for a particularly noxious brand of cigarettes called Belomorkanal.

"So far as I know," Marshall said, "she's never been on a date. Jeffries is about the mission. I mean, we're all about the mission, but . . ."

"Jeffries is *about* the mission," Wilson finished. "Speaking of which," he said, tossing the end of his sandwich in the trash, "duty calls."

Kay stayed late that night, as she did most nights, trying to catch up on everything she needed to know in order to be an effective counterintelligence Agent. And when she left—as always—the light in Jeffries's office was still burning brightly.

14

LUIS PUSHED his pawn forward a spot, leaving his knight unprotected.

Kay pursed her lips and thought for a while.

"Didn't see that coming, did you?" Luis asked happily. Close to seventy but still spry—handsome, even—silver hair and icy blue eyes, a smile that overflowed its mouth whenever he was with his niece.

"If you're trying to rattle me, Uncle," Kay said, "you're going to have to work a bit harder."

It was late afternoon on a Sunday. Kay had met her uncle earlier that morning and they had spent several hours walking through lower Manhattan, catching up on old times, ending up in Washington Square Park to enjoy the fading sunshine and get in a few games of chess.

"How is the new job?" Luis asked, putting another packet of sugar into his takeout coffee. He had always had a passion for sugar, as he did for red meat, alcohol, pretty girls, tobacco—really, the entire suite of things from which a person finds himself in a grave before old age, or at least some of the suite. He had given up most of the more egregious vices under the watchful eye of his wife, but he still enjoyed what sins were allowed him.

"It's all right," Kay said, trying to keep her mind on the game.

"Are you doing gang work? Like back in Baltimore?"

"Not exactly," Kay said. She castled, protecting her king, leaving Luis's knight hanging.

"Counterterrorism, perhaps? Tapping the phones of various Muhammads, listening in on the Friday-evening sermons to make sure they're within the acceptable bounds of anti-Americanism?"

Kay had long grown used to Luis's old-fashioned, quasi-radical sympathies, which she assumed to be a product of his having lived through the sixties and that she knew he only half believed anyway. "That's not really how we think of it," Kay said.

"It *is* counterterrorism, then?"

"No," Kay said, taking the knight.

Luis laughed and moved a rook to threaten her queen. "White-collar crime? Knocking down the next Madoff before he can cheat some poor old woman out of her last billion?"

"Not white-collar crime, thank God."

"I can only assume that your reticence to answer me is because they've taken to giving you the cloak-and-dagger."

"You know that I can't tell you, Uncle Luis," Kay said.

Luis smiled, reached out to take Kay's knight with a bishop. "You'll need to learn to lie better if you're going to work intelligence."

"The FBI does counterintelligence, Uncle. Just as a point of fact," Kay said, taking Luis's knight.

"I've never been entirely clear on the distinction between the two."

Which was understandable. In theory, it was Kay's job to defend America from infiltration and compromise by the intelligence organs of foreign governments, to act as a shield against potential malfeasance. In practice, doing so required the Bureau to adopt many of the tactics of its enemies: covertly gathering intelligence, actively recruiting informants from foreign governments and rival intelligence agencies. "We're the good guys," Kay explained half jokingly.

"I'll try and keep that in mind," Luis said.

"I saw Auntie last weekend," Kay said, shifting the conversation abruptly and without preamble.

"I see her every day."

"And a lucky man you are."

"Absolutely."

"Anyway, she told me something that I didn't know about Mom and Dad's . . . about what happened to Mom and Dad."

"Which was?"

"She said that after their funeral a couple of FBI Agents came by the house, offered their condolences and asked some questions about Dad's work. Do you remember anything like that?"

Luis pursed his lips, as if hyperfocused on the game. "I suppose, now that you mention it," he said, holding his hand over one of his pieces, then bringing it swiftly back to his side. Luis had raised her to play what was called "touch-move" chess, tournament-style, meaning that if you put a finger on a piece you had to move it. It had once made her cry uncontrollably in Washington Square Park at the tender age of eleven, but she had to admit that in the long run it had helped sharpen her focus.

"That didn't seem odd to you?"

"Not really," Luis grumbled, finally conceding to the inevitable and trading his rook for a bishop. "Maybe you didn't appreciate this, being so young, but your father had a great deal of status within his field. His death was in the *Times*, the *Post* . . . I suppose the FBI were just being thorough."

Kay had realized that, actually, indeed it was one of the things that, even as a child, she had associated most with her father: that he was, in some way that a ten-year-old girl could express only imperfectly, a good man, an important man, an important man who did good. But neither had he been a State Department Foreign Service Officer, and Kay still could not quite understand why the Bureau would have such an interest in him. Their resources were, God knew, far from unlimited, and for that matter the investigation into his murder in a foreign country would have fallen outside of their purview. "That's it, then? Just being thorough?" Kay asked, moving a piece.

"Remind me, Kay, which one of us is in the Federal Bureau of Investigation. I would think you would be better equipped to determine what interest the FBI had in the death of your parents than I would."

Which made sense as far as it went, but in fact part of being an Agent for the Federal Bureau of Investigation was that you didn't get to use the powers of your office for petty personal reasons; didn't get to pull the bank records of disliked neighbors or send out a SWAT team to torment old boyfriends. It was a clear breach of policy for her to be snooping into an old case, and there was no reason Kay could think of that her counterintelligence work would overlap with a twenty-year-old murder investigation.

"And how are your finances?" Luis asked.

"I didn't get into this business for the money," Kay said simply. In fact, wealth had never been a particular motivator for Kay—a legacy, she assumed, of her parents, both of whom had given up lucrative opportunities to work in the far less remunerative field of international development. As a federal employee, Kay was paid at a GS-13 rate, far less than some of her friends working in law or finance, but more than enough for her own needs.

"I've been . . . doing some thinking," Luis said, suddenly red-faced. "Perhaps your aunt and I could . . . help you out a bit. Just in these early years. You know we have enough," he said quickly. "It wouldn't be any trouble for us. We would be glad to do it, I mean."

Kay's hand hovered around her queen. Happy images flooded through her mind of renting an apartment in a part of town near where she worked, of avoiding an hour-long commute, of being able to order takeout without double-checking her bank account. She savored them for a long moment, knowing the entire time that they were only fancy. Aunt Justyna and Uncle Luis had done enough for her as a child—more than enough; indeed, she knew she owed them a debt she could never repay. There was no point in adding to it.

"That's very kind of you, Uncle Luis," she said, moving her queen to the back rank. "But I couldn't possibly accept. Incidentally, it's mate in three."

Luis laughed, looked down at the board and began to set up the pieces for another game.

15

H IGHLAND PARK at eleven thirty in the evening would
not have been Kay's first choice to meet a potential
recruit. It was secluded enough, in a distant corner of
not-quite-gentrified Brooklyn, close to an hour on the subway
from Manhattan, nearly as long by cab. Compared to Central
Park's enormity, or even Prospect Park's greenery, it was not very
large, a bare sliver of shrubbery interrupting the city's concrete
edifices. The area surrounding it was middle- and lower-middle-
class, a far cry from the slums Kay had grown used to during her
time in Baltimore, but equally distant from the tourist-thronged
neighborhoods of lower Manhattan.

Not, of course, that anyone had asked her. A bare month
with the squad, and so far mostly she had been trusted with
nothing more than routine work, most of her daily efforts going
towards digesting the immense, the seemingly infinite amount
of information required to bring her up to speed as a counterintelligence Agent. Likely she wouldn't have been tapped for this
duty, either, except that one of the other members of the squad
had been sick with the stomach flu.

"We need you for something, Kay," Marshall informed her
earlier that afternoon, walking briskly out of Jeffries's office after
a long chat. Marshall had a reputation, like everyone else in Jef-

fries's squad, for quiet excellence, for a cool and distinguished competence that did not draw attention to itself. He was also considered, within the office, to be one of the best handlers of assets—next to Jeffries herself, of course, although her position generally kept her out of the nitty-gritty of casework. Kay could see why Marshall was so highly regarded; he was amiable and good-natured but also gave the impression of a person who watched you carefully and closely, and remembered what he had seen.

"Of course," Kay said, there being nothing else to say. "What for?"

"I'm going to be meeting with a developmental recruit tonight, and we need you to fill in on the surveillance."

Not much information to go on there, and Kay knew that none would be forthcoming. A recruitment could take place over the course of weeks or months or even years, the process slow and torturous, like reeling in an oversized fish. Sometimes many meetings were required to convince a target of the wisdom of assisting the FBI with their operations. It took a deft hand with the right combination of stick and carrot to cultivate a recruitment in place, or RIP, the standard Bureau term for a double agent.

It also took a team of professionals assisting that deft hand. Kay and Wilson and the rest of the squad that had been assigned to assist Marshall had spent the hours beforehand prepping, in thorough detail, every aspect of the meeting: where in the park the meeting would take place and where the nearest exits were; where the members of the surveillance team would set up; and even the location of the nearest hospital in case something went terribly and unexpectedly wrong. One thing that was not discussed, for reasons of operational security, was the identity of the asset himself. It was not mentioned, and Kay did not ask.

Kay's part in the matter was a simple one, or seemingly simple. She and Wilson were posted in an unmarked car just outside of the main exit, tasked with keeping their eyes open, making sure that no member of the opposition had cottoned to their operation and was following close behind. Far from riveting, but Kay was enjoying herself all the same. It was the first time since joining the counterintelligence squad that she was out in the field. And for all that she often felt herself a step behind her colleagues, she felt more than confident in her surveillance skills, courtesy of her time in Baltimore.

And perhaps that was what alerted her to them: the long hours spent in grimy surroundings observing Rashid Williams and men like Rashid Williams. It was a warm September evening, still gripped tightly in an Indian summer, but the two boys lounging by the entrance of the park had their hoodies pulled up all the same, obscuring their faces, obscuring everything but two pairs of grim, voracious-seeming eyes. They shared a smoke, passing it back and forth between them warily, staring at the night and the things hidden within it.

"Anything about that seem strange to you?" Kay asked.

Wilson had worked counterintelligence for going on twenty years: a good Agent and a good team member. His attention was occupied on the interior of the park, on Marshall sitting on a wooden bench, patiently waiting for his contact to show up. "How so?"

Kay smiled grimly. "You've been working this so long, you can't smell regular old crime when you get a whiff of it? That's their second cigarette," Kay explained, "and if you had two anyway, why bother to share? Unless you want an excuse to stay where you are." Kay rolled down the window and inhaled deeply of the night air. "That ain't just tobacco, either."

"What are you getting at?" Wilson asked, turning to stare

at Kay full on. "I don't know how they do it in Baltimore, but here in the big leagues we don't get so worried about a couple of kids smoking a dime bag outside of a public park, leastways not enough to interrupt an ongoing operation."

"In Baltimore we don't get out of bed for anything less than a fresh corpse sitting on a half ton of heroin," she said, "but since we're already out here I might as well let you know that *those* two gentlemen"—she pointed at the men, who had just thrown aside their joint—"are about to try and rob *that* gentleman"—pointing now towards Marshall.

Wilson looked for a long time at the two potential trouble-makers, cursed, then leaned into his walkie-talkie. "Touissant, you there?"

Touissant was posted in a copse of trees close to where the meet was to take place. Kay could not see him, of course—the purpose of the dark clothes and the lack of movement—but he was there. "Yup."

"You clock those two coming in from the east entrance?"

Brief pause. "I do now."

"Malloy thinks they're trouble."

"I think she's right," he said, and a spare second later Kay saw him move out from his hiding spot: a big man, the largest in the squad, white teeth smiling but not friendly. After he took a few steps into the park itself, the two potential muggers looked at him, looked at each other, then turned and backtracked the way they had come. Touissant returned to his position, and a few minutes later their target, or so Kay assumed, walked swiftly from the direction of the subway and towards his meeting with Marshall.

"That was sharp, Malloy," Wilson said, not quite grudgingly.

Kay bit back a smile and returned to inspecting the night. Crisis averted.

16

G ENERALLY SPEAKING, Tom had found, it was not a very difficult thing to take apart a person's life: it was like pulling apart a warm roll at a nice restaurant.

They gave you a target; some background information, date of birth, education, marital status, a few pictures taken from a distance or, more recently, scraped off of Facebook. If it was possible, Tom liked to do the first bit of surveillance himself; of course, he had any number of underlings on his payroll but he had always found it useful to begin the operation on his own, rather than have his initial understanding of the target filtered through another person's eyes. After two decades in the business Tom had developed a sort of sixth sense for sin: he could sit down with someone for five or ten minutes, watch them out of the corner of his eye, ask them a few friendly questions, excuse himself and tell you with virtual assurance about drink, drugs, gambling debts, a pretty girl that his wife did not know about, perhaps a pretty boy.

Tom scratched at the garbled fat of his buttocks through his jeans, took a nip of vodka against the cold, wedged himself into his car seat. His size was the only thing that had ever kept him from being an absolutely first-class surveillance man. He had everything else required: cold, discerning eyes, a memory like a steel trap, the ability to ignore boredom, to concentrate for end-less hours narrowly on one particular point or individual. But he could do nothing about his size, and people tended to remember a six-foot-three completely bald man sitting on a bench across from their apartment. On the other hand, his size had been an advantage on those rare though not unheard-of occasions when he was called upon to do more than watch. He was over forty now, and some of his muscle had turned to fat—but not all of it. There had been a time when he had a reputation as a bruiser, and he still suspected, if it was necessary, he could remember which end of the gun to point.

His real name was Lev Telstei, although it had been a very long time since anyone had called him that. Sometimes late at night, alone in his bedroom as the clock face turned round its usual path, he would say it softly to himself—"Lev Telstei, Lev Telstei, Lev Telstei"—but never very loudly, never above a whis-per. It had a strange ring to it these days, like a lyric from an all-but-forgotten song.

Most of Tom's life was no different from that of any other American citizen. He owned a small store near Brighton Beach, a step up from a bodega, his pride insisted, although grim-eyed honesty admitted it was not a very large one. Still, it did not run itself, and at any given moment most of Tom's time was dedi-cated to all the many tasks required to keep his cover business operating: payroll and inventory, that sort of thing. Over the years he had acquired a trustworthy enough staff, but still, it was a rare day that did not see him behind the counter for at least a few hours, making sure things were running properly. His wife had died some years back, an Illegal like himself, the two of them set up with each other shortly before being shipped out to New York. It was more of a business arrangement than a love affair, but it was an amicable one, at least. He had been in a state of modest despair for some six months after her death, and still missed her sometimes, though faintly and without any great passion. Tom was an unsentimental sort, as much a part of his personality as it was a skill developed over long years working at his real job.

There were innumerable nuances and subtleties to the spy business, but most nations used the same rough structure. Within their embassies were embedded legal resident spies. These individuals were entitled to the same protection as other diplomats, and could not be prosecuted but only expelled back to their country. Although the FBI worked diligently to ascertain the identities of these individuals, and generally succeeded, they were still useful in coordinating or assisting in operations.

Beneath this network were a select group called, simply, "Illegals." Unknown, or at least undeclared, to their host country, they went about their business creating fictitious lives, as bartenders and cabdrivers, as businessmen and oil magnates, as housewives and hookers. For years and sometimes decades they burrowed into their cover stories, appearing to any outside observer to be no different from your next-door neighbor. All the while, of course, they were intimately involved in intelligence operations, trying to recruit potential targets or running surveillance. In practice, every side had an incentive to keep their people alive, and these days should an Illegal get arrested he was most likely to be swapped for a counterpart, the modern equivalent of a prisoner exchange. But not always: in the worst-case scenario an Illegal with his cover blown would find himself living out the rest of his life in a federal penitentiary.

Beneath even these Illegals were individuals cultivated to support them: a ring of small-time criminals, thugs, drug dealers, prostitutes and general lowlifes whom Tom had quietly and faithfully assembled during his nearly two decades in New York.

A few of the brighter and more senior ones might have had some idea that there was more to Tom than his cover as a minor criminal and fixer, although none could have pointed to any evidence of his being an SVR Illegal, and of course remained blissfully unaware of the existence of his superiors. Compartmentalization, after all, was one of the most critical requirements of the trade. No person should ever know anything about any other, or about any other operation with which he or she is not directly related. To do otherwise was to risk destroying the entire chain because of one weak link.

Tom sighed and scratched himself again and went to light a cigarette, remembering only after he had checked both of his front pockets that he had given up smoking six months earlier and made do with a stick of gum that he chewed through a snarl.

Tom had been born in Odessa back when it was still part of the Soviet Union and was trained by the KGB in all the different aspects of intelligence work: how to set up a network, how to recruit and train other agents, how to pass information without alerting U.S. intelligence, how to navigate the dangerous and dimly lit world of international espionage. And finally, how to kill: with a rifle or a pistol, with poison, with a length of twine or a piece of pipe or a bit of sharpened metal or his oversized hands.

When he had first stepped off the plane almost twenty years earlier he had thought himself properly trained to accomplish anything that would be required of him, and had soon realized how wrong he was. It had been Pyotr Andreev who had given him the master class in spycraft; who had made him, if Tom said so himself, as good at his job as anyone on earth; who had taught him to blend in seamlessly with American society, to operate inside it like a fish in water. To set up an organization of people you could control but must never trust; to use that organization to surround a target; to bend that person into the direction you required them to bend.

Yes, more than anything else, Pyotr had taught Tom to corrupt, to pervert—but there was only so much even a master like Tom could do with someone as morally blameless, not to say dull, as Kay Malloy. She went to work, she went home, she went back to work. Sometimes she met a friend for dinner. That was about as exciting as it got. These idealistic types, these young crusaders, they could be tough. Driven by work or advancement, lacking that happy hedonism that, generally speaking, made Tom's job so easy. A month now his men had been tailing her, searching quietly for some vulnerability to seize on, some way into her life. She did not do drugs; she did not gamble. She did not drink to excess—at least, she did not drink in such a fashion that made her act foolishly. She had not yet taken a man home to her bed—not that that alone would help them much in these days of frivolity. But at least it would have been something, some tangible trace of humanity to lock onto. Alas for both of them, he secretly thought, Kay's life consisted of work, sleep and an occasional visit to an aged relative.

Well, they were not always easy, were they? If they were all easy, then anyone could do Tom's job, and then Pyotr would not value him so highly. It was a source of pride for Tom, he could quietly admit to himself but no one else, that a man like Pyotr saw fit to leave large aspects of his operations in Tom's hands. Within the SVR, Pyotr was a figure of dark legend, his name whispered rather than spoken aloud. Most often he was referred to by one of his nicknames, the "gray man" or the "gray suit," both meant to indicate a certain vagueness, as if he could be seen only from the corner of your eye or in twilight. He was there but he was not there. He was the guy behind the guy behind the guy.

The *chop-chop-chop* of an engine snapped Tom out of his reverie, and a moment later a motorcycle made its way noisily into a parking spot across the street. A man got off it—unhelmeted, Tom noted casually, his eye for transgression as keen as ever. He had long hair and a handsome face and a worn leather jacket. He hooked his fingers into his pockets and strutted into a neighboring bar, and Tom did not think he was imagining the drunken roll to his gait.

Tom smiled. It was easy to break a person by their vices, but it was very nearly as easy to break them by their virtues. Kay Malloy was not a drunkard, not a gambling addict, not corrupt, not promiscuous or a fool. But she was a loyal sister, and in the end that would be enough.

17

KYRA MARTIN stood five foot seven, with dark hair and rather striking eyes. An academic, having received a doctorate in conflict management from an Ivy League university two years earlier, and she dressed like one: Her clothes were more conservative than stunning, but what could be expected of a young woman in an entry-level position at one of the innumerable think tanks that dotted the city? It was not as if she were a fashion consultant or arm candy for some Wall Street banker. No, perhaps her clothes left something to be desired, but the body beneath it was far from homely, and her lips were a bright and vivid red.

"Not bad for a woman that doesn't exist," Kay said, checking herself one final time in the mirror. Walking to the door, Kay reached for her regular purse, caught herself with a quick and severe rebuke, then grabbed the one hanging next to it. Inside were tissues, lipstick, a few sticks of chewing gum and a Florida driver's license and credit card with her fake name emblazoned on the front. Outside, she managed to flag a passing cab, told him the address—a venue on the Upper East Side—and settled into her seat.

Deep-cover FBI Agents were required to undergo elaborate training before being certified to enter the program, but more casual light cover, of the sort that would hold up to a brief investigation but not more than that, could be entered into by any Agent. It was not the sort of thing that had come up much when she was working violent crime: a young, pretty woman of her particular complexion would not have been very effective as a mole in the drug enterprises that blanketed the city of Baltimore. Here in counterintelligence, however, Kay's background and looks fit neatly into a far wider range of scenarios.

At least, that was the reason that Jeffries had given her the day before when she had explained the situation. "Tomorrow morning the Institute for the Advancement of Near East Relations will be having a talk, with drinks to follow. We'd like you to attend. We'll give you cover as an academic, get you an RSVP—not that you'll need one: these things aren't exactly velvet-rope events; most of the people going are there because they can't get out of it. Get a lay of the land," Jeffries said vaguely. "See if there's anyone worth talking to, and talk to them, and remember what they say."

Kay had wondered if there was more to it but knew better than to ask: Jeffries spent words like a miser does pennies, each weighed and measured and carefully chosen. If she elected to leave Kay's assignment vague, that was a deliberate decision. Asking for clarification would only serve to agitate her superior and leave Kay no more knowledgeable.

Kay stepped onto the sidewalk half an hour after she had gotten into the cab, adjusted the hemline of her dress and walked towards the entrance with what she hoped was confidence. The security guard—really more of an usher—scanned his list for the name Kay offered. There was no reason to be nervous, Kay told herself: surely her credentials could pass such basic scrutiny, and even if there was some mix-up, she could just walk off huffily. But she was nervous, and had to work to keep it off her face, and didn't let go of it until the guard nodded and waved her inside and even then not entirely.

She found a seat in the back and sat quietly for a few minutes before the lights dimmed and the panelists came onstage. The next hour and a half passed by slowly. The discussion was, if not painfully dull, then far from memorable: standard boilerplate about the importance of continued good relations between Russia and the United States. Few members of the audience seemed any more interested; there were lots of dulled eyes and slack mouths. The applause afterward was cordial but nothing more, and then the assembled rose and filtered out through the foyer and into an adjoining bar for the reception.

Kay got a drink at the bar and scanned the assemblage: intellectuals and would-be experts engaged in animated conversation, a hard core of diplomats and consulate functionaries and political players discussing business quietly. From one corner Kay heard the loud strands of harsh Slavic speech, sipped her wine and began to pay closer attention, her limited grasp of Russian insufficient to give her much insight into the conversation beyond that it was taking place. It was a small group, several men in not-quite-nice suits drinking slightly more vodka than the moment strictly required, and an attractive middle-aged woman with a well-worn look of boredom. Kay spent some time trying to remember how she recognized the man sitting next to her. After she remembered, she finished her glass of wine, gathered up her courage and went to make a new friend.

"*Privet,*" Kay said to the woman with what she hoped was ingratiating half awkwardness.

"*Dobry vecher,*" the woman said, smiling sweetly to assuage Kay's discomfort.

"*Mogu li ya sidet?*" Kay asked, with a slightly more tortured accent than she was capable of.

The woman waved at the vacant seat in offer and Kay dropped down beside her. "Where did you learn Russian?" she asked.

"I think 'learned' would be far too strong," Kay said. "I took some classes back in school, but . . ." She shrugged. "A lot of water under the bridge since then."

The woman smiled. "For you less than me. I'm Olga Stonavich."

"Kyra. A pleasure to meet you." Only the first half a lie. "You don't mind, do you? I don't really know anyone here. I suppose I feel a bit out of place."

All of which was true, actually, which was probably why Olga seemed to believe it. "Don't worry, that will wear off soon, and then you'll just be left with the mind-numbing tediousness of the evening." Kay laughed and Olga laughed also. "What are you doing here, exactly?" she asked.

"I'm part of the Fieldings Insitute," Kay said. "Just joined, actually. Moved up here from Virginia two months back. Still trying to get my sea legs."

"Don't feel bad, darling," Olga said. "I've been here four years and sometimes I still have no idea what's going on."

"And yourself? What brings you out this evening?"

Olga tilted her head at the man who had been sitting next to her earlier, now deep in conversation at the other end of the room. "Boris works at the consulate," she said. "And our attendance is . . . strongly encouraged at all of these functions."

"How lovely for you," Kay said.

Olga laughed again and shrugged.

The conversation continued easily, comfortably. After that initial bit of dishonesty, and a few sentences of deceit that Kay found rolled off her tongue rather more smoothly than she might have expected, there was little need for falsehood. Olga, like most people on earth, enjoyed talking about herself, and Kay made sure to keep the conversation moving in that direction. Nothing overt, nothing obvious, nothing interrogatory; just the casual empathy of one person trying to learn about another person, her life and history and habits and problems. Soon Olga's glass was empty, and soon after, Kay filled it and got one of her own. After forty minutes they were laughing and chatting like old friends, and Kay found that she was enjoying herself.

"How strange to have to move across the world," Kay said, "and to bring your entire family with you! It must be difficult."

Olga shrugged. "I knew it was a possibility when I married Boris. And it could be worse, far worse. You don't have much choice in where you get posted: I have friends that are whiling away their hours in third-world hellholes who would cut off a finger to spend a winter here in New York!"

"And your children?"

"They love it," Olga said, smiling. "Children take easiest to new environments, new settings. Our eldest, Vladimir, never wants to go back." The smile faded from her face, as if she had remembered something unpleasant.

If Kay were Kay and not Kyra, she would have ignored Olga's change in demeanor, recognizing it as one of those short moments of unhappiness that sometimes eclipse a good mood and are best left unremarked on. Instead she said, "Is something wrong?"

Perhaps it was the vodka, perhaps it was Kay's false good humor. Whatever it was, Olga found herself continuing. "Nothing, really. My husband's posting ends this summer; we'll all be traveling back to Moscow. Vlad is a senior; we were hoping that we could stick around long enough to see him into an American college. He's a very bright boy," Olga assured her, as if Kay might think otherwise. "But he's had some . . . learning problems.

They're not very well equipped to handle that sort of thing back home. We had very much hoped that Boris's posting might be extended but it seems unlikely now that it will happen."

"How unfortunate," Kay said, her face a mask of sympathy, consciously mimicking Olga's own. "There is no chance for him?"

"There doesn't seem much of one," Olga said. "It would be rather a difficult thing to acquire a visa for him."

"Of course, of course," Kay said, scribbling furiously in her mental notebook. "Keep up hope!" she said, patting Olga on the shoulder. "The world is a strange place, and fate sometimes lays unexpected plans."

18

K AY WAS in the office early, very early, earlier than usual, with a large cup of coffee for herself, two dozen do- nuts for the rest of the squad, and a minor intelligence coup for the Federal Bureau of Investigation writ large. She was smiling.

Jeffries was next, businesslike as ever. She greeted Kay and went swiftly into her office. Kay waited outside for a few mo- ments, feeling a curious sense of anticipation, childlike, as if she were back in school, about to complete an oral exam. She steeled herself and bit back her grin and got up and knocked on Jeffries's open door. "Do you have a moment?"

"Of course, Kay," Jeffries said, gesturing to an empty seat. "I assume you want to discuss last night's business."

"Exactly," Kay said, taking the chair.

"Everything went smoothly?"

"There were no problems with my cover. I get the sense that these panel discussions are not exactly high-security events. They seemed happy to have someone to fill the auditorium."

"I think you're probably not far wrong. And you? Did you enjoy yourself?"

" 'Enjoy' might be a bit strong. I believe that it proved . . . a valuable use of my time."

"How so?"

"Olga Stonavich and her husband, Boris, are worried about their eldest son, Vlad: a bright young man, apparently, though he has had some struggles in school. Olga does not feel that the Russian educational system will do much to nurture his particular cocktail of ability and would very much like to find some way that he could matriculate to an American university."

Jeffries didn't smile but for a moment it looked like she might. "Very clever, Agent Malloy."

"That's why you sent me, isn't it? To see whether I could sniff out anything new on Boris?"

"In part," Jeffries admitted. "Of course, anything which might further our objective with Boris is much appreciated. But, more than that, I wanted to see how you'd do in a more polished environment than you might have gotten used to in Baltimore."

"It was a test, then?"

Jeffries didn't answer, not for a long time, just stared at Kay with her arid gray eyes. "Do you like working in counterintelligence, Agent Malloy?"

Kay swallowed nervously, wondering if she had come on too strong, if her enthusiasm to present her findings had been misplaced. "I'm not sure I understand the question."

"It's not a complicated one. There's no hidden layer to it. I'm asking you if you enjoy coming to work in the morning. If you're happy being a member of the squad."

"If there's some problem with my work," Kay said, sitting up straighter in her chair, bracing for criticism, "I'll do my best to fix it."

"Quite the opposite, in fact. Yesterday evening was a test, as was your surveillance work the other week, and you acquitted yourself well in both. In six months or a year I believe you could be as good at counterintelligence as you ever were at violent crime and gangs—assuming, of course, that this is what you want. I'm well aware of the reputation that counterintelligence has within the Bureau, Kay, and I can even understand why. What we do doesn't end in a perp walk, doesn't end with drugs and money and a few AK-47s on a table for the evening news. It's a game in which the field, the players, even the outcome, never becomes entirely clear. You pit your skills against an opponent half a planet away, men and women you will never see or know, silently going about the business of corrupting our country. Your triumphs will go quietly unreported, unknown to anyone but a handful of brass inside the Bureau. Your failures will gain infamy. It is an exhausting and thankless task whose only saving grace is that it is absolutely necessary. My program is as good as it is because everyone here wants to be on it, understands its importance. Because they put the mission ahead of everything else, ahead of career advancement and often their personal life. Because they keep the good of the Bureau, and the country, front and center at all times."

It was far and away the longest speech that Kay had ever heard Jeffries give, and when it ended abruptly Kay was not sure what to say.

"Take some time and think it over," Jeffries said quietly. "I think that you could be good at it. I think you could be very good. But that's a choice you have to make on your own." Jeffries set aside her cup of coffee and turned towards one of the folders sitting on her desk. After a belated movement Kay realized that she had just been dismissed, and she stood and left awkwardly.

It was only twenty minutes before the start of the working day, but the outside office was already filled, the members of the counterintelligence squad at their desks, munching on the snacks

Kay had brought in, sipping coffee, sifting through information on their computers, continuing the tasks they had set aside the day before—set aside but not forgotten. After a long moment sitting at her desk, running through Jeffries's unexpected challenge, Kay logged on and got to joining them.

19

SIX GIRLS raised pink-colored cocktails in the air to match Kay's—more people than she would have imagined celebrating the anniversary of her birth into this benighted world, particularly as this was an occasion to which Kay herself did not attach any great importance. She laughed and sipped her drink through a smile that was about half genuine.

It was Kay's first night out in a month, and she wouldn't have had any trouble extending her isolationist streak, and quite frankly would have been fine spending her twenty-ninth birthday at home catching up on work. But Alice had been her friend since they were gawky, acne-ridden middle-schoolers sneaking cigarettes in the bathroom of their expensive prep school, and she had an app on her phone that told her anytime anyone was having a birthday. So she had called Kay the week before and all but demanded that she come out for a few congratulatory drinks, and Kay found herself unable to say no.

Which was what they were doing then, in a portion of Manhattan where a slice of pizza cost eight dollars and an alcoholic drink a grim fifteen. The last time Kay had been out celebrating something, it was her transfer out of Baltimore, and she could not imagine two less similar bars than Monaghan's, with its chipped tables and surly staff and cheap booze, and the half club that she was now occupying, which looked like someone's idea of a bondage dungeon: dim lighting and very loud music and a dance floor packed with what seemed exclusively lingerie models. For that matter she did not see many clear points of comparison between her Baltimore colleagues, hardened professionals, and her old friends, smiling, bright-eyed examples of bourgeois youth.

"Old friends" might be stretching the point a bit, Kay had to admit. They weren't bad. It wasn't their fault. Fair enough, Sandra's hemline would have been risqué had she been a dancer in the Moulin Rouge, and Anna had, since they had seen each other frequently back in high school, picked up the unfortunate habit of beginning every single sentence with the word "I." But that was about the worst you could say about any of them, and in the grand scheme of things these were far from cardinal sins.

No, Kay could admit it: the problem wasn't her sort-of friends, who were basically good-humored and who seemed to sincerely wish her well. It was Kay herself. It was Kay having just endured a week of digging through strangers' trash, trying to separate minor errors from outright evil, a week that seemed uncannily like the week before, and the week before that, and would almost certainly seem like next week as well. It had left her feeling rather nasty about the world and the species of bipeds that had come to rule it.

It was not an easy thing to turn off. The guy at the bar who had offered to buy her a drink, tall and dark and handsome and obviously, *obviously* married, rubbing the naked skin of his ring finger as if it were a good luck charm. In the back corner two girls were in the midst of some sort of a drug deal, probably ecstasy, although Kay wasn't certain; and, OK, it wasn't like she was going to run over and bust them, but for Christ's sake maybe show a little bit of discretion.

No, once you stepped into that labyrinth of mirrors, it became hard to leave it, hard to know if you'd left it. That fellow sitting quietly at the counter, nursing a vodka—had she seen him before, maybe somewhere in her neighborhood? And was he looking at her a bit too frequently, too frequently and too intently?

"Kay? Kay? Are you even listening?" Alice asked.

Kay turned swiftly from her paranoia to the woman who had been her best friend through much of the formative portion of her life. "Sorry, Alice—I'm a little bit distracted."

"I asked why you didn't invite any of your coworkers."

Kay stifled a laugh at the image of Jeffries out with the group of them, Jeffries having a casual drink, Jeffries flirting with someone at the bar, Jeffries relaxing her raptor eyes for a single solitary second. Marshall and Wilson were fine—she'd started to enjoy their company if not quite the way she had with Torres—but they had families to go home to, and had worked through as long a week as Kay had, or nearly, and she hadn't supposed any of them would be inclined to get drunk on sugary cocktails.

Kay shook her head. "I've got everyone I want right here!" she said, feigning an enthusiasm she didn't actually feel.

"Really, sister?" a voice from behind her asked. "You can't think of anyone you'd like to see?"

Alice gave that high-pitched squeal, and then she was up from her chair and taking Kay's brother in an embrace that some might have thought platonic, except that she had one hand on his ass and the kiss she gave him crossed over that undefinable boundary between cheek and neck. Alice had been carrying a torch for Kay's brother for the better part of twenty years, and Christopher's manifest disinterest as well as his lack of success since leaving high school had done nothing to extinguish it.

Christopher handled it with that grace that had always come naturally to him, that charm that was at once his most prized asset and the seed of his downfall, then spread it amongst the rest of Kay's friends, winning converts left and right. Alice and Sandra would be ready to kill each other by the end of the evening in an attempt to get her brother's attention. After all these years they still didn't understand that he couldn't keep himself focused on any one thing for any length of time.

But damn if he didn't look good in his tight jeans and black leather jacket and with his eyes that seemed not to give a damn about anything. And he was carrying a bright pink teddy bear which was the size of an overweight adolescent.

"What are you doing with that?" Kay asked.

"I went to Coney Island today," he said.

"One of the upsides of not having a real job."

"Absolutely. Anyway, I won it with my shooting ability."

"And what would I use that pink bear for, Christopher?"

"You could take it somewhere and use it for target practice."

Kay laughed and grabbed Christopher and pulled him into a hug, and he laughed and returned it.

"What the hell is wrong with you girls?" Christopher said, pushing her aside for the moment. "An hour into her birthday and my sister is still sober? No one's going to call you in to investigate a bank heist tonight, Kay," he said, signaling to the bartender, who brought over two shots of whiskey. "Tonight you're just one more sinner in a world full of them. So enjoy yourself."

"That's not my strong suit."

Christopher raised his glass. "Fear not, dear sister: your wiser elder brother is here to teach you."

Kay laughed and took the shot.

Christopher was a source of never-ending concern for Kay; kept her up long after her bedtime; wore lines into her face and into her heart. He could not be trusted to show up for interviews on time, to help her move, to act appropriately at family gatherings. His debts had just about risen into the five-figure range. He had more than a casual relationship with narcotics. He was selfish and reckless and foolish . . . but damn if he wasn't good for a laugh.

20

J EFFRIES CALLED Kay into her office one early fall afternoon, asked her to take a seat, then looked at her for a long while without saying anything. Kay knew better than to break the silence: Jeffries did not waste time with banter. She would speak when she was ready to, and not before.

"You've been up here several months now, Agent Malloy," she began finally.

It wasn't quite a question, but Kay answered anyway. "Yes, ma'am." Kay had fallen into a comfortable groove since her debriefing with Jeffries a month earlier. Her days were busy but productive, and she had started to feel she had transitioned out of her breaking-in period and was no longer figuring out the ropes so much as actively contributing to ongoing investigations. She had a better appreciation for the twilight world of counterintelligence, the feints and the trickery, the endless hidden motivations.

"How are you feeling about it?"

How to answer that question without sounding incompetent or immodest? "I'm doing my very best," Kay said, matching her superior's formality.

Jeffries grunted and looked down at the file on her desk.

"I suppose you've already figured that there's something in the offing," she said.

That morning Kay had spent several hours taking a polygraph test, being asked innumerable questions about her work, the polygrapher in charge of giving it tracking her heartbeat, pulse and respiration to make sure that she wasn't offering any false answers. The polygraph was a key tool in the counterintelligence arsenal, useful in ferreting out falsehoods. But it was a long way from perfect, which was part of the reason its results were not considered valid in the U.S. legal system or those of most Western countries. It could offer false positives, suggesting dishonesty where there actually was none. More important, it could be beaten, especially by those who had been trained to do so. The number of double agents who had managed to survive its stress without breaking was not insignificant. Indeed, the polygraph was something of a double-edged sword: it caught the vast majority of people who attempted to lie their way through it, but those who escaped the net were inevitably the most devious and dangerous and showed no deception on their polygraphs. Aldrich Ames, the CIA Case Officer who had been doubled by the KGB during the 1980s and remained undetected for years, had passed a polygraph test, laughing and lying through his teeth.

Although how exactly he had done so, Kay could not possibly say: she spent the entire test feeling nervous as all hell, and she hadn't even done anything. But it ended eventually with the polygrapher thanking her for her time and shuffling her out, and Kay assumed that she had done all right, otherwise she wouldn't be having this conversation with Jeffries.

"I had a hint of it," Kay said, trying unsuccessfully to match Jeffries's deadpan demeanor.

"HQ has assigned us a major case," Jeffries said simply.

Kay couldn't think of anything worth adding, so she remained silent.

"Looking into the identity of a possible CIA mole who's been wreaking havoc with their Russian spy networks." Jeffries said it like she was reciting a shopping list or informing Kay about some trivial bit of protocol, but to Kay it sounded enormously exciting. "I've been asked to put together a group of Agents with unimpeachable records and a hunger for the mission. I think you'd be a good addition to the squad. It'll be a full-time assignment. We'll have to take you off all of your current investigations. And the work won't be easy, and it might not get wrapped up anytime soon." There was a long and, to Kay's mind, rather dramatic pause while Jeffries stared out the window at the city below, drumming her fingers aimlessly on her desk. Just at the point when Kay thought she was going to burst from the tension, Jeffries turned back to her and said, "That is, if you think you're ready for it."

It was not a rhetorical question. A challenge was being put in front of her; it was up to Kay to decide if she would accept it. What if she decided she wasn't ready? Would she have a chance to return to criminal investigations, work she knew herself to be skilled at, and that she had enjoyed?

The mission came first: if this was what was required of her, then Kay would not back down now. "I believe I am," Kay said.

Jeffries nodded. "Welcome to Black Bear, Agent Malloy," she said. "Our first meeting is Monday morning down in Washington. Come ready to work."

21

THE FIRST meeting of the Black Bear investigation began at nine thirty sharp on a rainy autumn Monday in an unattractive side office in FBIHQ. In addition to Kay, Jeffries had selected Marshall and Wilson as part of her team of specialists, as well as a half dozen other Agents with whom Kay was less familiar but whose competence she had no reason to doubt. They had arranged themselves—perhaps deliberately, perhaps not—along one end of a long conference table. At the other sat two members of their sister agency, looking neat and serious and not altogether friendly.

One of them was Kay's age or a bit older, with skin the color of cocoa, handsome in an unassuming way, neatly but not expensively dressed. He had eyes of indeterminate hue and wore a soft smile like he knew something that you most likely did not. He had introduced himself as Andrew when she had walked in, giving each member of the team a friendly handshake, then sat back down and returned to his attitude of quiet observation.

"Don't bother asking for his last name," Jeffries had told Kay before the meeting, when the two of them were alone in the office. "He won't tell you, and if he did tell you it wouldn't be a real one. For that matter his first name will probably be an alias too. Also, virtually everything else that he tells us will be a cover."

"Everything?"

Jeffries shrugged, stood, slipped on her suit jacket. "Best to assume so. The Bureau trains you to investigate crimes, Kay. The Agency teaches them to lie. Remember to keep the ball in our court."

But as they walked out, Kay doubted there was much that anyone on the face of the earth could teach Jeffries about duplicity.

The older and senior of the two Agency men, Group Chief Mike Anthony, looked like the image of an intelligence officer you would have read about in John le Carré's novels. He was short and running towards fat, and he had thick owlish glasses and dark, penetrating gray eyes. He spoke slowly and evenly, as if every sentence were an elaborate algebraic equation that he was doing, neatly and with great competence, inside his head. He began the meeting with such little fanfare that it took Kay half a sentence before she noticed. "I'd like to start by thanking ASAC Jeffries, the rest of you, and the Bureau generally for . . . coming in and helping us out on this one."

The first story of the day, and the coffee was still warm. If there was one thing the CIA did not like, it was oversight. Oversight to the CIA was like garlic to a vampire, milk to the lactose intolerant, a razor blade to a hemophiliac. CIA case officers were like mushrooms, Marshall had joked with her earlier: they grew best in the dark. For that matter, there was no great love lost between the two organizations. They had the same rivalry as you could find anytime two organizations performed similar tasks, competing for funding and attention from the government. For the CIA to be approaching the FBI for help meant that things at their sister agency had gotten very grim, very grim indeed.

"Happy to help," Jeffries said flatly. Jeffries had many strengths, but a knack for pleasantries was not one of them. She would have been a very bad telemarketer.

"Recently we've lost several RIPs within the Russian heartland and we think it's time to take a good internal look," Mike Anthony said.

Looking around, Kay did not think that anyone seemed particularly shocked. The end of the Cold War had seen, happily for the planet Earth, a distinct downward tick in the likelihood of the United States and Russia fighting a tank war or, for that matter, a full-scale nuclear apocalypse. But neither had the intelligence services of the two countries shaken hands, packed up their radio transmitters, and headed home. Like every other major power in the world and most of the smaller ones, the United States was actively working to infiltrate the security services of modern Russia. The Russians, needless to say, were not slow to return the compliment. The KGB had changed their name to the SVR, but apart from that it remained essentially the same. The CIA had not bothered with a shift in nomenclature or in tactics, and in effect the low-grade conflict between the two countries continued unabated. It was, like Jeffries had said, a game that doesn't end, a chess match without a permanent victor, successes followed by reverses, but hopefully with a few more in the win column.

"This was Mikhail Valenko," Anthony said, and the large video screen over his shoulder shifted to display a grainy image of a man in his mid-fifties, eyes heavy, nose red from drink. "Born 1962 in Petrograd. At one point he was a top electronics man in the SVR technical service. At another, more recent point he was one of our top RIPs.

"This was Vladimir Dolstoi," Anthony continued, clicking a button on his computer, the screen shifting to show another man, slightly younger but otherwise more or less identical to the first. "Military background, moved into the SVR shortly after the end of the Cold War. Doubled him a few years back, after he got into some trouble in Berlin.

"This was Dmitri Ulyanov."Another click, another dowdy-looking Slav. "Worked counterintelligence for the SVR. Until recently, at least."

It seemed the show-and-tell portion of the meeting was over. Anthony sat back down in his chair and took a deep breath as if preparing himself for an unpleasant task ahead. "These three men represented the Agency's deepest penetration into the SVR, which is to say Mother Russia. They represented, on my part, personally, many thousands of hours of effort over a dozen years."

"And?" Jeffries asked quietly.

"And each one of them is now a corpse in some unhappy tundra grave. They have been rolled up. Dispatched. Disappeared. Fifteen years we have groomed these RIPs, and in less than six months every one of them was identified, tried and executed for treason. No doubt their final days were . . . unpleasant." No doubt. If the aims of the CIA and SVR were roughly similar, their tactics differed significantly. If caught, the Black Bear mole could count on spending the rest of his life in a federal penitentiary, but at least he wouldn't have to worry about spending any time being tortured in some subbasement at Langley.

Anthony pushed his glasses up the bridge of his nose. "The loss of one RIP could be explained as incompetence or bad luck. The loss of two might, less plausibly, be the same. At this point, unfortunately, we are left with one inescapable but unpleasant reality: the SVR has picked off our people because they have someone on our side pointing them out. We have a mole in our house," he said simply.

Kay felt a wave of self-doubt creep over her. She took a long sip of coffee to process the information.

"And what do we know about this mystery man?" Marshall asked.

"Unfortunately, damn little," Andrew said regretfully. They were the first words he had spoken since his greeting, and Kay was struck by the harmonious lilt of his voice. "We don't even know if there is only the one mole: it could be a number of people working in conjunction or separate recruits entirely, each offering the SVR just enough information to figure out who our people were."

"Word is that Susan has a number of RIPs within the Russian consulate," Mike Anthony answered.

There were long moments during meetings when, if you did not know Jeffries, you would think she was not paying attention at all—perhaps even that she had fallen asleep with her eyes open. Then she would make some casual aside in her too-soft voice, something that made it clear not only that she had missed nothing of what was said but indeed that she understood the subject better than anyone else in the room. "I'm afraid the identities of our RIPs are going to remain secret."

"Come on, Susan, how about a little bit of interagency trust?"

"I trust you fine, Mike," Jeffries said. "I just don't trust everyone working for you. And since I can't trust everyone who works for you, I can't trust anyone who works for you. Which means we're going to keep our cards inside our vest."

Anthony shrugged. Jeffries worked counterintelligence: it was a matter of principle and habit to play things close, and he couldn't have expected the Assistant Special Agent in Charge to suddenly break protocol. But then, Anthony was a spy, and it was in his nature to ferret out secrets, and probably he couldn't quite help himself. "Fair enough," he said. "But understand that at Langley this case has the attention of executive leadership. Anything that can be done, we'll do. Andrew here," he said, nodding to his colleague, "will head to New York to act as liaison and to render whatever assistance he can. Needless to say, he'll have no contact with our office there: his existence, as well as that of the rest of the Black Bear squad, will remain unknown to anyone in the CIA besides myself and a few of my immediate superiors."

Which made sense: it might very well turn out that their mole was operating out of the CIA's National Resource Office in New York, in which case it obviously wouldn't do to have any of them aware of Black Bear's existence or that Andrew was a part of it. They discussed a few other procedural matters and then the meeting broke up, Kay, Jeffries and the rest of the squad returning to another conference room.

"That was Mike Anthony," Marshall said. "I thought he'd be taller."

"He's a spy, not a basketball player," Kay said.

"Still, a man with his history, you expect a little more to it."

Kay had never heard of Mike Anthony before, but then, she was new to the world of counterintelligence. From what she gathered from her colleagues, in his own agency Anthony was held in a similar regard to that which Jeffries enjoyed internally: as a seasoned, old-school professional with more skeletons in his closet than a cut-rate embalmer. Relationships between the two agencies were often clouded by rivalry and distrust, but it seemed that Anthony's reputation had gone some way towards smoothing over such differences.

Feelings about Andrew, however, were rather more mixed. "The Agency couldn't have saddled us with anyone prettier?" Marshall grumbled, unhappy to discover that his dubious distinction of being the best-looking man in the office had come to an abrupt end.

"Word is he's a blue-flamer," Wilson said. "Supposed to be very sharp; spent some time out east doing top-quality work."

"That means we have to spend the rest of the investigation with him peeking over our shoulder?"

"We're all in it together," Jeffries counseled them. "One mission, one fight. We will, of course, give . . . Andrew our fullest cooperation. Keep him up-to-date on any information we think would be of help to him."

"So we ought to start turning over our RIPs? Just open up the company books and let the man peruse through?"

"Let's not exaggerate here, Agent Marshall," Jeffries said. "Andrew gets our output and whatever might be relevant to Black Bear. He obviously is not in that privileged inner circle that gets to know where exactly we are receiving our information." Protecting one's sources was one of the most basic elements of spycraft: information might be passed on to other intelligence partners, or to the political overseers, but where that information came from was a secret that a good Agent would be tortured without revealing.

"Lately we've been wondering why we keep you in it," Wilson said to Marshall, who laughed and shrugged.

"We don't need to get into a turf war with the CIA over protocol," said Jeffries, never one to let a moment of levity stretch out too long. "But let's not forget that they're here because they've got a leak they can't plug. Let's make absolutely sure that nothing that we're responsible for drains out through it. Beyond that, you don't need me to explain to you the seriousness of the situation. This mole is out there and he is very obviously quite active. We need to pick him up as soon as we can before he trades any more national secrets to the SVR."

"What now?" Kay asked.

Marshall and Wilson looked at each other. "Now we're going to introduce you to the matrix, Kay. The two of you are going to get to be very, very close over the course of the next few months. Years. Decades."

"That sounds ominous."

"Depends on how you feel about drudgery," Wilson said. "What can I tell you, Malloy? It's not fun but it's absolutely necessary."

22

I REGRET to inform you that, as of this point, direct surveillance of the target has been fruitless."

They were sitting in a Midtown diner, the kind that was increasingly priced out of the city by boutique cocktail bars and Asian fusion restaurants. They looked conspicuous sitting together, but there was nothing that could be done about that. Tom was six-two vertical and not half that in width, and he dressed like he was about to go to the gym, though a quick look at his belly suggested that he probably was not. Pyotr was a slim man, shorter than average, and he dressed in a charcoal suit that was just a bit too conservative to be described as exquisite.

"To be expected," Pyotr answered. He spoke Russian in hushed tones. New York City was the capital of the world, any given room might have a dozen people speaking English as a second tongue and caution was second nature to Pyotr. "She's young, idealistic, dedicated to her work. I hardly expected she'd turn out to be shooting heroin over her lunch hour."

"Perhaps nothing quite so dramatic," Tom admitted. "But still, most people have something they'd rather keep hidden. Some bit of vice, or sin, or simple foolishness. But this one . . ."

Tom paused as the waitress arrived. Pyotr, abstemious as ever, ordered a coffee, black. Tom had the menu open but had yet to make up his mind between the fruit cup and something more substantial. As was often the case, his ulcer and his tongue were in direct conflict. He ended up ordering a Western omelet with a side of bacon and french fries.

"White as cream," Tom finished after the waitress had disappeared.

"And the alternative we discussed?"

"That, however, shows some promise." Tom took an envelope out of his jacket pocket and passed it over. Inside were a handful of photographs, and Pyotr studied each one carefully.

"Christopher Malloy, age thirty-one. Unmarried, no children. Two arrests for possession of marijuana, one for drunk and disorderly, both quashed before trial. He lives in a sort of squat in what we used to call Bushwick, though I'm sure some clever real estate agent has given it a sexy-sounding acronym of which I'm unaware."

" 'A sort of squat'? What does that mean, exactly?"

"Twenty or thirty years ago it was a warehouse. Now it's a large, decaying structure to which the housing authority does not pay very much attention. In a few years, no doubt, when the next wave of gentrification breaks against its shores, it will be torn down and a glittering yuppie condo building will be put up in its place. In the meantime whoever has the deed on it makes a little bit of money by letting people occupy some of its square footage. It's not exactly legal, but"—Tom shrugged—"it is the sort of thing which has become popular with artist types."

"Is Christopher one of those?"

"He is rather unkempt, and doesn't hold a real job, and seems to think very much of himself, so in that sense, yes, I would say he is an artist type. As to having any actual creative ability? That would be up to the listener, I suppose. He plays guitar in some sort of"—Tom made a face—"metal band, and busks on occasion. I would not expect to see any of his music hit the charts in the near future."

"And what does Mr. Malloy do, other than not being a particularly skilled guitar player?"

"He pours drinks at a nearby bar a few nights a week. He walks aimlessly around the city. He has a motorcycle which he spends a great deal of time fixing. He has a number of different women that he visits. And he sells a small amount of cocaine now and again."

Tom had known that Pyotr would show no emotion at this happy piece of news, and indeed he did not. Tom was not quite sure what it would take to excite Pyotr; did not think in twenty years of working together he had seen him flustered or even particularly interested. He had a face like a block of ice left out in a blizzard. "Go on," he said.

"A sideline, dealing from behind the bar. Small quantities: a few dollars here, a few dollars there. Not the sort of the thing the police would likely be interested in, but . . ."

"A promising avenue of approach, at least," Pyotr said.

"Such was my thinking," Tom agreed. "The last month I have had some of my associates patronizing his establishment during the nights Christopher works. Apparently he is a garrulous young man, happy to make new friends. Two weeks ago he sold one of my people a gram of cocaine, just as a way of saying welcome to the neighborhood."

"What are you thinking?" Pyotr asked.

"I am thinking that perhaps Mr. Malloy, an American raised on rap music and dreams of easy money, might be interested in jumping up a few rungs in the world of narcotics distribution."

Pyotr chuckled. "You can arrange that?"

"Without difficulty."

"And what happens afterward?"

"Any number of ways to play the matter from there," Tom explained. "He could be threatened with arrest and prosecution, though I think we'd be better off with a rather more circuitous route. The first step is to get him buying from us, rather than the other way around."

"And you think he'll be up for that?"

"I don't see why not. Thus far his involvement in narcotics has been hand to hand, strictly small-time, baggies passed between friends. But from what I have seen of Christopher he is not a man prone to caution. The promise of money should be enough to convince him to ignore any qualms he has about moving up in the ranks. Yes," Tom said, feeling confident, "I think he would be amenable. As to whether his misfortunes will prove of sufficient concern to his sister for her to put her future on the line, I'm afraid I cannot speak so affirmatively."

"There is no question," Pyotr corrected him. "Kay Malloy feels a great sense of loyalty to her brother, would go . . . *will* go to great lengths to save him."

"I have had people watching your Agent Malloy for months now. In that time she has seen her sibling exactly one time, on her birthday. From what I can tell, her primary, perhaps her sole obsession is her career. Are you certain that she will be willing to jeopardize that for a no-good brother whom she rarely sees?"

"You'll have to go ahead and trust me on the matter," Pyotr said, smiling. "Christopher is her only living family, and their infrequent contact belies the ferocity of her loyalty."

"You sound certain."

"I *am* certain."

"Why, exactly?"

Pyotr smiled but did not answer. Tom shrugged, unoffended. He did not need to know everything. There were many reasons that Tom was very good at his job: he was industrious, he was clever, he had a sharp eye for human weakness. But part of this package—and not a small part, either—was that he was comfortable operating as a cog in the wheel, taking firm control over that aspect of an operation that was within his area of expertise and studiously avoiding looking outside of it. And of course Pyotr was the best; Tom was quite sure that Pyotr had never been wrong about something important. If Pyotr did not think that Tom needed to know the identity of his source, then this was certain to be the case.

The waitress returned then with their orders. Pyotr looked for a while at the black coffee in his cup but made no move to drink it. Tom threw himself into his own food with almost manic intensity, smearing butter onto his toast like he was trying to break the thing in two.

"What is wrong, my friend?" Pyotr asked, after Tom had put away half of his omelet and all of his bacon in around forty seconds.

"No disrespect, Pyotr, I am sure your source is reliable. All the same, I dislike such roundabout methods. It relies on too many contingencies, too much presumption. I agree, the brother angle seems our best, indeed our only potential point of access— but I'd still rather we had something firm to use on the target herself."

Pyotr laughed. "What can I tell you? Kay Malloy is a moralist," he said, brushing a bit of sugar off the table. "Like her father."

23

K AY SIGHED, scratched her head, drank a little bit of lukewarm coffee, clicked onto the next subject.

Bartholemew Ides, age forty-seven. Was he the CIA's secret mole? Was he the man responsible for the death of three double agents? Was he the fox in the henhouse? She spent a while digging through his files, every little nugget of information that the FBI had assembled on him, internal personnel reports, past history. Cross-checked this personal data against what little they knew of their spy, discounted him immediately. Clicked through to the next.

It was called the matrix, and it had quickly grown to take over the larger part of Kay's life.

A simple enough process. Start with everyone, literally *everyone*, who knew or may have gleaned the identity of the lost double agents. Next, identify those who may have had access to their compartmented reporting. If one was fortunate, there might be reporting from our double agents concerning the mole. Then start the arduous task of identifying any commonalities between the suspected mole and the lost double agents, things like similar postings abroad or foreign travel by the suspected mole. And then there was no substitute for good old-fashioned investigative work. In this way they might learn about the person who was betraying the country.

Of course, sometimes—often, in fact—the information was

contradictory, or confusing, or oblique. It was more art than sci-
ence, Kay was swiftly coming to realize, and there was always the
nagging fear that you had made the wrong decision, accidentally
gone ahead and knocked the mole off the list, set the investigation back months or years or maybe torpedoed it altogether.

Samuel Abondando, age fifty-nine. Was he the culprit? Had
he some hidden weakness that the competition had found a way
to prey upon, blackmailing or bribing him into treason? Had he
been squirreling away SVR funds, dead drops in the middle of
the night, burner phones to contact his handler, secret meetings
in obscure places?

The initial excitement of being involved in such an important
investigation had given way almost immediately to the reality of
the process, which was tedious and depressing. Kay was doing
her best not to keep an accurate count of how much time she
had spent in this exact position in the month since Black Bear
had begun, knowing the truth would only make it worse.

"Anything new, Malloy?"

Kay looked up from the pixelated glare of her monitor to see
Jeffries standing above her. Eight o'clock on a Wednesday but
she showed no particular signs of fatigue, the eyes behind her
glasses undimmed, sipping slowly from her ever-full thermos of
coffee.

"What do you think?" Kay asked, turning the monitor so
Susan could see better.

The ASAC spent a moment staring at the information Kay
had up. "Well, he doesn't speak Russian, hasn't been abroad for
twenty-five years. No operational experience, no obvious avenue
by which he could have been approached. Let's put him in the
'maybe' pile."

It took Kay a solid ten seconds before she realized that

Jeffries was making a joke, another five before she decided it was acceptable to smile at it.

"You need to stop doing this to yourself, Agent Malloy," Jeffries said, taking a seat, and was it Kay's imagination or had she heard Jeffries offer the slightest expression of relief upon getting off her feet? Was it possible that she might even be human, just like the rest of them?

An absurd suggestion. "What do you mean?" Kay asked.

But Jeffries didn't answer her for a while, turned her eyes like searchlights on Kay, sipped at her coffee. "Do you know who Robert Hanssen is?"

"Former Agent who approached the Soviets to become a spy. Sold out the identities of some of our own top recruitments, passed over signals intelligence. Hanssen had unfettered access to many of the espionage investigations, which provided him with a steady stream of intelligence for sale."

"And how many years did Mr. Hanssen spy for the Russians before we caught him?"

"Twenty years, if memory serves."

"Twenty-two, off and on," Jeffries said flatly. "And it was only after paying an SVR officer millions of dollars and setting him and his family up here in the States that we finally got our proof. Aldrich Ames?"

"CIA equivalent," Kay answered, enjoying the game. "Worked against the Soviets at the height of the Cold War. Nominally, at least, though in practice he spent the better part of his career doing the reverse. Responsible for the loss of dozens of RIPs and any number of deaths, including the execution of Major General Dmitri Polyakov, the highest-ranking Soviet RIP the CIA ever had in place. Passed two polygraph tests and, despite living a lavish lifestyle far beyond what his salary could afford him, was not arrested until almost ten years after he had begun passing information to Russia. The most significant CIA breach in history."

"Perhaps not anymore," Jeffries said. "Kim Philby?"

"The Brits' black eye, and one we still shouldn't let them forget. Became a Soviet double agent in college, before he had ever entered the intelligence world. Joined the SOE, or the Special Operations Executive, during World War II, then MI6. Postings in Turkey, the U.S. Worked for the Soviets for the entirety of his career; at one point was third in line to run Her Majesty's secret service, despite being an alcoholic traitor. Defected to Russia in the early sixties when the heat got too much for him; spent the rest of his life unpunished."

Jeffries didn't say anything after that, as if waiting for Kay to draw her own conclusions. Then: "We work in a business which prizes secrets, Agent Malloy, and which will pay a high premium for them. There's always a turncoat somewhere, whether you know it or not. You know I was part of the team that went after Hanssen."

Kay's ears perked up: the chance to fill in the blank spots in Jeffries's past with real data rather than gossip was not one to be passed up. "I didn't know that."

"For a long time we thought it was this CIA officer; spent months, years, tearing apart this poor guy's life, setting up false flag operations . . ." Jeffries shook her head sadly at the wasted effort. "It starts to get to you if you let it, digging through strangers' evils, walking around all day looking at your colleagues and coworkers, wondering which of them has decided to betray their country and their people for a little bit of money, or to get out of some difficulty, or for some other horrible, petty reason. And it's always petty reasons: they've been passed over for promotion, or they get made fun of in the break room, or they want cash to impress a woman half their age." Jeffries took her glasses off, rubbed at the wrinkles around her eyes.

It was, Kay felt certain, the longest conversation she had ever had with Jeffries about something that was not directly related to their work, which gave some hint of Jeffries's personality beyond the hyper-competent facade that she stood behind.

"But you can't let it get to you, Malloy," Jeffries said, her shield back up. "Because if you lose your mental balance, then you're useless to us; then all of your talent and drive becomes a liability. Staying here late every night, obsessing over the details of the case—it's counterproductive in the long run. It's going to dull your edge. This isn't a sprint; it's a marathon. You need to find a way to balance this with other things, whatever those other things are. You can't spend every night and every weekend in front of the computer—can't and still be any good to the mission. You have to put something else into your life besides counterintelligence."

Which was strange to hear coming from Jeffries: unmarried, no children, no hobbies that anyone knew about, came in earlier and left later than anyone else on the team—or at least had come in earlier and left later than everyone else on the team before Kay had arrived. "What do you do for recreation?"

"I go paintballing," Jeffries said flatly.

It occurred to Kay that she had no idea whether this was a joke, and she didn't think she'd have any luck in reading the truth behind Jeffries's imperceptible eyes.

"It's been a very long day," Jeffries said, finally, getting up from her seat. "Think about what I said. You have too much potential to burn yourself out so early."

"Thank you," Kay said, surprised as much by the sudden termination of the conversation as she was by Jeffries's unexpected moment of intimacy.

Kay sat in her chair awhile afterward, rubbing at her eyes. Thought about knocking off and going home, maybe grabbing a drink. Or giving Christopher a call; they hadn't chatted in a while, which probably meant he was into something he shouldn't be. Or Uncle Luis, maybe, or Alice. Kay was young, she was pretty, she had a little bit of money, she was in the greatest city in the world. There had to be something she could do, right? Right?

Kay sighed, stretched, clicked onward.

Joe Emanuel, age forty-seven.

24

DOING SURVEILLANCE on a potential recruit was not fundamentally different from doing surveillance on a drug dealer or crime lord. There was a lot of sitting around, drinking coffee, trying to keep yourself sharp despite the mind-numbing moment-to-moment boredom of the task. On the plus side, the surveillance that Kay was responsible for, a potential recruit at the Russian mission, at least kept her in nice neighborhoods. Surveillance in Baltimore meant angling down in a Bureau car in the dreariest and most impoverished portions of the city, watching crackheads fidget past aimlessly, staring at shiftless young men on stoops in the middle of the day, all of the ugliest aspects of American urban decay. Here in New York it meant being in the passenger seat across from Agent Marshall, parked on a lovely Manhattan residential block, towering apartment buildings filled with million-dollar condos. Middle-aged women kept young through shots of attenuated botulism and frequent plastic surgeries carried purse dogs to their weekly SoulCycle class.

"You ever think about what an odd job we have, Marshall?" Kay asked, shifting her legs about in an aimless effort to improve blood flow.

"Do it as long as I have, Malloy, and the whole thing starts to feel normal." He was fiddling with the lens on their long-distance camera, more to kill time than anything else. The better part of surveillance, Kay had long ago realized, was finding creative ways to make time a corpse.

"What's normal?"

"You got me," Marshall said. In a park across the street, a man had painted himself silver and was perched motionless atop a bench. A number of East Asian tourists were happily taking pictures of him. "In this city especially."

"You think we got a shot with this guy?"

"These living statues don't make very much," Marshall said. "I think if we pitch it to him the right way, he'll probably give us what he knows."

Kay made a motion as if to punch Marshall, and Marshall put his hands up apologetically. In the months since she had come to New York, Kay had grown closer to her comrades in counterintelligence, although she would have to admit that she had not yet found a friend to compare with Torres. Probably this was as much about Kay as it was them. She had come to Baltimore a fresh-faced new Agent, anxious for camaraderie. Here in New York she was, if not a hardened veteran, then at least not so desperately unsure of herself as she had been after leaving the Academy.

"Honestly, Kay," Marshall said, having avoided his beating, "it's hard to say. A recruitment is never a sure thing, as much work as you try to put in ahead of time to make sure otherwise. Of course, Jeffries thinks he's worth taking a look at, and Jeffries isn't wrong all that much. I mean, we're all wrong sometimes, but she's not the sort of person you'd want to make a habit of betting against."

Kay did not disagree.

Counterintelligence is not passive, and the investigation into

Black Bear included far more than simply staring at a computer. The information for the matrix, after all, had to come from somewhere. Some portion of it might be communications intelligence—or COMINT, as it was more popularly called—tapping phones and intercepting e-mails, the endless ongoing twenty-first-century game of encryption and decryption, of electronic cat and mouse. But COMINT was only part of the picture, and perhaps not the most important part, either. Human intelligence, or HUMINT, was still critical, and would remain so for as long as countries tried to spy on one another. An RIP, someone inside the enemy's operation who could provide not only specific details but background on the competition, was crucial to an effective counterintelligence operation. Identifying these potential recruits, tracking them, finding out their weaknesses, recruiting and finally running them, were key responsibilities of an FBI Agent working counterintelligence, albeit ones with which Kay was largely unfamiliar.

Over the course of the last few months, the Black Bear squad, spearheaded by ASAC Jeffries, had begun to assemble a complex dossier on the history, character and habits of one Artur Vadim, a Suspected Intelligence Officer, or SIO, working cover at the Russian mission. It was a strange sort of way to get to know someone. Kay did not know what Vadim's voice sounded like, or if he had a good sense of humor, or if he was the sort of person who would hold the door open if someone else was coming by, carrying a package. But she knew where he had been born and where he had gone to school and when he had started working at the Russian mission, and some of the intelligence work with which he was affiliated, and the contents of his bank account, and his spending habits, and dozens of other intimate, personal details.

It beat staring at the matrix, at least. "Artur Vadim," Kay said as if she had just heard it for the first time.

"Artur Vadim," Marshall seconded, because he was bored also and didn't have much else to say.

"What's our in with this guy?" Kay asked.

"Money," Marshall informed her. "It's almost always money. Back in the good old days, I suppose, you had the occasional recruit coming in for philosophical reasons. Like Polyakov."

Major General Dmitri Polyakov had been the crown jewel of the U.S. intelligence service's foreign assets throughout much of the Cold War, a high-ranking Soviet military officer who had passed on key secrets from his native country. Unlike the vast majority of placements, even during the Cold War, he had no interest in money, felt ideologically estranged from the regime of which he was a part, did his best to bring it down from the inside—until his identity was betrayed by CIA traitor Aldrich Ames, and he was tried, convicted, and executed for treason.

"Look what happened to him," Kay said.

Marshall grunted. "Vadim's no Polyakov, I'll give you that. But he's high enough in the Russian mission to be of real potential value, assuming we can hook him. And some of his habits— the cocktail bars, the opera tickets, that custom-tailored suit which we saw him walk out of work wearing—are difficult to indulge on his salary."

Kay nodded. "When do we make the approach?"

"Up to Jeffries," Wilson said. "But you only ever get one shot with these. If you blow it"—he drew a finger across his throat—"you're iced. Best to be damn well prepared first."

"So what you're saying is I ought to get used to sitting in the BuCar?" Kay used the slang for a Bureau-issued car.

"It ain't all honor and glory."

"You said that already," Kay said, trying without success to find a comfortable way to position her legs.

25

TWO MONTHS after the beginning of Black Bear, Kay met Andrew in the basement of New York's Penn Station, one of the busiest—and unquestionably the ugliest—train stations in the country. Kay was early, as she was to most things, and spent half an hour drinking coffee out of a Styrofoam cup and watching the departures board. Five minutes before nine and she started to get worried that she'd be making the trip solo, and then there was a tap on her shoulder and there he was.

"So sorry," Andrew explained, smiling that smile of his. "Shall we grab a seat?"

Before she could say anything, Andrew was off again, and Kay followed him through the mob and down into the bowels of the station, onto a crowded platform and then into the air-conditioned *Acela Express*. Kay was annoyed that he was late and also annoyed that his being late hadn't cost them anything, that they had gotten a comfortable seat without much trouble. Andrew was the sort of person for whom things worked out naturally: that rare, lucky breed that draws as much jealousy as it does admiration.

He offered her the window seat but Kay refused it, mostly out of pique, because she actually would have preferred it. Andrew didn't seem to mind. He headed to the dining car and came back with two cups of coffee. Kay grunted thanks and turned to her book.

Kay would have liked to think that representing the FBI in today's meeting with Mike Anthony was a select honor, although she lacked such a capacity for self-deception. This was a hassle, not a privilege. The train ride down to Union Station, a cab to CIA headquarters, a few pleasantries, then down to the meat of it—which was, in short, that thus far Jeffries's crack counterintelligence squad had come up with nothing firm as to the possible identity of the CIA's penetration. For that matter, they didn't have anything flimsy, either. Months of working the matrix; grueling months; months that Kay had not found overwhelmingly entertaining; months that had, unfortunately, gotten them no closer to the end of the Black Bear investigation. As the newest member of the squad, it had seemed only reasonable that she would be the one to make the haul to D.C.: seniority had its privileges, after all.

Andrew seemed cheerful enough about the whole thing. But then, Andrew always seemed cheerful. Whatever interagency tension might have been expected was swiftly soothed by his good humor, competence and willingness to handle the duller and more burdensome aspects of Black Bear. Indeed, it was hard to dislike Andrew. He smiled easily; he held doors for people in an unself-conscious and gentlemanly sort of way. He brought in donuts. In meetings he spoke succinctly, and what he said was worth listening to. Which was why Kay could not quite explain her own feelings towards him, which were somewhat more towards the negative side of mixed. Maybe it was that things seemed to come so easily to him, as if all of the props and levers of human existence had been greased and twisted to his advantage. Or maybe it was that she found him so handsome.

The train ride passed smoothly. Kay dodged all attempts at small talk, an evasion that didn't seem to bother Andrew, assuming he had noticed. They grabbed a cab from the stand at Union Station. Langley, Virginia, where the CIA is based, is only a few miles west of the capital, but with midday traffic it took nearly an hour to get there. The cabdriver was Pakistani and enormously entertained by Andrew's facility for Urdu, which Andrew claimed was fledgling but which seemed to Kay to be more than competent. By the time they were dropped off in front of CIA headquarters, the driver was shaking their hands vigorously and Andrew could add another name to his seemingly endless list of casual friends.

Kay and Andrew passed through security without any particular difficulty, and Kay was unsurprised at the good humor that greeted Andrew's return, the security guards laughing and waving, people slapping him on the back when they passed in the hall. The meeting with Mike Anthony went quickly and smoothly, primarily because there wasn't very much to report on. The Black Bear squad had identified a number of potential targets for recruitment, but nothing firm. An old hand like Anthony wasn't fool enough to expect results so swiftly, not in an operation like this. He listened carefully, asked relevant questions, thanked Kay and Andrew for their work and requested that they relay similar feelings to the rest of the team. Was he just the slightest bit brusque with his younger colleague, casually or not so casually unfriendly? Having only met Anthony once, Kay couldn't say with any sort of certainty, although she made a mental jot on the subject in the impeccable ledger that she kept stored between her ears.

Andrew and Kay had lunch at the CIA cafeteria, which honesty forced Kay to admit was way better than its FBI counterpart. She had a cup of coffee and an Italian sandwich. Andrew had sparkling water and a salad. It was not a fair thing to hold against him, but she found she couldn't quite help herself. They spoke little, and when they did it was about the case. Andrew was as up-to-date on the matrix information as anyone involved in the Black Bear investigation, despite the fact that he was kept entirely in the dark about how exactly the FBI had acquired their data.

The cab ride back to Union Station took longer than the one going out, and they barely made their train, cramming in with the rest of the evening commuters heading north back to Manhattan.

"You're from New York, aren't you, Kay?" Andrew asked on the way home. The train ride from D.C. to New York, the most heavily commuted portion of the country, is not what you would call particularly scenic: mostly gray suburbs and highways. But there is a short portion between Baltimore and Philadelphia that cruises north through the Chesapeake Bay, offering the occasional view of grass and water, one that Kay had been enjoying in the interim before Andrew had spoken.

"You pulled my file?" Kay asked, half kidding.

"It's the best part of being a spy," Andrew answered toothily. "We have files on everyone at the CIA. During the annual Christmas party we drink heavily and read from the funniest ones."

"That's interesting," Kay said. "We do the same thing. But I bet our jokes are better."

Andrew laughed. "Just office scuttlebutt."

"I spent my childhood years in Westchester," she said, then added, "but when I was ten I moved to the Upper West Side to live with my aunt and uncle."

"Why?" Andrew asked, shining those eyes on hers—eyes that Kay did not doubt had entranced many a woman into revealing her secrets.

"It's a long story," Kay said uncomfortably.

To his credit, Andrew knew enough not to push her. A brief silence, but not an awkward one, which Kay chalked up to Andrew's easy sociability. "And you? Where are you from?"

"I'm from outside of Dallas, originally."

"Do you get out there much?"

"Not really."

"No family?"

"Not for a while," Andrew admitted. "I'm an orphan, actually. My parents died when I was twelve." Said with that false casualness that Kay knew intimately, that she had mastered during her own long years of answering questions about why the couple coming to graduation looked nothing like her.

"I'm sorry," Kay said, knowing how hollow it sounded, because she was usually the one hearing it but not able to think of anything else.

Andrew received the condolences with more grace than Kay usually managed. "Thanks," he said. "It was a long time ago. I've turned the page."

"I hadn't . . ." All of a sudden Kay found herself feeling very foolish for her false assumptions about Andrew, for supposing his friendly manner was all there was to him. "I hadn't known."

"I don't really advertise it," he said, smiling.

"My parents died young also!" Kay found herself blurting out after a long moment of silence.

"Really?"

"When I was about ten."

Andrew's eyes lost some of their usual casual friendliness, that veneer of good humor that covered what went on beneath. "I didn't know that."

"That wasn't in my file?"

"We'll have to update it," he said.

Kay found she was smiling, their shared intimacies, tragic

though they were, bringing out some measure of good humor. "What happened to yours?"

"Drunk driver."

"Jesus," Kay blurted out.

"Had his license suspended, but that didn't seem to matter to him. Actually he had a number of outstanding warrants, should have been in jail, but . . . he wasn't."

"I'm sorry."

Andrew shrugged. "The world isn't always a nice place."

"No," Kay agreed. "It isn't. Is that why you joined the Agency?"

"Maybe. Who can say? Who knows why we do anything? Even the reasons we give ourselves are usually false, self-serving, comforting lies."

"I thought the CIA made a living off dishonesty."

"Is that what Jeffries told you?"

"Was she wrong?"

"No," Andrew admitted. "She wasn't. But it's one thing to sell a falsehood—it's entirely another to believe it yourself. I suppose in that sense, maybe what . . . Maybe what happened with my parents did play a role in my joining the Agency: the lies they feed you, the lies most children believe. I never really bought them. Didn't you ever feel that way growing up? All the 'Tomorrow will be better; things work out for the best.' You learn early on that none of that's true, that the certainties people cling to are nothing of the sort."

"Yes," Kay admitted. "I have often felt that way."

Andrew looked for a while like he was going to say more, but in the end he just smiled at her—not his usual smile but an authentic one, or at least one that seemed authentic, and turned back to his work.

They spent the rest of the ride in comfortable silence, Kay sifting through one of her Russian textbooks, or pretending to, although in truth she was spending very little mental effort on verb tenses and much more on Andrew's shoulders and on his clean, strong scent. They said good-bye at Penn Station, and when he asked if he could call her sometime, Kay did not say no.

26

K AY SAT at her desk a few days later, the matrix booted up on her desk computer, drinking a cup of coffee. These were not noteworthy activities; indeed, they were activities that Kay spent probably a rough majority of her waking hours engaged in. There could be no possible reason why the other Agents in the bullpen, most of whom were busily puttering away at their own work, could have any idea what she was considering. All the same, Kay found herself growing unreasonably paranoid, as if Marshall and Wilson and the others could read into the folds of her mind and know what she was secretly planning.

"For Christ's sake," Kay reminded herself. "*You* are a spy, essentially. You ought to be capable of a little bit of subtlety."

Besides, she was probably driving herself crazy over nothing. In the early days after Kay had moved in with Luis and Justyna, she had created all sorts of scenarios to explain the death of her parents, fantasies that offered her some comfort. Perhaps it had all been a mix-up, with the Colombian authorities misidentifying the bodies; elaborate dreams at the end of which the door to her room would swing open and the two of them would be standing there, holding hands and waiting to embrace her.

But they hadn't lasted long. Even at ten years old Kay was, if not a cynic, at least a realist. The deaths of her parents had taken what little naïveté had been left her. She did not believe in Santa Claus or happy endings. And she didn't believe in their reverse, in a devil or in the grand plans of evil men. Her parents had walked down the wrong street in the wrong part of the planet and crossed paths with some bitterly impoverished thug, some kid from the slums who had gotten his hands on a functioning pistol and recognized Paul and Anne as gringos and hoped to steal enough for food or drugs. And something had gone wrong, as things often did, and then there were two more corpses to be put into the ground. There was nothing more to it than that. The world was a grim and a dangerous place; the righteous remained unrewarded; greed and corruption and cruelty too frequently went unpunished. Life had no natural bent towards justice; it needed to be forced into that direction, forced by hard-eyed men and women with badges on their chests. A difficult job, one that no one did perfectly and that many did not even do well. But it was necessary all the same, to have someone standing by to push against the world's savagery. This had been the fundamental underpinning of Kay's thinking for twenty years, the reason she had joined the Bureau, the reason that she pushed herself so hard, day in and day out.

And yet . . . in a minimized window on her browser Kay had opened up Sentinel, the FBI's case management database. A quick search would reveal any information the Bureau had put together on her parents and their untimely deaths, and might clear up any last lingering mystery. Of course, performing that search was, strictly speaking, against Bureau policy. The vast agglomeration of data that the Bureau had painstakingly developed over the course of almost a century was not something that could be lightly perused by anyone. It existed to service active investigations, not so that Agents could use them for personal matters.

There was no legitimate reason that Kay could be using Bureau resources to investigate her parents' deaths. If anyone found out, Kay would get in trouble, and deservedly so.

An extremely unlikely possibility, Kay had to admit. She did not suppose that Jeffries was spending her afternoons looking over every keystroke logged onto each of her Agents' computers. But that wasn't really the point, not as far as Kay was concerned. She had not spent the better part of her life trying to join the FBI only to bend its protocol. A person either stood for something or they didn't, and Kay thought that she did, and that meant that you had to play by the rules that you'd chosen to uphold. Even a minor breach of regulations like the one Kay was considering made her feel guilty and out of sorts.

"Malloy . . . Malloy!"

"What?" Kay looked up abruptly.

"Going for sandwiches. You interested?" Marshall asked.

At the moment Kay found that she was not at all hungry. "No," she said. "Thanks."

For some reason the interruption seemed enough to push Kay into action. After Marshall had stepped out to get the order, she quickly tabbed over to Sentinel. She typed "Paul Malloy" in the text box, her heart beating with each keystroke.

The search lasted, or seemed to Kay to last, a very long time, long enough for Kay to replay in her mind all the reasons why this wasn't a good idea—indeed, was quite the opposite. When her father's name popped up with a "0" next to it, Kay wasn't sure whether to be happy or sad. A zero or "0" file was a control file in which information not acted upon for various reasons was stored. At least her breach of FBI protocol hadn't been pointless. The FBI had been in contact with her father for some reason. More than that she couldn't say without having her hands on the file itself, and it was only now that it occurred to Kay that her father's file—being an inactive case from twenty years ago—would not be in the database. Electronic record keeping only went back to around 1995; everything before that was stored in a huge warehouse near Washington, D.C., referred to within the Bureau as "Pickett Street." If she wanted to learn anything else, she'd have to find a way into it.

This was the problem with breaking rules with minor sins. This was why corruption needed to be guarded against so vehemently. No one started off planning to turn to evil, or at least Kay thought that very few did. One rubbed away a line, even a small one, at one's own peril. The relatively small breach of protocol that Kay had just committed would require a more substantial transgression if she ever wanted to find out what was in her father's file. "This must be how the RIPs feel," Kay thought. One act of malfeasance begetting a second, and then a third, and then at some point you looked up and realized you had no idea who you were anymore, that what had once seemed a bedrock moral code was as hollow as a rotted tree.

Kay sighed, closed down Sentinel. She stared at the matrix for a long time without actually seeing it. Then she headed towards the bathroom, stopping in the hallway outside of the SCIF to take out her cell phone.

"Torres?"

"If it isn't Ms. Big Leagues herself. What are you doing calling down to the minors?"

"I'm thinking I might be in Baltimore this weekend," Kay decided. "Can I buy you lunch?"

27

KAY AND Justyna were enjoying an elaborate dinner at a three-star French restaurant in Manhattan, the sort that Kay could not afford or could have afforded only if she had spent the next week fasting. She had made it a point of pride not to take money from her adoptive parents, not for years, not since she had finished college—but if ever there was anything that might tempt her fierce sense of independence, it was cassoulet and a red Bordeaux.

They had spent cocktails discussing Justyna's week. Like many women of her social milieu, she was involved in any number of charitable organizations, although unlike many of her peers Justyna actually cared about these charities beyond an excuse for social activity. When the appetizers arrived they had switched over to Kay's recent history, or what she could tell of it, which wasn't much. Life for Kay lately had been work, and obviously the specifics of Black Bear weren't the sort that could be made public knowledge.

"Yes, yes, you are a big important FBI Agent; we're all overwhelmingly impressed," Justyna said, although it was obvious that her sarcasm was feigned. "Let's talk about something interesting: How are the boys?"

Kay smiled. "I'm afraid being a big important FBI Agent doesn't leave me lots of time to cruise singles bars."

"Oh, Kay, you're far too young to have gotten so dull. Surely duty can't take up *all* of your time. There must be someone in this city of nine million who wouldn't mind meeting a beautiful young woman who is legally allowed to carry a concealed firearm."

Kay laughed. "I'll put out a Craigslist post, see if I get any responses."

"Seriously, Kay," Justyna said, laying one gloved hand on her niece's. "Life can't only be about work, however important that work is. You have to find some sort of balance."

Which sounded nice in theory, Kay had to admit, but which in practice meant less time with the matrix, less time looking over case files, less time doing her job. And meant the increasing likelihood of another death attributable to the unknown subject, or UNSUB, of the Black Bear investigation, more sensitive information filtering its way into the ears of the nation's enemies. For most people, extra hours at work, increasing dedication, meant a few more dollars to the company's bottom line, maybe a nice bonus at the end of the quarter. For Kay it was, quite literally, a matter of life and death. You couldn't turn that on and off like a switch.

"Well . . ." Kay began after an unsure moment, "there might be someone. Maybe."

Justyna gave an overdramatic clap of her hands. "Is he tall?"

"Yes?"

"Is he handsome?"

"He is."

"I like him," Justyna said. "You should marry him."

"It's nice to see where your priorities are."

"Handsome and tall you can't change. Everything else . . ." Justyna shrugged her shoulders, which were left uncovered by the small black dress she wore, one that would have been inappropriate for any sixty-year-old woman who was not her aunt. "A woman can work on. When I met Luis he used to wear sweatpants and sleeveless white T-shirts. He used to drop cigar ashes on the carpet and spit onto the street. But after forty years I've almost managed to civilize him."

"That doesn't sound much like my uncle," Kay said.

"I might be exaggerating slightly," Justyna admitted. "Don't try and change the subject. Tell me more about the potential father of my grandchildren."

Kay laughed. What was Andrew? He was handsome and he was extremely smart, a rising star within his own organization, obvious from the way they had treated him that day in D.C. Obvious just from meeting him, really. He gave off a strong impression of competence; of certainty, even; of a person who was going somewhere. He had taste and he had style, there was something cultured and almost grand about him. No, Kay had to admit, he had gotten to her.

Perhaps that was why Kay changed the conversation swiftly, rather than admit to any hint of softness. "I meant to ask you about something that you said on our last date: about that FBI Agent who came around after my parents were killed."

Justyna flinched, and immediately Kay regretted not putting the matter more tactfully. She had come, over the years, to be able to discuss the deaths of Paul and Anne Malloy with the detachment of someone whose job was intimately involved with death, and sometimes she forgot that other people did not have her professional discipline. "Can you remember what they asked about?"

Justyna sighed and poured herself another glass of wine. "It was a rough time, Kay, I don't need to tell you that. Those first few months we were so busy trying to set up a home for you and your brother that we barely had time to grieve. There were always people coming in, offering condolences, not to mention the practical aspects of it. Flying the . . . bodies home, all the logistics of the funeral. Honestly, it's been twenty years since I thought of that FBI Agent. As to the specifics of our conversation . . ." Justyna shrugged. "Not much. Sorry."

"Do you think it's possible that my father might have . . . contacted the FBI for some reason?"

Justyna narrowed her eyes. "Why?"

"I don't know why. I'm just wondering."

"Your father wasn't doing anything illegal," Justyna informed her. "He wasn't involved in money laundering, or racketeering, or smuggling endangered species. I'm sure I have no idea why he would have contacted the FBI, assuming that's what happened."

"Maybe something to do with his new job?"

Justyna wiped her upper lip with her napkin, then set her hands at her side. "What is this about, Kay? What are you getting at?"

Except that Kay still wasn't sure, didn't have anything firm. For that matter didn't have anything shaky, only the vague smell of malfeasance, an uncomfortable itch that there was more to the matter than seemed clear to her at this point. But then, suspicion is not evidence, and there was no point in worrying Justyna unnecessarily.

"Don't worry about it, Auntie," Kay said, smiling and trying to change the subject. "Shall we split the crème brûlée, or do you think one dessert alone is insufficient?"

"We can split it," Justyna said, unsatisfied with Kay's answer, but knowing she wasn't going to get a better one.

28

TORRES PICKED Kay up at Baltimore's Penn Station, drove her east out towards the city line, stopped in front of a strip mall just past Canton that housed a Dollar Store, a Vietnamese nail service, a takeout joint advertising pizza/subs/Chinese food, and a restaurant that Torres informed her confidently served "the best goddamned crabs that ever got steamed to death in service of my stomach." Hard-shell crabs were a specialty of the Chesapeake Bay region, and the best of them were inevitably found in seemingly unhygienic holes-in-the-wall, the sorts of places a person would drive past swiftly and not think twice about. Torres, needless to say, had an encyclopedic knowledge of the best dives and takeout places in the greater Baltimore area, and in this as well as many other things Kay trusted him implicitly.

They sat at a booth in the back, started with a dozen extra large and some Natty Boh, both of which were brought out swiftly. Half the crabs and all of the beer were spent without touching on anything serious. Mostly sports news. Did the Ravens have a chance this year? Was it possible that the Jets suffered from some sort of curse, and if so, could it be removed? They argued for a time over the virtues of soccer, Kay being an early convert to the sport by way of Aunt Justyna, who was a mild obsessive, Torres adamantly asserting he would rather be beaten about the face and neck with a claw hammer than forced to sit through any game allowed to end in a tie. It was an old argument, and progressed in the standard fashion.

"How's your wife?" Kay asked.

Torres shrugged. Torres didn't like to talk about Eileen, and when he did he liked to paint her as a shrew. Neither of which did anything to fool Kay, of course. She had seen him slip away from too many stakeouts to call her before she went to sleep; did not have any trouble recognizing the clear signs of affection that her ex-partner tried so hard to hide. "She's fine."

"How's the office?"

Torres inserted his thumb into the carapace of a bright red crustacean, split it neatly in half, poured some butter on the meat and wolfed it down happily. "We muddle along without you, Kay, though the warmth has gone out of summer."

"How poetic."

"Thank you. I've been thinking it up for most of the afternoon."

"And the job?"

Torres shrugged. "It's the job. We're hot on the trail of the next Williams, based out of the west side, but other than that, essentially identical. Not quite so nasty, maybe, but very nearly. The drug war continues, Kay, us on one side, them on the other. How about your end? How's counterintelligence?"

"Kind of the same," Kay said, "except that the enemy is better trained and meaner."

"You enjoying it?"

Kay thought this over for a moment. "I think 'enjoy' might be a bit too strong. Some days involve staring at a computer screen until your eyes start to freeze over." Kay shrugged. "Hard not to miss the day-to-day excitement of gangs. But I'm good at it; that's something. It's necessary."

"How's Frowny?"

"We don't really call her that, up in New York."

"I'd hope not. She's not one who minds cracking the whip now and again, our Jeffries."

"No indeed."

"She cracked the whip on you at all, Ivy?"

Kay laughed. "We've come to an understanding, Frowny and I."

Torres laughed also. "So what are we here for? Because that train ride from New York to Baltimore is a long one, and I don't imagine it'll go any easier with a bushel of crabs in your belly."

"Look, Marc . . ." Kay began, then fell silent.

"Oh, shit," Torres said, smiling, "this must be serious if we're using first names."

"I need a favor."

"I've got two kidneys, Ivy, and you're welcome to one of them, if that's really what you're interested in."

"It isn't," Kay said, but then fell silent again. Asking for help had never been her strong suit. Quite the opposite.

Torres came to her assistance. "I don't really need to remind you, do I, Ivy, that you literally saved my life last year?"

Kay blushed. "Don't make so much of it. You'd have done the same as I did if I'd been the one who caught that bullet."

"It was my leg, Kay, and it was your pistol that saved the rest of me. So tell me what you need and I'll see if I can do it."

But it took Kay a moment to get started. "Did I ever tell you about what happened to my parents?"

"No," Torres said, setting his crabmeat down on the newsprint covering the table. "Not in detail."

Kay did then, flatly and without any excess of emotion. The straight facts as she knew them. Paul and Anne Malloy met as residents at Johns Hopkins. Specialized in global health, trying to cure those pesky third-world diseases that seem old-fashioned, even rather quaint, here in the Western world: tuberculosis and polio, things our grandparents or great-grandparents used to die of. True believers, the two of them, gallivanting all across the planet, trying to do some small measure of good. Namibia, Cambodia, Colombia. During a seemingly routine visit to the last, they were both killed in a robbery gone wrong, some thug losing his cool or just reveling in sadism. A few words about the godparents who took her in: good people, people who kept her on the straight and narrow. The story recounted as if it had happened to someone else, as if Kay were just repeating something she had heard, rather than trauma that she had experienced.

"I'm sorry," Torres said afterward.

Kay grunted. "You did some work down in Colombia as part of some joint task force, right?"

"Years back. Maybe you've heard this rumor, Ivy, but they actually have some cocaine in Colombia. Hard to believe, I know."

"You make any friends while you were down there?"

"Like, how friendly?"

"Friendly enough to get their hands on the file relating to my parents' death."

"Why?"

"Can we call it curiosity for the moment?"

"For the moment," Torres agreed, less than happy. "You so sure you want to go picking at scabs?"

"They're my wounds, Torres," Kay said. "I'll pick at them if I want to."

Torres nodded. "Fair enough."

The waiter came back, and they ordered more beer and more crabs, although they still had a fair quantity of both left. Torres started up again after he was gone. "Shit, Ivy. All that buildup, I was at least expecting you were going to ask me for something a little more substantial than a phone call to an old colleague."

"That was part one," Kay said cleanly.

Torres cleared his throat loudly. "Then I suppose lunch is on you?"

"I see how deep your well of loyalty runs. Yes, yes, lunch is on me."

"And what do you need?"

"I ran a search for my father on the Sentinel database."

Torres wedged one thick finger into his ear canal, wiggled it dramatically. "I gotta get my ears checked," he said. "Because it almost sounded like you just told me that you used Bureau resources for a personal matter, which last time I checked is a big no-no."

"It came up as a zero file."

Torres's good humor slid right off his face. "Shit," he said.

"Yeah."

"What else did it say?"

"Unfortunately, I have no idea. He died just before we started switching our paper files over to digital."

"So then the file is located in—"

"Pickett Street. Exactly."

Torres scratched at his jowls.

"You got any friends down there?" Kay asked.

Torres thought it over awhile. "Not exactly," he equivocated. "Friends of friends, maybe. I'll have to think about it. What you're asking, Kay, it could get a fellow in trouble. A fellow . . . or a lady."

"I know it's a lot to ask," Kay said. "If you don't feel comfortable doing it, I can understand completely. It's just that—" But before she could say anything else, Torres cut her off with one motion of his thick hand.

"You think I'd forget the turn you did me so quick? If this is what you need, this is what you'll get." He poured half a Natty Boh through a smile. "But I'm ordering more crabs."

Kay smiled. "That seems fair," she said.

29

I T WAS something of a shock, having watched him through a telephoto lens for so long, to get a face-to-face view of Mr. Artur Vadim. He looked younger in person, and sunnier, a handsome and well-kept forty. He was even fairly tan for a Slav in late autumn. He wore a suit that was nice-looking but not quite new, and his hair was salt-and-pepper and had started to recede.

"Mr. Vadim," Jeffries said, and as always Kay was impressed with her absolute sense of composure, as if this were a routine task in a routine job, a librarian stamping a book, a bank teller examining a check. "Please, have a seat."

Vadim looked at Jeffries with something like a smile on his face. He did not seem particularly surprised, although whether that was because he had somehow become aware of their surveillance or he just didn't display shock easily, Kay was not sure. "I'd just as soon stand."

"As you prefer," Jeffries said, "though this might take a few minutes, and I don't see any reason that they should be spent with you in discomfort."

Vadim shrugged and took a seat. A small victory, Kay thought, one to build on.

They had arranged a meeting with him on false pretenses, through the auspices of another one of Jeffries's contacts, a Russian businessman who had long been amongst her stable of assets. The surroundings felt appropriate to the moment, the sort of faceless institutional hotel room that is indistinguishable from a thousand just like it scattered across America. They had made an elaborate security sweep of the premises beforehand, almost certainly unnecessary but then there was that pesky "almost," wasn't there? The margin for error in this kind of game was razor-thin; Kay had learned that much already. The smallest mistake, the tiniest detail overlooked, was enough to sink an entire operation.

"Do not feel overly compelled to say anything," Jeffries had warned Kay after they had finished setting the stage, in the nervous half hour before Vadim's arrival. "It can be useful to have several people in the room when you make the pitch. It gives them the vague sense of being outnumbered, of playing against forces with whom they're overmatched. But I'll take the lead on everything. Listen, watch, remember."

Kay hadn't really needed the warning, but she nodded her head all the same.

"My name is Jeffries. This is Agent Malloy. We're with the FBI."

"I know who you are," Vadim said.

"I thought you might."

"And I know why you're here." Although, to Kay's mind, this wasn't a very impressive piece of prognostication. There could be only one reason why two FBI Agents were sitting quietly in a hotel room, waiting for him, and it was not to trade stock tips.

"Then I suppose my job should be very easy," Jeffries said cheekily, although her face maintained its inimitable flat affect.

"I'm afraid I'm not so sure that's the case," Vadim said, even though the fact that he was still there—that he hadn't run off as soon as he'd entered—at least suggested some interest on his part.

"We've been watching you for some time, Mr. Vadim. And in

that time we've come to recognize you as an individual of taste, of discernment, of class. An individual whose appreciation for the good life, unfortunately, is not adequately being served on his SVR salary."

"How kind of the FBI to notice this manifest injustice," Vadim said. His English was perfect, with just the slightest hint of a Russian accent as garnish. "You have not such a reputation for softness."

"The Director's heart weeps for you," Jeffries said. "Fat, salty tears. It's become quite the scandal. We thought it might be wise to do something about it, just so he stops breaking down at meetings."

Kay stifled a laugh.

"And what exactly would I be doing in exchange for this . . . honorarium?"

"It would seem to us that there might be all sorts of things that an individual in your position would be able to do to ensure that our relationship is a mutually beneficial one," Jeffries said, keeping her cards close against her vest. "Of course, the reward for any piece of information would need to be assessed on a case-by-case basis, but that assessment, I can assure you, would be generous."

This much was true, at least. Good double agents were worth their weight in gold, not only for the information they could provide but for the insight they could provide about it. This was one area where the Bureau couldn't afford to be tightfisted.

"Being a double in the SVR is a dangerous occupation these days," Vadim said. "They have an unfortunate habit of disappearing into unmarked graves."

Kay's heart caught in her throat. If Vadim knew that the SVR had rolled up the CIA's network, what else might he know? The identity of the Black Bear mole, perhaps, or at least information that might lead them to him? After all of these months staring at the matrix, like plowing the desert, Kay literally salivated at the thought of getting something more substantial to work with.

Jeffries gave no indication that she had heard anything of any particular interest, and Kay cursed herself for her relative lack of self-control. "Being a double in the SVR, Mr. Vadim, is a dangerous occupation, period, I would think."

"Indeed!" he said, smiling. "A man would have to be very foolish to consider it."

"Or extremely well compensated," Jeffries added.

"Or extremely well compensated," Vadim agreed. "And yet, even the greediest of men would not suggest that a dollar value can be put on life. On their own lives, at least," Vadim amended. "We are sometimes prone, particularly in our line of work, to estimate the lives of others as a few cents on the dollar."

"Some of us are," Jeffries said noncommittally. "But others of us—and here, to dispense with false modesty for a moment, I would include myself—know the value of a friend and understand that loyalty runs two ways. Should you choose to avail yourself of our assistance, know that it would be wholehearted."

"You seem very sure of yourself."

"Do you know who I am, Mr. Vadim?" Jeffries asked.

Vadim laughed. "Who works in our field and does not? You are ASAC Jeffries, the American bogeyman. You have ears on every phone, eyes in every window. The birds sit on your shoulder and whisper the secrets they have heard on the wind. The rats gnawing wires in the bowels of the Kremlin are on your payroll. Russian spies frighten misbehaving children with your name."

If this flattered Jeffries, she gave no sign of it. A stray tangle of graying hair came loose over her glasses, but she brushed it back and continued. "Then you would know that I work for the FBI and not the CIA."

"As long as I have been in this business, I think that I've picked up on the distinction between the two, thank you."

"I'd hope so. You wouldn't be much good to us if you hadn't."

Vadim chuckled again. Kay wasn't quite sure yet whether his deliberate jocularity was a cover for fear or if he simply had ice water running through his veins. Somehow she suspected the former. "And what is your point, exactly?"

"We're not the CIA. You would report directly to me and my handpicked team. Absolute compartmentalization of information. No one outside of my office would ever know who you are."

"You can promise this?" Vadim asked.

"I don't speak flippantly," Jeffries said. "You can count everything I say as a promise."

"I'm sure that someone told Dmitri Ulyanov something similar."

"I'm sure someone did," Jeffries said. "But that someone wasn't me. I did not earn my reputation through lack of caution. I did not get it by being foolish, or unobservant, or unprofessional. My recruits are well protected and sleep at night as soundly as if a battalion of U.S. marines waited outside their door."

"That seems a bit of an exaggeration."

"Perhaps it's nudging the corner," Jeffries admitted. "Then again, if the job were so easy, we wouldn't need to pay you a very large sum of money to do it."

Vadim went silent for a moment. Behind his eyes SVR info was converted into dollars, dollars converted into luxury automobiles, expensive suits, trips to foreign locales, an entire life different and better and happier than his own. A trace of saliva pooled at the corner of his mouth. He brushed it away with the cuff of his cheap suit. "How large a sum of money?"

Jeffries shrugged, and Kay detected a trickle of enthusiasm leaking through her facade. To discuss a specific financial situation was to move the recruitment from the realm of theory into, at least slightly, the realm of fact. You were no longer arguing about whether a recruit *would* do something; instead the question became "How much?" "We have deep pockets," Jeffries said vaguely. "And long memories for friends."

"Those are attractive qualities."

"We imagine them to be," Jeffries said, cool as ever. "Though of course, neither of them are offered unreservedly to anyone. We'd need to be convinced of the value of our new friend before we are willing to open our pocketbook, deep as it is."

Vadim smiled. "You do not need to tell me of your standards, ASAC Jeffries, nor do I need to tell you of mine. The information I can provide would be invaluable in any number of ways, not the least of which is in determining the identity of the mole in your sister agency."

"Can one put a price on the invaluable?" Jeffries asked.

"I can," Vadim said. "And it is not a low one."

They had reached the nitty-gritty of the matter. Vadim didn't promise anything, but what he did do was agree with Jeffries on an elaborate clandestine method for remaining in contact, a system of call signs, paroles and secret messages that should ensure that Vadim could get information to them even if he was being monitored closely by the SVR. In theory, of course, although nothing was infallible.

"It was a pleasure getting to meet you, Mr. Vadim," Jeffries said, standing and shaking his hand. "I look forward to any number of other, similarly productive meetings."

"The next time we have one, *Comrade* Jeffries, I would hope you would have more than papers in your briefcase. Or perhaps I should say I would hope the paper is green and comes in large denominations."

"That would depend on the contents of your own briefcase,

Mr. Vadim," Jeffries countered, "although, as I've said before, we're generous to our friends."

Vadim nodded at Jeffries, then at Kay, then slipped out the door.

"We got him," Kay said, managing to hold in her excitement for a full twenty seconds or so after Vadim had left. She felt like she had just finished running a marathon or staked a year's wages on one turn of a roulette wheel, watching the ball *click-click-click* across wood, coming up on her desired colors. "That was . . ." Kay cleared her throat, tried to regain some of her composure. "That was fantastic."

"Maybe," Jeffries said, remaining as imperturbable as ever. "Or maybe he'll head back immediately and report our contact with him to his superiors. Perhaps they're already aware of it and, far from today being a great success, it's been step one of a mammoth failure in which Vadim, dangled out falsely as a potential double, is anything but, and any information he chooses to provide us is carefully vetted in Moscow and intended to cause us nothing but harm." Jeffries turned her cool, distant gray eyes towards Kay. "It might be a little early to break out the champagne."

30

CHOOSING AN outfit on a first date was like deciding on an order of battle for a general: a question that required careful and nuanced consideration. It was Kay's first in months—not the first time she had been asked on a date in months, needless to say, but the first time she had decided that it was worth her effort to actually go on one. She finally settled on a red strapless thing that Alice had insisted she buy one afternoon in SoHo: a bit much by Kay's standards, but then, Alice had reminded her, Kay's standards had died during the second Eisenhower administration and could perhaps do with some updating.

And she was gratified to see Andrew's reaction when he saw her coming up the stairs of the Houston Street subway station, his jaw not quite on the floor but at least some level below his shoulders. For that matter, Kay had to admit some mild disturbance of her own perfectly smooth manner on seeing his wide shoulders and deep, one might even say piercing eyes. "You look lovely," he said, and smiled when she smiled. Then he presented his arm in a way that would have allowed Kay to ignore the offer without embarrassment, part of the casual grace with which he did everything. But Kay took it, and the two walked comfortably to the Village.

The restaurant was old and stylish and served Italian cuisine. Andrew knew the owner, a friendly, moustachioed sort who complimented Kay's beauty in thickly accented English, then took them swiftly to a corner table. Andrew thanked him in what sounded to Kay's ears like competent Italian, then looked over the wine list. "Shall I choose a bottle?" he asked.

Kay was, if not an expert, at least something of a wine buff—courtesy of growing up around Aunt Justyna—but she found herself acquiescing all the same. When the waiter came around, Andrew ordered them a bottle and a mixed tray of appetizers.

"And how proceeds Black Bear?" Andrew asked a few minutes later, after pleasantries had been dispensed with. "Any burning leads?"

"Yes. I forgot to mention, just this morning, we cracked the case wide open. We've got a team of Agents about to fall on our unfortunate traitor at just this very minute, put a knee in his spine and drag him off to a federal penitentiary."

"Yikes," Andrew said. "Sucks to be that guy."

Kay laughed.

"I've been reviewing some of the matrix results," Andrew said, taking a bite out of a piece of *arancini*.

"The matrix?" Kay said quizzically. "Now that you mention it . . . yes, yes I do think I recall the matrix. You mean the focal point of my daily existence for oh so many months?"

"I'm not sure I trust this Deputy Chief that you've got your hooks into over at the Russian mission. Have you considered that he's being used as a dangle?" "Dangle" was slang for a false double who planted false information from one side to the other, part of the endless selection of tricks that made up the intelligence officer's toolkit.

"You mean the Political Officer?" Kay asked, finishing off her first glass of wine. "It's not like they come with their intentions written out on their back. Jeffries is keeping a close eye on the matter, you can be sure of that, at least."

"No doubt," Andrew said. "She's a rare talent, your Jeffries. You should hear some of the stories they tell about her down at Langley. Not just Langley, either. The competition holds her in a special sort of reverence—a red, white and blue monster hiding in closets and ferreting out secrets."

"That's kind of how we think of her too," Kay admitted, "though mostly she wears gray."

Over the rest of the wine Andrew regaled her about some of his earlier postings. Two years in Kiev, two more in Moscow. He spoke affectionately of the people, the great literary and artistic traditions of the nation, those who survived several generations beneath communism's tread, and those who had started to flourish in the years after the fall of the Soviet empire. He was funny and insightful, and unlike most men on first dates he didn't feel the need to expound indefinitely, instead turning the conversation comfortably back onto Kay.

"Where have you been assigned, Kay?"

"Quantico, Baltimore, then back up here," she replied. "But I spent two years in Namibia after college."

"Namibia? What were you doing there?"

"I did a term in the Peace Corps."

"Did you have dreadlocks?"

"Everyone sort of had dreadlocks in Namibia. I lived in a hut, and water came from a pump a mile and a half away. Hair washing ceases to be a major priority. One of the benefits of the first world."

"I'm sure they looked flattering," Andrew said, smooth as ever. "What pushed you into the Peace Corps?"

"My parents were . . . interested in foreign development," she said lamely. In fact they had been more than interested, it had been their passion, the most important thing in their lives, apart from their children.

"And what made you get involved in law enforcement?"

Their murder, Kay wanted to say but didn't. "I watched too many James Bond movies when I was a kid," she said.

"For me it was reruns of *The Man from U.N.C.L.E.*," Andrew admitted.

The entrées were delicious. Almost in spite of herself Kay realized that she was having a rather marvelous time. Andrew was handsome and charming and seemed genuinely interested in what she had to say. After dinner they ordered two espressos and split a cannoli.

"Best in the city," Andrew assured her.

"How could you possibly know that?" Kay asked. "You just moved here."

Andrew wiped a bit of cream off his chin. "The Internet says so. And when has the Internet ever been wrong about anything?"

"Never, to the best of my knowledge." Kay looked longingly at the last bite, one which Andrew was kind enough to push in her direction. "It is . . . reasonably delicious," she said.

Andrew laughed. "I think that's the nicest thing that I ever heard you say, Kay."

Kay smiled and forked another bite of dessert. The conversation, in its slow and effortless way, turned back to Kay. She found herself speaking offhandedly of some casual incident from her childhood, and from there on to adolescence generally.

"How old did you say you were when . . . ?"

Andrew didn't finish but Kay knew what he meant. "Ten or so."

"How did it happen?" Andrew asked.

As a rule, Kay did not speak casually about her parents. Not to anyone but her brother and her surrogate parents, and not even very much with them. "They were murdered," she said.

Andrew didn't say anything for a long time, as if observing an honorary silence. Then he smiled.

"Is that funny?"

"No, that's terrible. That's absolutely terrible. I think it's also the first time I ever lost the my-childhood-was-worse-than-yours game."

Kay found herself smiling as well. "What's my prize?"

"A lifetime of therapy?"

And then Kay was laughing also, and they were ordering two shots of *limoncello*, Andrew waving to the owner, who came by swiftly, happy to further what seemed a budding romance.

"To shared misfortunes," Kay said.

"They make us what we are."

"You think so?"

"Of course. I'm not sure if what happened to my parents is the reason I joined the CIA, but it's certainly part of what made me a good case officer."

"How so?"

He thought for a moment before answering. "You learn a lot of things, growing up on your own. But mainly what you learn is that you have to be responsible for the creation of your own character. There is . . . There is a certain terrible freedom in the thing: I had no one to shelter or define me, no one to tell me who to be or how to act. But I had no one to hold me back, no one that I had to pretend for. I was solitary, but . . . it made me strong."

"You're wrong," Kay found herself saying, more forcefully than she perhaps intended. "I mean . . . that's never been how I felt. If it hadn't been for my godparents—for my brother, even, all the trouble he is—I'd have been lost. Without people caring for me, without people to care for, I'd have been lost. I don't know what would have become of me." Belatedly she realized that this was exactly what seemed to have happened to Andrew and that it might have been better to keep her mouth shut.

But he didn't seem to mind, leaning back in his chair as if seriously considering it. "Some of the situations I've been in, Kay, overseas and undercover . . . Attachment of any kind is dangerous and can even be fatal. You have to be sharp and quick and clean and think clearly, without anyone around you to confuse the situation. You can't hold yourself back for anything."

"It sounds a lonely way to live."

"I don't know any other way," he said, with something like regret.

Neither of them seemed to want the dinner to end, but there was no category on the menu for "after-after-dinner drinks," and anyway the restaurant was closing. When the bill came, Kay made an effort to split it, as she always did on dates, but backed down in the face of Andrew's unwavering refusal to go dutch. They took a leisurely walk back to the Houston Street station and in the awkward moment after the good-bye Kay leaned in and kissed him.

31

PRODUCTIVE EVENING, Malloy?" Jeffries asked, appearing, as she had a tendency to, unexpectedly above Kay's shoulder.

It was a late evening in November, and like a lot of those, Kay and Jeffries were staying late in the office.

"Not particularly," Kay admitted, rubbing at her eyes. "Actually, I was just about getting ready to push my head through the monitor."

"That's government property," Jeffries said, taking a seat next to Kay, sipping from her thermos, which seemed bottomless. It was one of the lesser parts of her legend, that a woman weighing all of a hundred and ten pounds could drink her weight in caffeine every day without getting the least bit jittery. "And the Bureau does not look fondly on the destruction of its property."

Humor was so rare from Jeffries that, when it came, it always took Kay a few extra seconds to decipher it. "Maybe I could just pick a spot on the wall and launch my skull against it."

"That helps with the computer," Jeffries acknowledged, "but I don't imagine a severe concussion would be of much benefit to the good work and sharp thinking of our Agent Malloy."

Kay looked down at her desk and tried not to blush. Compliments from Jeffries were even rarer than humor. "I'm government property?" Kay asked.

"You're a Special Agent," Jeffries responded, taking a long sip from her thermos. "So more or less."

"I don't feel like it lately," Kay confessed. She had come to recognize these rare moments when Jeffries would drop her guard ever so slightly and was quick to take advantage of them. "Shuffling aimlessly through the matrix, like Alice lost in Wonderland."

"I told you these things can last years. Right now it seems like the focal point of existence and requires every waking moment of your time. When we wrap it up, you'll feel the same way about the next one, and the one after that. It'll take a while, but you'll get used to it."

A sudden burst of courage, brought on by exhaustion or too much coffee, and Kay asked, "How long did it take you?"

"You mean back when I first got involved in counterintelligence?" Jeffries repeated, as if struggling to recall halcyon memories of a half-mythical age. "When I started we did the matrix with a pencil. A 'folder' was not something you double-clicked to open; it was something that you had to drag out of a giant metal cabinet and then drag back in when you were done. Imagine everything that you hate about the matrix, and now imagine it being several times worse."

Kay shuddered. "You paint a nightmarish scenario."

"It was never easy," Jeffries said. "It's not an easy business. When I started out, we still had the KGB and the GRU. Remember the Cold War?"

"I think I can remember it coming on sometimes between cartoon shows."

A hint of a smile creased Jeffries's face, but she swallowed it quickly. "In some ways it was easier. The Soviets held down their half of the world, and we held down ours. Mostly we had a shared interest in making sure that things didn't blow up completely. They were the enemy, but they weren't so radically dissimilar from us, for all their talk about the proletariat. You could put yourself in their head space. It's a whole new ball game these days. After 9/11 . . ." Jeffries shrugged. "You can probably imagine."

There was no question that the events of September 11, 2001, had been a watershed moment for the Bureau, as it was for every intelligence agency and for the country at large. Terrorism had swiftly become the FBI's top priority, and forestalling another major attack their raison d'être. Not for the first time it occurred to Kay what an extraordinary breadth of experience Jeffries had acquired over the course of her long service to the nation.

"What was it like back then?"

"The clothes were worse but the music was better."

Kay had a sudden image of Jeffries in a disco suit, bobbing her head to a Bee Gees tune, but it was too absurd to stay firm in her mind for more than a split second. "I meant the job."

"I know what you meant, Malloy," Jeffries said. "That was a joke."

"Oh."

"The Bureau was . . . different in some ways. When I joined there were other women in the FBI, but not many. You know we didn't get our first female Agent until 1972?"

Kay did, of course. They hammered FBI history into you in Quantico, along with investigative techniques and weapons training and legal theory and the dozens of other things you needed to know to do your job. It was more than personal curiosity: the history, the lore, was part of what made one an effective Agent. An appreciation for the mission, for how it had evolved and developed over the years and how the Bureau had grown to deal with it. There had been women serving in the FBI back in the 1920s, when it was still a fledgling organization, but they were retired once J. Edgar Hoover had taken over as Director. A brilliant organizer whose passion for the Bureau had created the modern FBI, Hoover was, at the same time, a dyed-in-the-wool misogynist, and it wasn't until after his death that women could again become Agents. Two were recruited for Quantico's class of 1972, one an ex-nun, the other a former U.S. Marine—which, Kay had always felt, spoke to some indefinable part of the job that was somewhere between a military duty and a religious calling. These days there were more than two thousand women serving as Bureau Agents, in posts across the country and the world. For Kay the days of the FBI being a "boys' club" were far distant, but they wouldn't have been for Jeffries.

"It was . . . different," Jeffries said blandly. It was the closest that she would ever come to an outright complaint about the matter. Jeffries was a stoic through and through. "There were still a few holdovers from the old days, people who couldn't quite wrap their heads around the idea that I was a woman *and* an FBI Agent. The ratios were still skewed: I can't tell you how many times I looked around the room to see I was the only one in it with long hair. Not everyone thought that a woman could do the job."

"So?"

"I cut my hair," Jeffries said neatly. "And I outworked every one of my detractors. It's not about showing that you can beat the rest of the office in an arm wrestling competition or drink anyone under the table. I made sure that I was the best Agent in the room that I was in, whatever that room was—not loudly, not in a way that called attention to itself. But at the end of the day I wanted my supervisors, when they had something important that needed to be done, something critical, to look around the bullpen and find themselves staring at me."

Kay could appreciate that sentiment.

"That's the thing about the Bureau, Kay: the mission comes first. The mission always comes first. I suppose there was the occasional holdout here and there who never got over the fact that I had two X chromosomes. But most of them came around quickly enough once they saw that I could further the success of our mission. The protection of the country, the safety of its citizens—that's too important a thing to let prejudice get in the way. Most of the Agents understood that. Most understand that now. Enough with the matrix for tonight, Agent Malloy," she said. "Go home. Black Bear will be waiting for you tomorrow."

"Is that an order?" Kay asked cheekily.

"I suppose, if it needs to be," Jeffries said.

Kay smiled a little, and shut down her workstation, and followed Jeffries out.

32

THAT MORNING he had been called into the office of his superior, Alexei Rossokov. A casual request, his secretary coming by to ask if he had a few minutes, which of course Vadim did. And Rossokov had been friendly, as he usually was, with no hint of menace in his dark brown eyes. There was some course of training that the brass back in Moscow was demanding of all their Agents overseas. Unnecessary, probably, but what could Rossokov do about it, or Vadim, for that matter? Annoying to be taken away from one's work, but it should only be a week or two, and it wouldn't be such a terrible thing to be back in the old country for a little while.

Vadim played the role of the competent subordinate well. He was extremely busy with his own work at the moment, but if Moscow wanted him to come for a visit, then of course he would find a way to get it done. He smiled and made a joke about Russian winters starting in American autumns while feeling his heart fall through his chest and down his pleated pants to rest uncomfortably in his left loafer.

The rest of that day continued as usual. He went about his work with an easy attitude, or at least the easiest attitude that he could fake. The next day was Thanksgiving, obviously not a holiday in which anyone in the Russian mission had particular interest, although as a practical matter it made sense to shut down. He said good-bye to his neighbors when he left that evening, told them he would be heading back home Friday, to keep his seat warm until he came back. Then he went to a bar and began to drink heavily.

"Called back to Moscow for new training." It was plausible. It was not outside the realm of possibility. And yet it was not true, Vadim knew—knew the way a fisherman might know that it was going to rain before evening, hang the weatherman. A spy's business is paranoia. He swam in it, he breathed it through his nostrils, he exuded it through his pores. Despite all her guarantees of secrecy, Jeffries or someone on Jeffries's team had blown it. The SVR knew that he had been approached by the FBI and that he hadn't reported that contact. That Vadim had not yet actually given them anything valuable would not be any sort of affirmative defense, he knew: ironic but irrelevant.

Equally ironic was the fact that, having created this difficulty for him, Jeffries and the FBI were also the only ones who might solve it. Had that been the game all along? he wondered, his paranoia level rising sharply. Had they made preliminary contact with him, expecting that he would play it coy, all the while planning to somehow alert the SVR and thus force him into defecting? Put a pin in that one, Vadim told himself. Paranoia might be the only defense one had in this business, but still it could drive you mad if you let it. And anyway, it didn't matter. However they had found out, whatever the plan was, Vadim had only one potential out, and he knew it.

He woke up early the next afternoon with a splitting headache but absolutely clear on what he had to do. On his personal phone he found the number for Antonio's Flower Service and dialed it. He let it ring three times, then disconnected. Five minutes later he called the number again, but this time he let it ring.

It was called a parole, after the premodern military practice by which soldiers on watch would repeat two halves of a given password as a call-and-response, thus ensuring they weren't about to fall victim to a surprise assault. Antonio's Flower Service was, needless to say, not a real business but rather part of the elaborate game by which Vadim informed the FBI that he needed to talk to someone on their end.

• • •

It was bad luck that Marshall had pulled duty over Thanksgiving, but he tried not to let it bother him. It was part of the job; there was nothing else to say about it. He'd rather have been in Boston with his wife and his two children, but he wasn't, so Marshall resigned himself to whiling away the hours with a Ludlum novel and a frozen turkey dinner. With Vadim's recruitment still in play, someone needed to be around to man the station at all times, even though it seemed unlikely that it would end up being necessary.

The drawer rang once. Snapped out of his boredom, there was a brief moment when Marshall thought he might have imagined it. When the drawer rang a second time he opened it with a curse, revealing a sea of cheap cellular phones attached to a power strip.

A "hello" phone was called that because names were never exchanged over it, not real ones, at least. An Agent might have dozens sitting in their desk drawer, each keyed to one specific asset, each with its own peculiar set of code words that needed to be memorized by the user.

"Hello?" Marshall said breathlessly.

"This is Mr. Conrad," Vadim said, as calmly as he could make himself. "I was supposed to stop in and pick up a floral arrangement you're putting together for me, and I was hoping I might be able to come in a bit earlier than we had planned."

Long pause. "When were you hoping to pick it up?"

"Today. Tonight. Immediately."

"I'm going to talk to our staff on-site," Marshall said, thinking as quickly as possible. "This is a very busy weekend, after all."

"I assure you, I would not be bothering you were the matter not . . . extremely urgent."

"We'll handle it," Marshall said, trying to sound more confident than he was. "Call back in an hour."

Marshall hung up the phone, allowing himself one brief moment of horror-tinged confusion before grabbing his own phone off his desk and dialing Jeffries's number as fast as he could.

33

AFTER KAY had finished baking her carrot cake, and frosting her carrot cake, and putting her carrot cake in Tupperware; and after she had finished applying her makeup; and even after she had put her shoes and her coat on, and pulled her keys out, and turned off the lights in preparation for leaving, she sat down on the couch.

It would have been thirteen years—or perhaps fourteen—since they had all had Thanksgiving together, midway through Christopher's first and only semester at college. Struggle though she did to date it correctly, Kay had no difficulty in remembering why their tradition had come to an abrupt end. It had involved drinking (Christopher's mostly), and anger (here Christopher and Luis shared the honors), and yelling (everyone), and afterward Christopher slammed the door and headed back to school—but not for very long: they had rules at college like everywhere else, and like everywhere else, Christopher had proved steadfastly uninterested in abiding by them. By Christmas he had been expelled from campus, and by New Year's he had vacated his room at Uncle Luis's—to go on tour with his band, if she remembered correctly, or perhaps that had been the winter he ran off to Buenos Aires. There had been so many misadventures, so much disappointment,

Christopher's youthful foolishness stretching into his mid-thirties, at a time when most people settled down to careers and families.

Kay checked her watch. Four thirty: if she didn't leave now she'd be late, although of course Christopher wouldn't show up on time, and in fact she found the idea of skipping the event not at all unappealing. She even spent a brief moment considering trying to come up with some sort of work emergency, but the thought of leaving poor Aunt Justyna alone to deal with Christopher and Luis was a step too far into outright villainy. Sighing, she slipped downstairs and found her way into the subway.

Aunt Justyna had an apron on that said "Kiss the Chef" in Polish, and enough pots and pans on the stove to feed a small army, and the relief in her eyes when her niece came in was enough to make Kay feel guilty for thinking about not showing up. Luis was not, to judge by the way he stumbled as he came over to give her a hug, on his first tumbler of whiskey; but then again, it was a holiday, and Kay was not in the mood to be judgmental. She herself was thinking the evening might well prove more tolerable with a large glass of wine in hand.

Uncle Luis and Aunt Justyna lived in a gorgeous apartment on the Upper West Side, only a couple of blocks from Central Park. It had been Kay's home during the eight years of her life between the deaths of Paul and Anne Malloy and her leaving for Princeton, but she had never really thought of it as such. Home had been her parents' house in Westchester, three stories with a big green backyard, a dog they had to give up, the sort of suburban bliss that most people can only dream of, and indeed that Kay often dreamed of in the long years after it had been taken away from her.

But they'd done the best they could—that was what Christopher never seemed to be able to understand. If it hadn't been a very easy thing to be uprooted from your home and moved into the city, into a different environment, Kay didn't think it had been any easier from the opposite end. As a child you suppose that adults have all the answers to everything—or should have them, at least—and feel betrayed when your parents or guardians fall short of these impossibly high standards. But you get older and you realize that's nonsense; the sudden arrival of two adolescents in Luis and Justyna's pleasant, childless existence, the responsibilities and burdens of parenthood forced upon them unasked—it couldn't have been easy. Perhaps Luis had been too harsh at times, too quick to dismiss Christopher; but raising children doesn't come with a playbook, and he hadn't had much practice before being thrown into the deep end.

Kay spent a while sort of pretending to help Justyna in the kitchen but mainly just gossiping and drinking while her aunt did all the hard work. Kay had a little flutter in her chest that the white wine was not helping with, as if she were back in Quantico, about to sit down and take a test she hadn't prepared for. Of course, Kay was the sort of person who had always prepared thoroughly for tests, so the metaphor wasn't entirely apt, but it was close. Something unpleasant was coming, and there was nothing Kay could do to head it off, nothing but smile and play at ignorance.

Luis came into the kitchen, swaying slightly from drink while trying hard to hide it. "So?" Luis began in a deliberately off-handed way. "Shall we eat?"

Kay didn't say anything. Justyna clucked unhappily.

"What? What is that about?"

"Christopher isn't here," Kay muttered.

"It is Christopher we are waiting for?" Luis said, as if the idea had just occurred to him. "Then perhaps you will not mind if I go back into the den and watch some television. Or take a nap. Or perhaps order some takeout, because if we're going to be waiting for my nephew's arrival to eat, I'm afraid I may never get a crack at that turkey."

"A bit of an exaggeration, don't you think?" Kay asked. "It's five thirty; I'm sure you won't starve for at least another hour or two."

Luis chuckled and went back into the den.

Although of course Christopher actually was late by about thirty minutes, minutes during which Kay at least half hoped that his arrival would be canceled rather than postponed. It would be a very nice thing if they could all sit down and enjoy one another's company, this small ad hoc family that was now all that Kay had left. But, barring that, it would be a welcome change not to have to sit through another dispute between her brother and her uncle, one which she would unavoidably be called upon to referee.

But then the buzzer rang and a few minutes later Christopher was at the door, a bottle of wine under his arm and another in his stomach. At least a bottle, to judge by his flushed red face. "Sister," he said, kissing her on the cheek, then hurrying over to his aunt. "Aunt Justyna," he said, kissing her as well.

Prelude over, he turned suddenly towards Luis, who was not quite grinning around his unlit cigar. "Dearest Uncle," he said, "how long has it been?"

"A while."

"You look magnificent, Don, just magnificent. Aging like a monarch, and not one of the French ones who always had trouble with the gout."

"Dinner's served!" Justyna said brightly, hoping food might head off trouble. Wishful thinking, but Kay couldn't blame her. They each took a place at the large, rarely used dinner table, in front of china plates and white linen that were brought out just as infrequently. Justyna had gone all out, as if the prepared feast and elegant table setting could ameliorate any potential unpleasantness. All the classic Thanksgiving foods were in attendance: turkey and mashed potatoes; cranberry sauce, freshly made and canned, because Justyna knew that Christopher had always preferred the latter; cheesy broccoli and creamed spinach.

It looked beautiful and it tasted even better, and no one seemed to make any particular effort to eat any of it. Christopher grouped a few slivers of canned cranberry sauce onto his plate—to placate Justyna, Kay suspected—but mostly he just drank. Luis crammed his plate to near overflowing but then left it there as if he had forgotten to eat it. Kay did her best to swallow a few bites of turkey, as much to hold down the wine as anything else. Even Justyna, Kay felt, was only going through the motions, all of them playing at being a well-adjusted family, inexpertly and not for very long.

"And how is your band, Christopher?" Justyna asked brightly, and as was often the case Kay was impressed at her easy grace, at the natural ability she had to focus on happy things, although she thought for once it wouldn't be sufficient.

"It's all right," Christopher said, eyes bloodshot from whatever he had drunk before coming to dinner. "We've got a showcase in Bushwick coming up next week."

"Straight on to the top forty," Luis began, and Kay's heart sank down into her gut. "Remind us again, Christopher, what's the name of your brilliant ensemble?"

"Chicken Shit," Christopher said to Luis around a mouthful of greens. "Captain Swill and his Chicken Shit Extravaganza."

This was a lie, as Kay well knew, a cheap and rather petty attempt to infuriate their adoptive father, and one which Kay had hoped Christopher might avoid making, at least until the second course.

"An apt sobriquet," Luis said, as always happy to give as good as he got.

Justyna shot Kay a quick, sad, helpless look, then took another sip of wine. There wasn't much else to do, and a little more alcohol probably wouldn't change anything.

"And what are you up to apart from that, Christopher? What occupies your time, as an adult male in the prime of his years? What other accomplishments can we expect from you?" Luis's sarcasm permeated his string of questions.

"I do a lot of drugs," Christopher said cheerily, "and I've gotten pretty good at Super Nintendo. Old-fashioned, I know, but then, the classics are the best, right?"

Kay's phone chirped like happy release, and she pulled it from her pocket and herself up from her chair in one swift motion. "Could be the office," she explained, excusing herself from the table and the combat that was swiftly to arrive.

Her exit was not long lamented, a brief interruption before Christopher and Luis threw themselves back at each other. Kay ducked into her uncle's study. "Yes?"

"Agent Malloy? Agent Malloy?" The connection wasn't great, but Kay could recognize Jeffries on the other end. There was a faint quiver in her voice, enough for Kay to know something serious was going on, although Kay did not miss that Jeffries still insisted on "Agent Malloy" rather than "Kay." The apocalypse itself would need to descend on the city before Jeffries broke formality. "Are you in New York?"

As the volume of the yelling grew louder, Kay had to shove a newly painted nail into the ear that she didn't have the phone against. "Why? What's going on?"

Jeffries said something but it was lost in a sudden sharp spike of profanity from the other room. Kay was about ready to go in and start doing some yelling of her own when the front door slammed shut, Christopher's part in the dialogue coming to an abrupt end.

"I didn't catch that," Kay said, turning her mind back to work. "One more time?"

"Are you in New York?"

"Upper West Side, why?"

"Kay, I need you to listen to me very carefully, because there isn't time to go through this twice. Our friend contacted Marshall twenty minutes ago. They may have gotten wind of our conversation, and before they do something unpleasantly permanent, he wants to come to the side of the angels."

Kay felt guilty for feeling so relieved, but the truth was that she could have kissed Jeffries at that moment, she was so grateful for the interruption. "Fantastic!" she said, although in the back of her mind she could appreciate that Vadim might not see things in quite the same way. "What's the problem?"

"The problem is that I'm in Atlanta right now, Agent Malloy. And Wilson is in Boston, and the rest of the squad are out of pocket also. It's just you and Marshall, and since you're the only one who was in the room when we made the approach, you're now also the person responsible for coordinating the retrieval of our friend, and for doing so before the trap pulls shut. Are you up for it?"

Kay peeked through the crack in the doorway, at the Thanksgiving feast growing cold on her aunt's table, at the aftermath of a holiday brawl, another in a long list of gatherings that had ended in a similar fashion. "Extremely," she said.

34

KAY HAD drunk half a bottle of wine over dinner two hours earlier—at the time she had not anticipated going from the Thanksgiving table directly back into the world of international espionage—but she felt absolutely sober; had felt that way as soon as she picked up the phone and heard Jeffries's voice. Family was maddening, and impossible to get a handle on, and an open sore—but this? This came naturally, came smoothly. Kay had never felt so certain that she was doing what she was meant to do. She could feel herself rising to the occasion, making decisions and giving orders with calculated thought but no hesitation.

Kay managed to hail a cab outside of her uncle's apartment building, told the driver to take off to the Bureau's downtown office, resisted the temptation to encourage him to speed. Then she sprinted through Security and into the office that had been set aside for the Black Bear op, greeted Marshall with a peremptoriness bordering on rudeness, then hovered over the drawer of "hello" phones, waiting for Vadim to make second contact.

She did not have to wait long. The phone buzzed and Kay snatched it.

"Hello?" Vadim said.

"Mr. Conrad," Kay said calmly, using Vadim's code name.

"Where the hell is Ms. Galway?" Vadim asked, likewise using Jeffries's own.

"Perhaps you've noticed, Mr. Conrad, that today is a holiday. Ms. Galway, like most of the rest of the country, is off celebrating it, and unfortunately not in a position to assist you. I assure you, however, that Ms. Galway has placed her unreserved confidence in me and that I'm in a position to handle your situation just as adeptly and competently as Ms. Galway would." "Hell, I hope that's true," Kay thought.

"This isn't the way this is supposed to occur," Vadim said, and Kay could hear the way his fear had eaten him down.

"And yet this is the way it will," Kay said smoothly, doing her best to radiate a subtle blend of comfort and absolute confidence, as if the matter were already settled. Handling an asset was, in some ways, similar to interrogating a subject. The important thing was to retain control at all times, never to act surprised by any unexpected development, as if everything were unfolding according to a plan that you alone were aware of. "Trust us, Mr. Conrad. We know what we're doing; we'll keep you safe. Of course, should you be disinterested in availing yourself of our hospitality, you're more than welcome to throw yourself on the tender graces of your colleagues . . ."

Vadim cursed awhile, Kay's limited grasp of Russian insufficient to follow the nuances, though it sounded serious. Russian is quite a language for swear words, Kay had long ago realized. "All right," Vadim said. "Where are we meeting?"

"Are you familiar with the Sixty-Fifth Street entrance to Central Park?"

"East side or west?"

"West. On the third bench in from the entrance, in one hour, you will find a white woman with dark hair wearing a gray trench coat. That woman will be me, and I'll be in a position to bring you home."

"My new home or my old one?" Vadim said, rather cheekily for a man about to defect to a foreign country.

"Home is where the heart is, Mr. Conrad," Kay said. "And on behalf of the American people, let me say just how thrilled we'll be to see to your repatriation."

Vadim barked out a laugh. "Central Park, one hour," he said, then hung up the phone.

But Kay was there in half an hour, she and Marshall doing a lap around the area, keeping an eye out for anything unexpected, anything out of place. It was here, Kay knew, that they would miss Jeffries's expertise, not to mention the assistance of the rest of their Black Bear colleagues. The entire thing had happened so quickly—between Vadim's contacting them and the defection only a couple of hours had elapsed—that it seemed unlikely the SVR would have had time to get wind of it. Although, on the other hand, it seemed more than unlikely that the SVR could have sniffed Vadim out as a potential traitor, it seemed all but impossible, and yet here they were.

Still, when Kay took a seat at the bench, ten minutes before her meeting with Vadim, she felt reasonably confident—confident, at least, in how she had handled the situation so far, if not necessarily at the outcome. She had been thrown a hell of a curveball, but with a little bit of luck she might end this chilly Thanksgiving evening with an intelligence coup that could provide the answers to their Black Bear investigation. Kay rubbed vigorously at her legs to try to keep warm, checked that the microphone attached to her lapel was working. "Marshall, you hear me?"

"Five by five," he echoed back in her earbud. "You ready for this?"

"You tell me."

"Hell, from where I'm sitting, you look like you could take care of this with one arm tied behind your back."

Kay appreciated the vote of confidence but wasn't sure that it was deserved. She focused intently on the surroundings, tried to bite down tight on the flutter of nerves from her stomach. Central Park was quiet, all but silent, the usual pedestrians inside celebrating the holiday or just avoiding the dark and the cold. Apart from the occasional transient passing through, and one late-evening jogger trying to make up for a Thanksgiving feast, the park was empty. Kay made Vadim out almost before Marshall alerted her to his arrival. "Subject is crossing up Central Park West," he said.

Vadim, as sharp-eyed and nervous as Kay, noticed her as well, giving a little motion with his head that was not quite an acknowledgment. Kay responded with a shake of one hand that might have been simply a woman trying to keep her extremities warm, and the SVR double began to walk rapidly towards her.

Kay's heart was in her throat. Coming towards her, at this very moment, so close she could almost grab him, was the potential key to the Black Bear operation, an intelligence coup of the first order. So close that she could almost smell the reek of his after-shave; so close that she could nearly make out his chin stubble.

Distantly, from someplace beyond her excitement, Kay heard the sound of tires screeching, noticed something moving swiftly from outside her field of vision. She screamed a warning into her microphone and leaped off the bench, heading for Vadim at a tear. Vadim noticed it a moment after Kay had, turned his head to see the van speeding towards him. Kay screamed a second warning, turned her run into a sprint, knowing all the while that she wouldn't be able to make it, watching furiously as a burly man ripped open the sliding door of his vehicle, stepped forward and placed something against Vadim's neck. The spark of light that came next revealed it to be a Taser, as did Vadim's reaction, his knees collapsing out from under him as he fumbled forward to the ground. He'd have received a nasty wound if the thug in the van hadn't grabbed him by the shoulders and hauled him inside, the entire operation taking no more than a few seconds.

Just as Kay made it to the park entrance, the door of the van slammed shut, and her last images of Artur Vadim were ones of blind and horrified terror. Then the van streaked off downtown and was lost in the night, leaving a furious Kay behind, screaming in futility at the exhaust.

35

K AY WAS back at her apartment, staring blankly at a wall, running through the events of the second-worst day of her life, when an unknown number came up on her phone. She let it ring awhile, because who could possibly be on the other end of the phone who would make her day better? Perhaps it was Vadim, calling to announce that he'd found his way free of his SVR captors, was safely ensconced in a nearby McDonald's, a vanilla milk shake in one hand, and could Kay spring over and pick him up so he could tell her the secret identity of their mole?

"Hello," Kay said into her mouthpiece, with no particular enthusiasm.

"Is this Kay Malloy? Agent Kay Malloy?"

"I don't want to be part of any survey, and if you're selling something, I don't want to buy it, either."

"This is Officer Talloway, NYPD, at the Eighteenth Precinct. Do you have a brother named Christopher Malloy?"

He had overdosed in a hallway in Bed-Stuy, Kay thought. No, he had put back a fifth of gin and gone for a long drive down Eastern Parkway, clipped a janitor coming back from a long day of work, two bodies for the beleaguered NYPD to scrape off the asphalt. "Yes," Kay said flatly.

"We've got him in lockup, awaiting processing. He was intoxicated outside a club, acted belligerent with one of our officers. He asked that we give you a call. Normally we'd run him through booking, but as a professional courtesy . . ." Officer Talloway left the rest of the thought unexpressed.

Afterward would come the slow swelling rage like a boil, but right at that moment there was only an enormous sense of relief. "I'll be down in forty minutes," Kay said.

She did not ask Officer Talloway for any favors, but she had not made a point of refusing them, and he had agreed to write Christopher up for drunk and disorderly while looking the other way on whatever else Christopher had been up to. Afterward Talloway asked if she had a phone number, and she told him it was classified to try and keep the conversation professional. He smiled and said maybe he'd try and suss it out, but Kay had no more notion of romance with him than a rattlesnake. She hadn't seen it coming, but Andrew was a presence in her life.

He came out of lockup whistling, his hands in his pockets and his shoulders slumped, looking like an eight-year-old boy caught with his hand in a cookie jar. He made some sort of joke when he saw her, although she didn't really hear it, her eyes hard on his, walking him out of the station and out to the parking lot and into her car. Kay drove six blocks without saying anything, saw what she was looking for, pulled a hard right into a small parking lot, got a ticket from the automatic machine; it was five dollars for twenty minutes, but at that moment she felt willing to pay the fee.

"Where we going?" Christopher asked, but Kay didn't answer, just headed up to the top floor and parked in a distant corner of the lot and shut off the car.

She opened the door and got out of the car, stretched down to her toes, then stretched back up and from side to side. Christopher lit a cigarette just about as soon as he was outside, and she let him drag off of it for a second before punching him hard enough to send his American Spirit spinning off into the darkness.

"Are you out of your mind?" she screamed, and there was a moment when she had to stop herself from going after him on the ground, she was still so choked with rage. "ARE YOU OUT OF YOUR MIND?" she screamed again, louder, loud enough to wake the neighbors. "You get busted drunk and you drop my name! It's not enough you shit all over *your* life, you've got to scrap mine in the process. You're a leech, you're a goddamned leech," she said. "And one of these days you're going to push me too far, Christopher, I swear to God you will, and I'll drop you. And who will you have left after that, huh? Is there anyone else in your life that you haven't pushed away entirely?"

Christopher sat up straight, rubbed at his jaw for a moment. Then he smiled and lit another cigarette. "Rough day?" he asked.

And somehow that did it. She could feel the evening's hysteria seep through her pores and out with her breath. Suddenly she was drained of rage, like a lanced boil. Her shoulders slumped. She reached over and helped Christopher to his feet.

"You might say that," Kay said. Kay held on to him awhile after he was upright, maybe even leaned against him a little.

"Feel like talking about it?"

"Over a cup of coffee, maybe."

"My treat," Christopher said, holding his sleeve to his nose and leading the way to the car. "By the by, can I borrow five dollars?"

She laughed and opened the door and slipped inside.

Another car had come in after them—odd, given how late it was—but Kay was too exhausted to notice.

36

W HEN KAY finished her briefing on what had happened with Vadim, Jeffries tensed her hands on her
desk ever so slightly. All the time and effort they had
put into trying to recruit him, all the subtle maneuverings, all
the future plans, gone completely. Not to mention the human
element: Vadim had not seemed so terrible, for a traitor to his
country, and even so, he had been Jeffries's traitor. The bond between a handler and an asset was not a friendship, and certainly
Jeffries had been in the business long enough to know that, but
still, certain feelings begin to creep in. Now Vadim was in some
basement in Moscow, an SVR officer working him over with a
length of rubber pipe or subjecting him to some other, more
ingenious and terrible method of torture. His next destination
would be an unmarked grave, his family pawned off with some
obvious falsehood or other.

It was a heavy thing to carry. Apart from the brief fluttering of
her hands, however, Jeffries proved as steady as always. "Thank
you for your efforts," she said evenly. "Of course I'll expect a
formal report as soon as possible."

"Of course," Kay said, standing and plodding miserably to
the exit.

"It's like baseball," Jeffries said suddenly, just as Kay was about to exit. "You get more outs than hits."

Which was the general tenor of the office. It wasn't like the Rashid Williams case: no one blamed her. Marshall and Wilson had been openly complimentary: for an Agent with her relative lack of experience, she had done excellently; the damn SVR had just done that little bit better. Andrew had spent a few furious moments after he had heard almost theatrically angry, but had calmed himself down quickly and even in the midst of his tantrum had not called out Kay for incompetence. No, there was broad agreement that Kay had done the best she could with a difficult job, thrust into an unexpected and uncontrolled situation. Things hadn't worked out, but things sometimes didn't.

The only person who did not accept this comforting explanation was Kay herself. In the days and weeks after the event, she went over that late Thanksgiving evening again and again, in intimate detail, running through every moment in her memory. If she had been a step quicker, a few IQ points smarter, some tiny bit luckier . . .

When Kay wasn't berating herself for her perceived failure, she was eating, breathing, sleeping the matrix. She would fall asleep to vivid dreams of boredom, sitting in a cubicle and clicking through personnel files. Sometimes in the dreams she found that somehow she herself had been put in the matrix, or sometimes Christopher, or Andrew, or Luis, or Jeffries. She scrolled through histories of their past misdeeds, sifted through their various venial sins for something outright cardinal. She would wake up the next morning more drained than when she had fallen asleep, then grab a cup of coffee and go right back to work.

But the new year rolled around without any success, Kay's nocturnal investigations no more productive than waking. Jeffries put the best face she could on it, but the simple fact of the matter was that the investigation had stalled. They were out of recruits—the SVR had eaten up each of them—and there was no new information to add to what they were already using. They would need to start over from the beginning, search for another potential RIP, go through the long, slow process of researching him. Meanwhile the matrix beckoned, and Kay gave in to its siren's call, not only while at work but on her off hours—lunch breaks, late evenings, the occasional weekend afternoon—trying to seize on that one critical piece of information she had missed that would crack the whole thing wide open and would redeem her failure with Vadim.

That winter was long and cruel for many people in New York, but it was longer and crueler for Kay than most.

37

B Y THE end of February, over three months after Vadim's abduction, Kay and Andrew had crossed over that
nebulous twenty-first-century divide between casually
seeing each other and being in a relationship. Theirs was a dis-
creet, almost old-fashioned sort of courtship. They ate at quiet
restaurants with pleasant service, far away from the bustling
crowds of Manhattan tourists. They shared quiet confidences in
candlelit bars. They went to the movies or sometimes to galler-
ies. Once, on a whim, they stopped in to see a musical but they
left during the intermission, laughing and looking for a place
to drink. She had yet to introduce him to her aunt and uncle,
but the morning after having drinks with Alice she received a
text reading, in all capital letters and with too many exclamation
points: MARRY HIM!!!!!!! And if Kay wasn't quite ready to start
shopping for rings, she had to admit that Andrew had become
one of the few bright spots in that long, dreary winter.

It was a Tuesday much like other Tuesdays that winter, which
was to say that when Kay left the office, night had long since
fallen, leaving Manhattan in the grip of a dank, misty evening,
the streets slick with black ice and the snow heavily leavened
with grit. Her mind on Bureau matters, she neglected her due
diligence, found herself ankle-deep in a puddle a block away

from Andrew's, used some epithets that she admitted were un-deserving of her upbringing and occupation.

But she cheered up as soon as she saw him coming out of the foyer at something near to a jog, smiling and solicitous as ever. "Rough day?" he asked after they'd exchanged a kiss somewhere between comforting and passionate.

"The usual."

"That bad? Somehow I had an inkling. Come on, Joo-won says he'll hold a table for us if we hurry."

Joo-won ran Joo-won's, appropriately enough, a little hole-in-the-wall near Andrew's apartment that, to Kay's estimation, served just about the best Korean barbecue in the city. It wasn't until he'd suggested it that she remembered she hadn't eaten since breakfast, and then only a protein bar, and that her stomach was doing that thing stomachs do when they haven't been filled in a reasonable period of time. Andrew took her arm during the short walk over, and Kay found herself ignoring her wet shoes altogether.

Over a few glasses of *soju* and a platter of well-cooked meat, Kay felt the strain of the day slough off her. Andrew was good company as ever, charming and attentive. He had a rare talent for conversation, which made you feel comfortable opening up to him, no doubt part of what had made him such a skilled case officer. Kay found herself speaking of Christopher, or more ac-curately, of his absence—three months since she had sprung him from lockup on that horrible Thanksgiving evening—despite two phone calls this week alone and a flurry of increasingly ag-gressive texts.

"Are you worried about him?"

"Always," Kay admitted, smiling. "Though not any more than ever. This is true to pattern. He's ashamed about what happened over Thanksgiving and afterward. He feels humiliated, and he feels like he's a burden. It'll probably be another three months before he forgets about it enough to let me see him."

"So you help him and he bites your hand?"

"People are like that sometimes," she admitted. "It's paradoxical, but people don't operate logically. He's punishing me for doing him a favor."

Andrew shrugged. "If I were you, I'd enjoy the hiatus while it lasts."

Kay laughed awkwardly. "There's more to him than I've made out. I'm not sure that I'm giving you the right impression of him. He's not all bad."

"I haven't met him, so I can't say for certain, but I think probably you're giving me exactly the right impression of him—you just wish that that wasn't the case."

"What's that supposed to mean?"

"He sounds like a parasite," Andrew said. "I'm sorry, but that's the person you've described to me."

"He's family," Kay said, flatly and with some force, as if that were enough to end the conversation.

Andrew disagreed. "The one does not exclude the other. People take advantage of their family all the time, Kay. There are men who make entire lives out of it. Let's be honest: all of this kindness you've done him, has he ever reciprocated any of it? If you needed him, would he be there for you?"

"He would," Kay affirmed. "I know he would."

"And why are you so certain?"

"I just . . . am," Kay said confidently, although she wasn't sure why exactly. "After our parents died, we were all each other had."

"What about your aunt and your uncle?"

"They were great," Kay said quickly. "They were . . . I'll never be able to repay what they did for me. Never. They weren't blood. Christopher and I—we were all that was left. For the first year after we moved in with Uncle Luis, he slept in the same bed as me. Every night I used to have the most terrible nightmares, wake up shivering and choking, and he'd sit awake with me until I could fall back to sleep. We were all we had. You wouldn't understand," she said finally, with more force than she intended.

"Because I didn't have anyone left?"

Kay turned her green eyes down to her plate. "I didn't mean that," she said after a moment.

But when she looked up again, Andrew was smiling. "Yes you did. And you're probably right: I don't know what it was like to have that sort of support. It's no insult to recognize that as being the case, and it's not anything so terrible to say so. Honestly, I'm not sure that you were any better off."

"You don't really mean that," Kay said after a moment. Andrew spoke very rarely about his youth in an orphanage, and even then only to gloss over it as being not nearly as bad as people seemed to imagine.

"I think I do. Though of course you never really know. We only live our own lives; it's a difficult thing to make a comparison. Things weren't always easy in the orphanage, I suppose. You were . . . There were times . . . Well, sometimes I felt very much alone. I *was* very much alone. There was no one else there but me. I admit now, though, looking back on it, sometimes I just feel like I traded some solitude up front for an easier time of it as an adult. At least there's no one holding me back."

"That's all people are?" Kay asked trying to maintain her good humor. "Things that hold you back?"

"Of course not," Andrew said, reaching across the table and setting his hands on hers. His eyes were deep and dark and soothing. "That wasn't what I meant. Our choices define us, whether it's the people we care for or the causes we espouse. But at least I know I've chosen those people and causes for appropriate reasons, and not just as vestiges of past history."

" 'Past history'?"

"This sense of loyalty that you have towards . . . It's admirable. It's certainly understandable. But it's also misguided. Who are you loyal to? A brother you've seen a handful of times in five years, usually to hit you up for money or for some other assistance? No, you're loyal to the boy you used to know, a boy who helped you fall asleep when you were scared and sad, who made your tragedy a little easier to bear. That boy sounds like he was probably all right—but the man he turned into . . ." Andrew shrugged. "People don't stay the same, Kay, and neither do you. We weave in and out of each other's lives; we hold different positions and different levels of importance. Holding on to old loyalties, past affections—you might as well walk around in the same clothes you wore in high school."

"So what are you saying? That people only matter insofar as they can help you? That you should toss them aside once they're no longer useful?"

"Isn't that how your brother treats you? Picks up the phone when he needs some money or some . . . extra-legal assistance, otherwise you've got no idea what's happening with him? Say you walked out of here and got hit by a car: Would he come visit you in the hospital? How would he even know about it, since he won't answer your phone calls?"

"You don't know my fucking brother," Kay said hotly.

The curse wafted into the air, mixing with the acrid smell of kimchi and the cooking fat from the burner. Kay swallowed hard. Andrew smiled. "You're right," he said. "I don't know Christopher, and it's really not my place to criticize. I'm sorry."

"No, I'm sorry," Kay answered after a long moment. "That was nasty. It's been a long day, I shouldn't have snapped at you."

"Forget it," Andrew responded, touching her knee softly under the table. "Chalk it up to the weather. Let me get the check and we can head home."

Which in that moment seemed an appealing enough prospect to earn Kay's silence.

38

K AY GOT a call from Torres one miserable, slushy morning a few days after her date with Andrew, but she was
too busy to answer, and when she tried him over her
lunch hour he didn't pick up; and so they didn't manage to speak
until Kay was back home from work, in her little one-bedroom
apartment, making herself pasta with tomato sauce from a jar.
A step up from packaged ramen, but that was as much as you
could say for it. Kay could do a lot of things, but cooking would
never be her strong suit.

"You too busy locking up spies to answer your phone?" he
began with feigned gruffness.

"Today Jeffries and the head of the SVR had a boxing match
determining the future of the free world," she said. "So that took
up a lot of our time."

"Whole different world, counterintelligence," Torres admitted. "Who won?"

"Jeffries on points," Kay said, boiling water.

"Odds-on favorite."

"I take it this isn't a friendly call."

"Much as I love hearing that drawl of yours, no, it isn't.
I heard back from my guy in Colombia about that thing you
wanted to hear about."

It was not lost on Kay that he had not called her "Ivy." She steeled herself for unpleasantness. "And?"

"My guy, he says that your parents' file wasn't where it should have been. Wasn't with the rest of the murders. That was why it took him so long to find. Their state security had flagged it as suspicious; he had to spend a while snooping around for it."

"Suspicious? Suspicious, like, how?"

"The way it was done, it didn't . . . didn't seem accidental. Some of the specifics . . ." He fell silent.

"I can take it, Torres. You don't need to worry about sparing my feelings."

"Your father got two in the head. Some thug hoping to pull a watch off a couple of gringos—they might get scared or angry, pop off in the heat of the moment. Maybe, if they were really crazy or they were hopped up on something, they might have even managed to catch your mother with some flak. But two in the head? That's something that someone does to make sure of something."

Kay's face was steady as the pulse of a corpse. "Indeed it is," she said.

"You got any idea why someone would have wanted to have your father assassinated, Kay?"

The line went silent while Kay considered this question, mentally examining a number of different angles, dismissing them one after the next. Her parents had been doctors, do-gooders; there was no percentage that she could see in anyone deciding to kill them. It didn't make any sense—at least, not as far as Kay could figure it.

"How about the zero file?" she asked after a while, rather than answer Torres's question.

"I know a guy who might be able to get us a copy, but he's on temporary duty assignment, won't be available for a while yet. I'll get back in touch with him when he's in a position to help us."

"Thanks," Kay said blandly. "Thanks for everything. I appreciate it, Marc, I do. Really."

"Don't worry about it," he said; then, stopping her before she hung up, he added, "My guy down in Colombia, he's always been pretty solid. I mean, anyone can make a mistake, but he's always been pretty solid in my experience."

"Yes," Kay said flatly.

"If you need anything else," Torres said, being deliberately oblique about what the "else" could be, "whatever it is, you get back in touch with me, OK? We'll figure out the way to play it."

"You bet."

"There's a bit too much of the loner in you for my liking. This isn't the Wild West, Kay. You're an FBI Agent; you have responsibilities. You took an oath. We're already stretching the bounds of protocol as it is here, stretching and more than stretching. You understand what I mean?"

"I'm sure that it's just a strange coincidence," Kay said after a moment. "But if we find anything, I'll make sure to go through proper channels."

"That's what we're here for," Torres said, sounding relieved.

After she hung up the phone, Kay spent a moment thinking about the last things she had told Torres. The first had been an absolute lie. And as to the second . . .

39

OR TWO-BIT thugs, for a-dime-a-dozen hoods, for men who had velvet pictures of Scarface hanging above their mantelpieces, Sergei and Vlad were almost trustworthy. Not trustworthy in the sense of being decent or honest, but trustworthy in the sense that if they told you they would be at a certain place at a certain time, they would most likely show up with some pretension of punctuality. It did not sound like much when you put it that way, but the truth was Tom had long since learned not to expect basic competence from anyone.

And they *were* competent: they could handle a situation without having their hand held every moment of every day. Given clear directions—frequent the bar where Christopher Malloy works, become friends, buy cocaine from him, suggest that you have avenues by which he might easily acquire larger amounts—they could be expected, generally speaking, to follow through. And they were big men, with thick shoulders and fat guts, and neither was unused to doing violence. This was not the first time that he had made use of them, of their connections to the New York–based Russian mob, large men in tracksuits eating caviar out at Brighton Beach, bringing in tens of millions a year in automatic weapons and sad-eyed foreign girls.

Although sometimes, Tom had to admit, this bare facade of competence was not enough to make up for how unpleasant he found their actual company to be.

"Is easy, bro," Sergei said. He had already polished off two beers and a shot of vodka in the twenty minutes that they had been sitting at the bar, but he waved around for another. "Chris is your typical Brooklyn pretty boy, always looking for an easy out. We slip him the coke on retainer, we get a few of our boys to snatch it up from him . . ." Sergei rubbed his hands together. "Is easy."

"Is not problem," Vlad added.

"And Christopher . . . trusts you?" Tom asked, thinking as he said it that this Malloy would need to be very different from his sister to be capable of such mammoth foolishness.

"We are friends," Sergei said, faintly offended. "He is fun guy, Christopher; we have good times together."

"Good guy to get a drink with," Vlad confirmed.

"Women love him," Sergei added.

The irony seemed to be lost entirely on the two of them, but then, Tom suspected they did not know what irony was. Certainly it was not his place to explain it to them. "And these . . . other friends of yours. The ones who will make the snatch. They can be relied upon?"

The waitress came by with two more shots, swiftly made empty. "To stick up a hipster?" Sergei asked. "Yes, I think they can handle that."

"To keep their mouths shut afterward."

"Who will they tell?" Sergei asked. "What would they tell? They will sell the coke off and never think twice about the matter."

"And what will Christopher do?"

"Piss his pants with fear," Vlad said nastily.

"He will not be sprinting off to the cops, I can promise you that much. He will disappear on a fear bender for a few days, drink until he cannot stand, and then he will come to us desperate to explain his situation, begging us to take it easy on him. And then we will introduce him to you, Tom," Sergei said knowingly. "And you will do with him whatever it is that you do."

Most of the time Tom was a perfectly ordinary sort of fellow, running his little shop out near Brighton Beach. Occasionally, he was the head of a small cell of thugs responsible for taking care of various shady deals as directed by Pyotr or one of Pyotr's colleagues. Very occasionally Tom would be called upon to take care of some task that required one further level of removal from the "official" SVR, one more layer of covering. For these tasks he turned to what he thought of as his "collection": members of that network of lowlifes, fixers, thugs and minor criminals whom he had cultivated over the course of his time in America. Sergei and Vlad were minor members of the feared Russian Mafia, as violent and brutal a branch of organized crime as existed in America, the sort of men who made the more famous Cosa Nostra seem like a class of kindergartners. Not full-fledged initiates; more like hangers-on, as expendable to the bosses as they were to Tom, looking to do something that might gain them some attention. Most likely they would both be dead before thirty—earlier if they met someone tougher or more brutal than they were; otherwise their drug use, heavy drinking and general foolishness would probably put them in a coffin. They were big men, dangerous-seeming, well practiced in violence. Compared to some of the SVR hitters he had known, they were fierce as little kittens, though both of them imagined they were some combination of Al Capone and Biggie Smalls.

"And what is it that you will do, exactly, Tom?" Vlad asked. Three drinks had done little to counteract the no doubt significant quantity of cocaine that Vlad had snorted before coming to the meeting, and beneath the table his foot, clad in hideous off-white tennis shoes, tapped arrhythmically.

Sergei shot him a worried look, then turned fretful eyes back to Tom.

"Excuse me?" Tom asked quietly. It was one of his rules, one of the many little things he had picked up from watching how Pyotr handled himself: the nastier things start to turn, the softer and sweeter one ought to speak. "I am not sure I heard you."

Somewhere in the mass of pink pulp that served Vlad as a brain, the dim realization that he had overstepped his bounds warred with his own implacable sense of arrogance, ending in some sort of stalemate. "I'm just wondering what part you will have in the operation," he mumbled meaninglessly.

"Why, Vlad—do you have aspirations of moving up the ladder? Feel like taking on my job? Think that's something you can handle?"

"Nothing like that," Sergei said. The brighter of the two, smart enough to recognize that Tom was a bad man to make angry, although you hardly needed to be a rocket scientist to put that together. "Vlad is just talking."

"This is the problem with this country," Tom said evenly. "Everyone talks. Talks all the time. Talks to make themselves feel strong and powerful, talks to make themselves feel important. Talks to impress pretty girls and strangers at bars. Talks and talks and talks." Tom could feel himself getting angry, tamped down most of it but let enough leak out to bring Vlad and Sergei to a state of tension. "I have no use for a talker. I need thinkers and I need doers. There is no question that neither of you are the former: all that is left, should you wish to continue in my employment, is to show that you are the latter. And you show that by doing exactly what I tell you, exactly as I tell you to do it, without ever asking any questions as to the why. And if you ever, *ever* speak to me disrespectfully again, Vlad, I am going to be forced to do something to remind you why I'm the one who gives orders in this operation and you're the one who follows them."

Vlad opened his mouth to speak, to explain or excuse himself, but Sergei astutely and somewhat roughly elbowed him into silence.

"He is sorry, Tom," Sergei added quickly. "You must forgive him: he does not know you like I do."

It had been a long time since Tom had needed to get his hands dirty, years and years. There was some part of him that was happy to see his reputation hadn't entirely faded in that time, that he was still known as a man to fear. "Stick to the script and do not forget who wrote it," Tom said, finishing off his can of beer and then crushing it in a fist the size of a cinder block. A bit too blunt for his tastes, but with men the likes of Sergei and Vlad one needed to eschew subtlety. "I want Christopher Malloy wrapped up in a neat little bundle, ready to be plucked up anytime I feel like doing so. Understood?"

"Is no problem, bro," Vlad agreed quickly.

"Is no problem," Sergei echoed.

"It had better not be," Tom said, then left a C-note on the table and disappeared into the evening.

40

THEY WERE lying in bed late one night, listening to the city sounds from outside Andrew's window, enjoying the soft mattress and the thick covers and the warmth from each other's bodies. "Our UNSUB is important enough to have access to all of this classified knowledge," Kay began, "but not someone in a leadership position or likely to get there."

Andrew laughed. It was an old game of theirs. Andrew was very sharp and had more experience in the intelligence world than Kay did. He was a good person to bounce thoughts off, and he didn't seem to mind that Kay took her work home with her and never got annoyed at having to spend dinners discussing tradecraft.

"He's stalled out in the middle ranks, bitter that his genius isn't recognized. Sees an easy way to make a few hundred thousand dollars and stick a finger in the eye of everyone who ever passed him over."

"Maybe, maybe," Andrew returned. "That's the most common profile, but not the only one. Philby was well liked, moved swiftly up the chain of command. If it hadn't been for the rest of the Cambridge Five being drunken buffoons, they might have made him head of MI6. But then, Philby was a fanatic, a true believer. Hard to imagine, but there was a time when people gave their lives for the ideal of international Marxism."

"I'm not sure there ever was," Kay corrected him. "Not for most of them, at least. Here and there, maybe, in the beginning, some of them might have really believed in Bolshevism, 'Workers of the World Unite' and all of that. But for most of them it comes down to a personality defect, pure and simple, a psychological tic that mandates their misbehavior."

"Playing armchair Freud again? I studied the Classics in college, but you don't see me constantly quoting Homer."

"Philby was a drunken manic-depressive with daddy issues. If MI6 hadn't been such a chummy old-boys' club, he'd never have gotten in, and if anyone over there had been doing their due diligence, they'd have caught him long before he defected to the East." Kay sucked at her teeth, went back to thinking about the Black Bear UNSUB. "Our guy is different: sharp as hell, sharp enough to stay hidden just beneath our noses. If it wasn't for the SVR being so anxious, overplaying their own hand, rolling up our networks left and right, we wouldn't even know he existed."

"Oh my God!" Andrew said, sitting up suddenly and slapping his hand to his forehead with deliberate melodrama. "It's Mike! All this time, how could I have failed to see it! It's been Mike this whole time. I feel so betrayed!"

Kay laughed and pulled him back down against her. "I'll let Jeffries know: we can pick him up tomorrow."

"Poor Mike," Andrew said. "I guess he needed the money."

"Money's part of it," Kay said. "But not all of it."

"Why, then?"

"Narcissism," Kay replied. "The excitement of feeling like he was smarter than everyone else around him. A strange sense of self-importance he must have from running both sides simultaneously."

"Good thing it isn't really Mike," Andrew said.

"Good thing," Kay agreed.

Andrew went silent awhile and Kay did the same, though just when the conversation seemed over he began to speak again. "Our first double to get picked up was a signals man, right? Tapping phones and reading e-mails?"

"Yup," Kay said, having long ago memorized every detail of the Black Bear investigation.

"Maybe that's the way in: go back and take a look at everyone in the CIA who matches the profile you've worked up and was doing signals work over the last few years." He shrugged rather deliberately. "Might get lucky, at least."

"Just might," Kay said, the wheels inside her head turning.

Andrew fell asleep shortly afterward, his snoring in an even and pleasant rhythm. But Kay stayed awake long after, running through what Andrew had told her, pulling strands together, trying to force connections. She went into work early the next morning and sat down at her desk with a fire in her eyes that had been missing for months.

41

THE FIRST thing to keep in mind, the main thing, the crux of the matter, at least as far as Joseph Sadler was concerned, was that it was not his fault.

Not really. A little bit, perhaps—obviously he was not entirely uninvolved with the matter—but in the main, by and large, he had not done anything that anyone else wouldn't have done. It was just a question of circumstance. He was convinced of this. He was absolutely certain.

Whose fault was it, then? There were lots of culprits; there were many fingers to be pointed. If he had been appreciated properly, if *they* had treated him better—they being the Agency, his wife, the world—he would certainly not be in this situation. Twenty years he had given to the CIA, a man of his obvious intelligence and drive, two entire decades. Had they appreciated his efforts? Had he been rewarded according to the merit he had demonstrated? No, not at all, not a bit of it, watching as underlings became colleagues became superiors, men and women—women especially: with the PC cops ascendant, the only requirement for promotion was an XX chromosome.

And his wife, Janet—had she ever really tried to understand him? Understood the pressures he was under, the stresses? No, of course not: he had come home from long days of strain to longer evenings of the exact same. There was never enough money—and why hadn't he gotten that promotion they had both expected?—and she did not like their landscape crew or the maid. Always complaining, never satisfied.

Not like Indre. He had noticed her the first time she had walked into McKeever's. McKeever's was a neighborhood dive bar that Sadler had been to a lot back in those days, slipping out of the office a bit early, not too early, and he had put in his time; no one could say otherwise. But anyway Sadler was in McKeever's a lot back in those days, and of course he noticed her as soon as she came in, a body like that you'd have had to be blind not to, blind and deaf also, because there was a collective sigh from the patrons inhabiting the bar at five in the afternoon when the door opened up and Indre stood there.

But, being neither blind nor deaf, Sadler didn't have any trouble noticing her; indeed, found himself blushing and turning back to his drink. Would you believe it, a man of his age? And then there had been the scent of perfume, sweet but not cloying, and then she was *standing right next to him*. Was the seat taken? No, he assured her, the seat was not.

She was new to the city, she told him, born in Vilnius. Her name was Indre; she'd come over to study fashion design. She seemed simple and kind and slightly lost. That night he rolled her name over in his mind, whispering each syllable while his wife slept soundly beside him. Of course he would never see her again. Beautiful women did not have trouble meeting men in a city like New York. Not in any city, probably.

But then she was there the next day, blushing and looking away from him as she walked in, but then looking back and taking the seat next to him. She asked about his day and he found himself telling her, not in thorough detail but more than he should have, given that he worked for the world's foremost covert organization. She seemed fascinated, asked insightful and interesting questions, questions that elicited more answers, one after another like pieces of bread in a fairy tale, leading him home.

He came back to McKeever's every day afterward, every workday, at least, and she came back nearly as often. She would tell him some about her struggles being an immigrant to the country, trying to navigate her new life, and he would tell her a great deal about what he did, skewed in a way to make him seem heroic, rather than one more bureaucrat in the largest bureaucracy in the history of the planet. He saw her five days a week or at least four, and she always laughed at his jokes, and she always smelled delightful.

Finally she came in one day and she looked worried, and he asked her if there was anything he could to do help. And as it turned out, there was, in fact. Her sister had been dating a man, was supposed to marry him, and Indre was nervous: there was something a little bit off about him, something she didn't quite trust. And she loved her sister so, and couldn't Sadler just take a little peek at his records, see if there was anything in the databases or whatever it was that they used—Indre wasn't sure of the terminology—but if he could just take a look and make sure that her soon-to-be brother-in-law was on the up and up, take a look, maybe bring her back the file? She hated asking him, she was quick to explain; she felt terrible about it, just *terrible*, her red fingernails brushing against his leg.

Life drags most of us down slowly, bit by cruel bit, in savage wars of attrition. But some of us are given a choice, a moment— left or right, up or down, white or black—even if we don't realize it at the time. Sadler had another beer and told Indre that he would take care of it, no problem, and the noose was pulled tight around his neck.

There was more to it, of course: hotel room liaisons, lunch-hour romances, paid for by her—she said that she did not want him to think she was taking advantage of his wealth, and since in fact he did not have very much, he did not complain. If he did not know it when she had asked for the first file—and on some level he did, because Sadler was not a fool, though he often acted like one—then he certainly knew it when she asked him for the second, because there could be no reason why she would need to know the background of her best friend's new boyfriend also. No legitimate reason, at least.

So he was not exactly surprised when he walked into the suite for their weekly session and found a thin Slavic man in a not particularly nice suit sitting on the bed, clear-eyed but not smiling.

He had been frightened, of course. Anyone would have been. But Pyotr was calm and affable: no nasty words, the soft sell all the way. They were both professionals, Pyotr reminded him; there was no need for any of the usual intelligence tricks. Sadler had already been working for them for two months, effectively—at least, the CIA would see it that way, should they be alerted to his having stolen information. And had it really been so bad? Had his quality of life suffered? Was he struggling to sleep at night? Had he turned towards the bottle? Indre would remain his usual contact. She liked him, Pyotr mentioned, but did not insist. Moreover, Pyotr was authorized to offer Sadler a reasonable gratuity, extremely reasonable. And what was a case officer's salary, after all, these days? Not enough for a boat or a second house or a yearly trip to Tuscany. Everything that Sadler had done for them over the years, the hard work, the sacrifices, and here he was passed over again and again, stuck in middle management, a wage slave like any other.

Strange to say, but in the short term, at least, his work improved. Sadler was so nervous that some slipup would draw attention down on him that he regained a motivation he hadn't possessed since being fresh from training, making sure to dot every *i* and cross every *t*. Six months after he had become a double agent, his boss had called him into his office, told him that he had noticed his renewed effort, thanked him and gave vague promises of some future reward. On his way home Sadler had started to laugh so hard that he couldn't breathe—laughed so hard that he nearly lost control over the steering wheel and ended up splattered against a highway barrier.

He gave the SVR anything that came across his desk that he thought might be of interest to them, which was to say that he thought might result in them giving him more money. He slept fine at night. The Cold War was over, after all. Not like the old days, when any moment the Soviets might decide to storm over the Rhine. The Russians were a spent force, the bear toothless and old; nothing Sadler's tidbits would do would change the balance of power. And if any of these secrets were so important, then they wouldn't be so easy to sneak out, would they? Hell, security was so bad down at the shop, security was such a joke, they were practically asking for a breach! Looked at that way, which is the way that Sadler looked at it, he was practically doing the CIA a favor. Could you imagine if the SVR had gotten their hooks into someone really nasty?

Of course, the thrill had gone out pretty quickly, as the thrill tends to do. A year became three became five, and in time Sadler began to find his espionage banal: "Have to call a plumber, have to pick up dog food, have to put out the call sign to let Pyotr know that I've got something to slip him." The SVR wasn't any different from the CIA, when it came right down to it: it was staffed by the same set of self-obsessed incompetents unable to recognize Sadler's quality no matter how frequently he demonstrated it. Of course, Pyotr was all right; at least he appreciated

Sadler, realized all the things he'd done for them, pushed to get Sadler just compensation. But the higher-ups, Pyotr explained— well, if it was up to Pyotr, Sadler would get twice as much as he was getting, but he had people to answer to, just like everyone. Just like everyone.

The second week of April, Sadler began to get antsy. Faces repeating themselves in crowds, strangers or apparent strangers paying slightly too much attention to him. Paranoia, Indre insisted, lying naked next to him in their room at the Sheraton, the same one they had been sharing for years now. Why would they start looking at him now? Why indeed? Sadler wondered, uncomfortable.

But the third week he was certain that he had caught the same unmarked car prowling around his neighborhood, spending two hours pretending to read beside his upstairs window, flipping a page every so often to keep up the charade but actually staring through the blinds like his life depended on it. Was he going mad? After all these years as a double, quietly gliding by without drawing attention, had his number finally come up?

Pyotr understood, at least. He wasn't angry when Sadler contacted him, even though it was two weeks before their set meet, and it was against protocol to approach him directly. But Pyotr was one of the good ones; there were few of them on either side of the divide, few of them regardless of which acronym you worked for. They talked for a long time, forty-five minutes or so, starting with Sadler's worries about being followed, though by the time he had unspooled these to Pyotr he got the distinct sensation that they were nothing but the product of paranoia, a sensation aided by Pyotr, who, if he was too polite to scoff outright, nonetheless helped Sadler realize that it was just his nerves getting him into trouble. He hung up the phone thanking his handler and meaning it. And why not? Five years they'd been working together, and he liked the Russian more than he did any of his other colleagues.

Sadler went into the office that morning smiling, as he did most mornings, a man happy with his life and comfortable with the choices that had formed it.

42

THIS IS Joseph Sadler," Jeffries said, pressing a button and throwing his face up onto the display board, "and he's been a very naughty boy."

Seated around the table were Kay and the rest of her squad, plus Andrew. Standing at one end and running the presentation, Jeffries looked as cool and unimpressed as ever. At the other end of the table sat Mike Anthony, who had caught the train up the night before. There was a feeling of hushed anticipation, one that Kay had not enjoyed since she left Baltimore. All that buildup, the endless hours with the matrix, the grim suspicion that her efforts would lead to nothing, but here they were.

"Two months ago Agent Malloy identified Joseph Sadler as someone to whom we ought to be paying attention. Forty-six years of age, worked for the Agency for nearly twenty of those. His personnel files reflect competence but not brilliance, as well as occasional difficulties in his relationships with his colleagues: drunken misbehavior at the Christmas party, that sort of thing. He lives quietly in a house in Pelham Bay with his wife, Janet, two years younger. No children."

"So far I'm not hearing much justification for your suspicions," Mike said.

Jeffries continued without acknowledging the interruption.

"This is Mr. Sadler visiting Tuscany, May of last year." She clicked again. "This is Mr. Sadler in Vegas in January. We pulled these both off of social media."

"Facebook," Andrew said. "A spy's best friend."

Kay smiled but didn't laugh.

"You check into his financials?" asked Anthony, who found Andrew as funny as ever, which was to say not much.

"With a fine-toothed comb," Jeffries confirmed. "Nothing firm: his accounts don't show any large payments, no obvious red flags. His wife's were clean as well, though that's not to say that Mr. Sadler couldn't have an account in the Caymans or Switzerland."

"Or have a few hundred grand buried in the garden," Andrew added.

"Absence of evidence is not evidence, Susan," Mike said. "In fact, it's the opposite."

"This," Jeffries continued, "is the hotel room that Mr. Sadler has occupied nearly every Thursday afternoon for, so far as we can tell, the last several years. This"—a picture of a pretty Eastern European woman taken with a long-distance camera—"is the woman he shares it with. Indre Askovitch is the name which she goes by towards Mr. Sadler, though we believe her name is actually Katarina Golov, formerly of St. Petersburg. We identified her years ago as a likely SVR Illegal and have been keeping tabs."

The room went quiet. As a practical matter, working in intelligence meant being the heir to an old-fashioned sense of morality. In a normal business, one's sexual misbehavior was no particular source of concern for anyone. But in the spy game a personal sin could too easily be turned against you, a chink in the armor through which the enemy could strike. Sadler's affair would have been enough to sink him even if the object of his affections hadn't been working for the SVR.

"Does he know it?" Anthony asked.

"We think he does," Jeffries continued. "We think that she's part of his compensation, along with the money that he's been using to finance these foreign excursions. We think that he was turned years ago and he's been working as an active double ever since."

"Any firm proof of this?"

"As it happens, there is," Jeffries said, not quite smiling but happy to be laying down a trump. "We found bits of a dead-drop cheat sheet detailing where Sadler is to receive his cash pickups."

In fact, that had been Kay's doing, a task that had tested the limits of her dedication to the Bureau and the mission by requiring her to drive out to the Bronx once a week to sift through eggshells and dirty newsprint (Sadler did not recycle) and rotting chicken carcasses. But it had not been in vain: after several months of trash covers, nestled in a bottom corner of a black Glad bag, she had found pieces of a map of Central Park with a number of black *X*'s marked on it—*X*'s that, upon investigation, turned out to be the locations of trash cans scattered around the park, trash cans that were far from any prying eyes and could be used conveniently as spots for leaving money.

Anthony took off his glasses, cleaned them with a bit of cloth, put them back on. He bent his head over his hands as if seeking an answer inside his palms, then looked up. "Level with me, Susan," Mike said. "You really think this is Black Bear?"

Jeffries shrugged, ever cautious to commit. "It's too early to make that assessment. I think he fits our profile."

"He's getting that money from somewhere," Andrew said, more confident. "And unless we've picked up something about Mr. Sadler having a burgeoning career as a professional model . . . No? Then I think it would be wise if we continue to take a good hard look at the man." He turned to face Kay and the rest of the team. "This is great work, guys—really top-notch."

"So what happens now?" Mike asked. He had begun the conversation skeptical, but Jeffries's explanations had swung him around. "Do we have enough to move?"

Jeffries looked at Kay for a moment, the sudden attention—the implication that Jeffries valued her opinion so highly—almost enough to make her blush. "He's dirty," Kay said. "There's no doubt about it. But is he our Black Bear UNSUB?" She shrugged. "It's too early to tell."

"My assessment as well," Jeffries echoed. "Suspicion isn't certainty: when we go at Sadler it needs to be airtight. We don't want any wiggle room, and if he isn't the Black Bear UNSUB, then we don't want to spook our real target."

"He's gotta be our guy," Andrew insisted. "Fits too neatly into everything we know. He has means, he has opportunity. If he didn't learn the identities of our doubles in his professional capacity, he'd know enough to game the system and find out on his own."

"Maybe," Jeffries said, equivocal as always. "Maybe not. Either way, there's no point in moving prematurely. We've got him under our thumb; he won't be going anywhere. Once we've got the rest of the pieces together, we can snap him up whenever you want."

"This is excellent work, Susan," Mike said. "You ought to be congratulated on it, and I don't see any reason to be second-guessing you at this point. But neither do I like the idea of leaving this . . . traitor out there to wreak any more havoc on our operations. Get whatever proof you need," he said, "and get it quickly."

Jeffries nodded. "We're on top of it," she said.

43

SADLER WAS walking into work the next morning when he saw, in the window of an apartment building a few blocks from the office, a paper sign reading: LET'S GO METS! Not, in and of itself, particularly ominous, but noticing it, Sadler blanched white as bonemeal and stopped abruptly, earning for himself a shove and some uncomplimentary words from the pedestrians whose passage he had impeded. He ignored them: he had more to worry about just at the moment than the ill will of random strangers.

It took him twenty minutes to find a functioning pay phone—these days everyone carried a cell, even the poorest and most miserable inhabitants of the five boroughs had one; Sadler had once been asked for change by a homeless man holding an iPhone series 3—and then dialed a number to a cleaning service in Chelsea.

"This is Mr. Kosczyisko," he said. "I was wondering if Mr. Simon is available to speak?"

A brief pause from the other end. "He's out on a delivery right now," the voice said. "I can have him call you back at the usual number."

"As soon as possible," he added, then slammed the phone back onto the receiver.

The LET'S GO METS! sign was part of the elaborate code that Sadler had worked out over the years with Pyotr. So long as it wasn't in the window, as it had never been these five years that Sadler had been working for the SVR, everything was fine: he could head into work as normal. But if it was there, then that meant that a net had surrounded him and was closing fast—that Pyotr or his people had reason to believe that Sadler's cover had been blown.

A transient filtered past, muttering to himself, made like he was going to enter the phone booth. Sadler gave him a ten-spot and convinced him to find somewhere else to urinate. He checked his watch, near frantic. He came into work early most days; in a few minutes his absence would be noticed. A very minor change in his schedule, but if they were watching him, then any small shift in his habits, any alteration in his routine, would be swiftly registered and might even be the signal for them to shut the trap. Which of course assumed that they hadn't already decided to close it, that his arrival at the office wouldn't be followed immediately by a swarm of FBI Agents spiriting him swiftly away, the first step in a legal process that would inevitably end in a life sentence in a federal penitentiary and the perpetual condemnation of his family, friends and colleagues.

The phone rang and an instant afterward Sadler had it up to his ear. "Hello?"

"Mr. Kosczyisko?" Pyotr's voice asked.

"Who else would it be?" Sadler asked, anxious and impatient. "I saw the sign. What's going on?"

"I'm afraid we were rather too sanguine in our estimation of the situation," Pyotr said, in the same tone of voice with which a doctor delivers bad news: "The tumor has spread," "That boil needs to be lanced," "Your cholesterol is three times what it should be." Part regretful, part disappointed, but mainly with a sense of professional detachment that made it clear that, at the end of the day, there is only so much a person can concern himself with the problems of another.

"What the hell does that mean?" Sadler asked.

"It means that your earlier suspicions were not unwarranted. Your superiors have eyes on you and will likely make their move soon. We need to get you out of New York immediately."

On some level Sadler had known that this was the case as soon as he had seen the sign, but still, hearing it out loud, having it confirmed . . . He spent a moment gasping for air, trying to swallow his fear, and then he asked, "What do I do?"

"Go into work today. Act completely normal. They have suspicions but no proof. You are in no danger so long as you don't do anything foolish."

Sadler's heart was racing fast enough to be of concern to his cardiologist. It was steaming hot in the booth, but he dared not turn around to face the street and instead hunched his back against any passersby. "How can you be sure?" Sadler asked. He realized he was raising his voice but didn't care. "How can you be sure of any of this? The last time we talked, you said I was being paranoid and that there was nothing to worry about; now I need to slip onto the next plane for Moscow!" This was not the way he should be acting, he knew, not the way a man of his experience and abilities, of his long practice as a double agent, should be behaving. But he couldn't help himself: everyone had a threshold, and Sadler was just about at his.

"With whom exactly do you imagine you are speaking?" Pyotr asked, without any hint of anger or annoyance. "Because this is not the way that a drowning man ought to address his lifeline. Unless you feel comfortable going for a swim on your own?"

"I've got plenty that might be of interest to my superiors,"

Sadler said, knowing it was foolish even as he said it—that if he was caught, nothing he could do, no information he could provide, would be enough to save him from a lifetime in federal prison.

"What exactly is it you think you know? Your arrest would be a . . . difficulty, might injure some of our ongoing plans. But somehow I can't help but feel it would be more of an inconvenience for you. Perhaps I'm wrong. It's true your country's process for dealing with traitors is rather less . . . savage than ours. I'm told these federal penitentiaries are the best that the prison system has to offer. Movie nights, ice cream on weekends. I hope this is true at least, seeing as how you will most likely be dying inside of one unless I help you."

"No," Sadler said after a moment. "You're right. I'm sorry. Of course you're right. I'm just . . . I'm a little nervous," he admitted lamely.

"Natural, but entirely unnecessary. Don't worry, my friend. We have it all under control. This is not our first time in this situation. As I said, we still have a window in which to facilitate your escape. They are preparing to move on you, but they aren't in position quite yet."

"How do you know all this?" Sadler asked belatedly. "You've got someone else in place, don't you?"

"Not at all your concern," Pyotr said, a hint of annoyance breaking through his usual steady equanimity. "Not your concern at all. The important thing right now is not to let anyone know that you know that they know. Understand?"

"I understand."

"I'm in the process of arranging your extraction. By tomorrow morning you'll be on your way to Moscow and a hero's pension."

"What about my wife?" Sadler asked.

"What about your wife?"

Upon consideration, Sadler did not have an answer.

It was the longest and most uncomfortable day of his life, and there was not a close second. He sat at his desk and pantomimed working, although he was so distracted he could barely hold on to a coherent thought, and found himself reading and rereading the same sentence for minutes on end. He was unable to shake the sense that everyone in the building knew his terrible secret, that every minor tic from every coworker was a silent prelude to his capture. Which was absurd, of course. The investigation into his conduct would have bypassed his colleagues altogether: some special operation put together by the higher-ups, probably with FBI collusion; there was nothing that the Bureau liked more than digging up dirt on the Agency. But still, he couldn't shake the feeling that the whole office knew of his secret sin and was staring at his back hatefully, waiting for the door to swing open.

For lunch he went to a nearby deli, ordered a Reuben, fries and a vanilla milk shake, thinking that this might well be the last time he could eat a credible New York sandwich and he had best enjoy it. For all he knew, he'd be spending the rest of his afternoons devouring borscht. When the sandwich came, he took two bites and pushed the thing away, the pain in his stomach searing and unwilling to share space with corned beef.

The phone at the corner of Third Avenue and Fifteenth Street rang exactly at one fifteen, as Pyotr had promised, and Sadler was there to rip it off its handle a moment later. "It's me," Sadler said self-evidently.

Pyotr laughed at the other end of the line, kindly and unworried. "Calm down, my friend, calm down. We've got everything neatly in place," he said.

"What's the plan?"

"Finish out your workday," Pyotr instructed him. "Be your usual amiable, congenial self. Go home as normal. Eat dinner with your wife—"

"I never eat dinner with my wife," Sadler said, petulant despite everything.

"Then do whatever you would normally do for dinner," Pyotr answered, unruffled despite Sadler's unpleasantness. "Continue on as normal. Do nothing which might alert your . . . colleagues. At eleven o'clock, leave your house as if you were going for something at the corner store. Pack no bag and take nothing with you but the clothes you are wearing. We'll provide everything for you, don't worry. Do what you need to do to shake anyone tailing you, and then find your way to the Kings Highway subway station."

Sadler had lived in New York half his life and had no idea where Kings Highway subway station was. Pyotr, as ever, was quick with an answer. "It's off the N line, in southern Brooklyn. It should take you about an hour and a half to get there from your home. You can be trusted to shake off anyone following you, I assume?"

"I'll handle it," Sadler told him.

"Excellent. Two blocks from the station is a bar named the Blue and Gold. Order a beer and go sit in the back. I will have a man waiting there for you."

"And then?"

"And then, my friend, your years of service to the Russian Federation will be amply rewarded. Moscow is lovely in the spring," Pyotr assured him. "Better than Leavenworth, at least."

Sadler did not doubt it. He hung up the phone and went back to his office.

• • •

The rest of the workday went by at an excruciatingly slow pace, or at least it seemed so to Sadler, but it passed. Not wanting to be the first person out the door, he waited until six thirty before closing down his workstation and preparing to leave.

His wife was sitting at the kitchen table, on her third or perhaps fourth glass of wine, and she gave him a vague greeting once he arrived home. For one brief moment he had an almost overwhelming urge to confess to her his long years of infidelity, both against her with Indre and against his country with the SVR. But it passed quickly, and indeed as soon as it was gone it seemed absurd to Sadler that he had ever considered it.

Janet went to bed early, aided by the bottle of wine that she had put away, and here, for the first time, Sadler deviated from Pyotr's instructions. Standing by the bedroom door, there was a brief moment where he considered saying good-bye to his wife of thirty-odd years; but after a moment he shrugged his shoulders and went into his small office, pulling a jacket off the coat rack. He then violated the second of Pyotr's directives, heading to his desk, pulling out a small .38-caliber revolver and putting it into his breast pocket. The weight felt reassuring against his chest. He stepped outside of his house feeling an odd sense of lightness, a moment of exhilaration: the die was cast now, for better or worse.

He walked to Pelham Bay Park station, bought a new Metro-Card with cash, took the 6 line to Union Square. He didn't think that they had anyone tailing him, but just in case, he got on the L train, waited until the doors were about to close, then disembarked, quickly checking to make sure no one else did the same. But the train pulled out of the station as normal, and Sadler felt confident that he was now free to continue on with his rendezvous.

Forty-five minutes later he climbed up out of the subway,

looked around, then very nearly climbed back down again. Like everyone else who lived in New York, he was familiar only with his own small section of the city, Manhattan mostly, a few neighborhoods in the Bronx. He had never found any particularly compelling reason to investigate the far corners of Brooklyn, and looking at it now he did not think this had been foolishness. The neighborhood looked grungy and dull, the side of New York that the tourists never got a look at. He touched the .38 in his pocket, felt reassured. If some thug thought him easy prey, they would be quickly disabused of the notion. Sadler was deskbound, had no direct experience with violence, personally or professionally, but he knew which end of the gun to hold. Casting a glance about warily, he began to walk south, towards the location Pyotr had given him.

What would life be like in Russia? Sadler wondered. It had been years since his time there, just immediately after the fall, and he did not suppose it had remained the same. He hoped so, at least; in fact he had not particularly enjoyed Moscow, finding the city dirty and crowded, freezing in the winter, absolutely sweltering in the summer and uninviting year-round. But then again, Russia was the largest country in the world: there had to be some corner of it that he would find more enjoyable.

And it was better than being hauled in by the damn FBI, his secrets sweated out of him, the humiliation of a trial, the rest of his life in a cage. Probably there wouldn't even be an announcement of his defection, it was not as if the CIA would want to alert the public to their incompetence.

He noticed the men but did not think anything of them, thickly set white guys dressed poorly, indistinguishable from a few million others living in the city. He brushed past them and headed towards the Blue and Gold, the neon sign bright in the distance, speaking of hope, of a fresh start, of salvation.

"Joseph Sadler?" one the men asked in thickly accented English.

Things clicked into place for Sadler then, too late to go for his weapon, too late to run, too late for anything but regret—and not even that for very long.

44

TOM WAS drinking a beer at a dive bar near Coney Island, trying to ease his nerves. All of these years and they never quite went away, even for an operation like this, which ought to be easy as cake. The entire thing set out in advance, the man walking blindly down a side alley in a part of town where people sometimes did, for no very good reason except bad luck, find themselves shot several times in the chest. Not a young man, Sadler; no match for thugs practiced at violence. Even Sergei and Vlad shouldn't have had any trouble with it.

On the counter in front of him his phone lit up for a moment, vibrated against the wood. He flipped it open, saw the message in Cyrillic. He nodded contentedly, turned the phone off and removed the SIM card. On the way out he would drop the phone itself into a trash can; he had many of these, burners they were sometimes called, to be used and discarded after an operation.

From inside his pocket he picked out his real phone—one of the new iPhones; one needed to keep up with the times—and sent out a message.

. . .

In his apartment in Forest Hills, Pyotr sat quietly in his armchair. The television was on but muted. He found the flickering images somehow soothing, although the noise that normally accompanied it was unutterably annoying. He was not quite nervous— Tom had never botched an operation in all the years Pyotr had been using him—but still, he was happy when his phone beeped and he opened it to find happy confirmation that the operation was complete.

Pyotr rarely drank these days, but he got a bottle of good Polish vodka out from under the table and poured himself a shot. "To Joseph Sadler," he said quietly, then let the clear liquor slip down his throat.

PART 3

Hateful to me as the gates of Hades is that man who hides one thing in his heart and speaks another.

—HOMER

45

KAY DROPPED a stack of files into a brown cardboard box with a thump.

"You know, Kay," Marshall began, "given my highly developed observational skills, a prerequisite and specialty of an FBI Agent, I'm almost getting the sense that you're upset about something."

"But, Marshall," Wilson pointed out, "we found the target of operation Black Bear; if memory serves, we found it in part through the hard work of Agent Malloy."

"This is a mystery which even my abilities seem unable to solve."

Kay scowled, closed her box, sealed and marked it. "You two are just adorable. You should put together a vaudeville act, take it on the road."

"I don't really think there's such a thing as vaudeville anymore," Wilson said regretfully. "For real, Malloy, what's your problem? You can't tell a win when you get one?"

"What kind of a win is this? Our suspect dead in a ditch?"

"That such a terrible thing? You shedding a lot of tears at the unfortunate fate of Joseph Sadler, likely spy and all-around scumbag?"

"I didn't wring any teardrops out of my pillowcase this morning," Kay seethed. "Although while we're on the subject, we don't actually know for certain that he was a spy."

"Come on, Malloy, his afternoon rendezvous with a known Illegal? That cold-drop cheat sheet you picked up out of his garbage? That man was guilty as sin."

"We don't know that he's *our* spy," Kay amended. "Because we never got to pick him up and interrogate him, because he was murdered in an alleyway in a part of Brooklyn where he never should have been."

Marshall looked at Wilson. The joke didn't seem so funny anymore. "Things happen, Kay. There are no neat endings in this business."

"This is the neatest ending imaginable," Kay said. "This is the sort of ending which, if one was a paranoid sort of person, one might suspect had been deliberately engineered by people disinterested in our digging further into the identity of the Black Bear UNSUB."

"You think that the SVR gave us Sadler to distract us from the real mole?"

"Why not? Wouldn't you? Isn't that the clever move? Something thick enough to satisfy us, lull us into a false sense of certainty? Who's to say he's not still out there, lying low until our attention is elsewhere?"

"That's a fascinating hypothesis," Marshall said, starting to get heated. Marshall had worked as hard as anyone in the investigation; had been one of the unfortunates who had joined Kay on trash duty, week after week. Like most of the rest of the squad, he'd been, well, perhaps not happy to hear of Sadler's demise but at least satisfied. "Unfortunately, it has a hole big enough to drive a truck through. How did the SVR know that we were onto Sadler? No one in the CIA knew that, just Mike Anthony and the Black Bear squad. What you're suggesting, Agent Malloy, whether you've thought it through like this or not, is that one of the people on the team is a traitor to the Bureau and their country."

Kay sighed, pulled her chair out and sank down into it. "Sadler could have sniffed it out on his own," she said, although she didn't really believe it. Their surveillance on Sadler could have been a case study at Quantico. After being burned with Vadim, everyone on the team had made damn sure there would be no screwups; they'd done everything exactly the way it was supposed to be done. "Maybe he let his handler know what was happening and they decided it would be easier to offload a corpse than go through the trouble of a defection. What do you think, ma'am?" Kay asked. Jeffries had appeared unexpectedly—in the way that Jeffries was prone to do—from her office and was leaning quietly against a spare desk and drinking from her cinder block–sized mug of coffee. "You aren't buying this nonsense, are you?"

Jeffries looked at Kay for a long time before speaking, then pushed her glasses up the bridge of her nose. "I think that the CIA is satisfied that they got their man, even if they don't have him any longer. I think that Operation Black Bear was officially ended by order of the Special Agent in Charge. I think that the plaque on my desk reads Assistant Special Agent in Charge, which, if the 'Assistant' part didn't tip you, ranks beneath the Special Agent in Charge. And I think you, Malloy, don't even have an 'in Charge' as part of your title, and therefore ought to learn to follow your marching orders a bit more closely."

Which, of course, wasn't an answer—not really. Jeffries caught Kay's eye after she delivered the rebuke, shrugged, then headed back to the office.

"She doesn't like it, either," Wilson said, continuing with the packing.

"No, she does not," Kay agreed.

46

NEW YORK, in Luis's estimation, was a very good place if you were young and poor or if you were old and rich—otherwise it was probably not worth the candle. The young, of course, could flit about the city, drinking and laughing and generally looking beautiful, taking advantage of the infinite opportunities that the metropolis had on offer. The old, by contrast, could sit in the parks and in the bars and watch the young go about their foolishness, as the old had watched the young since the species had stepped out of the primordial ooze.

There were pleasures to be found in age, and Luis enjoyed all of them: enjoyed dressing up in a nice suit and strolling through Central Park as the city swirled around him; enjoyed watching each face quietly; enjoyed the endless churn of the loudest, greatest, wildest city since the fall of Rome. Enjoyed sitting on a bench on a warm afternoon, scattering bits of popcorn to pigeons, strutting about arrogantly, distinguishable from the passing pedestrians only by their wings.

That was what he was doing that morning when the world bit down around him, when he was finally forced to pay for a long life of sin. Thirty years ago Luis would have noticed him immediately, would have smelled him in the air even before his arrival, instincts sharpened by long years of professional paranoia.

As it was, Pyotr was nearly on top of him before he looked up, and even then it took Luis a long time to recognize him. He had changed in the many years since they had first met, withered from thin to shriveled, his hair gone, his skin wrinkled and his pallor sallow. But his eyes, those cold little eyes like black dots in a swirl of pink, those Luis remembered, those Luis could never forget.

"What the hell are you doing here?" Luis croaked, the question sounding weak and vacillating even to his own ears.

"Is that any way to treat an old friend?"

"Friend?"

"Acquaintance, at least, and anyway old." Pyotr leaned back on the bench, stretched his legs and groaned. "Of course, I have not yet taken to feeding pigeons. A bit cliché, don't you think, Luis, both as a septuagenarian and a spy?"

Luis closed his bag and put it down next to him. "It isn't enough that you dragged me back into this after twenty years of peace? I gave you what you wanted: her background, insight, as you called it. I'll have nothing more to do with it. I'm out."

"I admit," Pyotr continued, ignoring what Luis had said completely, "I never understood the point of pigeons. Rats with wings, isn't that what your people say about them? They carry disease, you know." Pyotr reached into his coat pocket and pulled out a battered box of cigarettes reading BELOMORKANAL, a brand you couldn't find in the local supermarkets or gas stations: nasty, unfiltered things unique to the poorer portions of Russia and Eastern Europe. "Would you like one? No, of course, you quit smoking ten years ago. Justyna demanded it."

"I'd think the KGB would have better things to do than torment an old man just to show that you can," Luis grumbled.

"You demonstrate your age again, my friend," Pyotr said, striking a match off the bench and bringing it to his cigarette.

"We haven't been the KGB in twenty-five years. It's the SVR these days."

"Shit by any other name would reek as foul," Luis muttered in Spanish.

Pyotr treated the end of his cigarette, lit it, puffed out a few good gasps, then answered in perfect Spanish, the accent oddly international, some curious and uncertain amalgam of the South American continent. "You are a seventy-year-old man, Luis. You quit smoking too late, you eat far, far too much red meat and you never lost your taste for whiskey. Your heart is bad and will not get better. I am at the peak of health. I run two miles each morning. For a Russian I barely drink vodka. Apart from the odd cigarette here and there, I hardly have a vice these days."

"There are worse sins than overindulgence."

"No doubt, but that's hardly the point."

"What is the point, then?"

"The point is that I will live to see your funeral, Luis. A lovely affair, I'm sure, your wife and your friends and old colleagues, your surrogate children"—and here he paused for a moment before continuing—"all of them strung out in black and trying to hold back weeping. The reading will be lovely; Justyna always had fine taste. Perhaps it will be in the spring and the leaves just budding. Perhaps it will be in the autumn as they change color and fall. I'll stand near the back during the service, and afterward I'll approach the coffin and offer my condolences. I'll tell everyone I'm some sort of old work acquaintance—certainly you had enough of those, a diplomat with all of your gray shenanigans; I will not be pushed too hard. I will say good-bye to you in your grave, and then I will go to whatever reception is held afterward, telling properly expurgated stories of you, and take a shot of vodka in your honor. And on that day, Luis Jorge Cristobal Alvaro-Nuñez," Pyotr hissed nastily through the thick fog of his cigarette, "on that day you will be free of us, released from your fetters. On that day and not on any day before."

Luis had stopped feeding the birds, was holding the bag of popcorn numbly. The flock of pigeons, ravenous as ever, made brave by their endless hunger, had collected about his feet, brushing up against his sharp khaki pants and cooing expectantly.

"Really, Luis," Pyotr said, by all impressions again as calm and friendly as ever, "you are too old for me to be explaining these things to you. This is the sort of foolishness that I would expect of a man half your age, of a stud just taken to bit. The things that we have done for you, the things that you have done for us?" Pyotr shook his head. "These are things which cannot be forgotten, which mark you forever. Or do you disagree?"

"No," Luis said, seeming small and very tired. "You are right. They mark us forever."

"Excellent. Now let us speak about Kay . . ."

47

W HY THE hell was Sadler in Brooklyn at two thirty in the morning? That's what I'd like to know," Kay said, angry the next morning, as she had been every day of the two weeks since Sadler had found himself dead.

Andrew was midway through the process of making Kay breakfast. On her counter, eggshells shared space with exhausted orange rinds. He was cutting up a green pepper, each movement swift and certain. Andrew was as good a cook as he seemed to be at everything else to which he set his hands. "Who knows? Maybe he was an insomniac."

"You have trouble sleeping, you pour yourself a glass of warm milk, you make yourself a sandwich, maybe you go for a walk around the block. You don't take the N train to Brooklyn and wander aimlessly in alleyways."

"Maybe he had a girl he was seeing there. Or a boy. Maybe he had a sweet tooth for nose candy, was looking to cop his fix." He turned and offered her a lick from the spoon he had been using to spread Nutella. He was wearing a pair of boxer shorts with a hockey logo on them and a pair of her old slippers.

"I've gone through Joseph Sadler's life with a fine-toothed comb. I know him better than his wife, better than his mother, better than his confessor. The only woman he was seeing was the Lithuanian at the Sheraton—who, curiously enough, has also dropped clean off the face of the map. He didn't do drugs, he didn't go for midnight rambles. He was in Brooklyn for the simple reason that someone called him there, and I'd trade three fingers off my right hand to find out who."

"I like your hands," Andrew said, taking one and kissing it absently. "Please don't do that."

"I'm serious, Andrew," Kay said, pulling free of him. "I don't care what the suits say, I don't care if the CIA has decided this entire thing has been wrapped up for them with a pretty red bow. There's something here we're not seeing, but I'll be damned if I can figure out what it is."

Andrew pulled the chair out and sat down beside her. He stroked her arm for a while, like one might a lapdog. "Look, Kay," he said, his voice dripping with concern. "I've been there. You've been chasing after this bastard almost a year. You've eaten with him, you've slept with him. Now he goes and slips the noose. I get it, I get it. But things happen. You can't let it grind its way into your soul, and you can't go mad seeing a conspiracy in every shadow."

"Our prime suspect in the Black Bear investigation killed in a mugging gone wrong weeks, days, before we were ready to move on him? This doesn't seem suspicious to you?"

Andrew shrugged. "Maybe you're right. Maybe the SVR figured we were onto him, decided on snipping a loose thread rather than give us the opportunity to interrogate him. Sucks for us, but unless you're planning on consulting a medium—and I'll have to check, but I'm pretty sure there isn't a line in the budget for that—then we're out of luck."

"But why would they move on him now?" Kay asked, half to herself. "How could they have known that we were on his tail?"

"What are you suggesting?" Andrew asked, raising his voice a bit.

Kay shrugged and looked away. "Nothing," she said. "You're right. I'm just being paranoid. I can't let go of the case."

Andrew nodded, content. "It's part of what makes you such a special Agent, Kay," Andrew said. "It's part of what makes you special, period."

It was early June; in a few weeks the city would turn muggy and miserable, and everyone who could get to the Hamptons or out into the country would do so, and everyone who couldn't would clog the parks and public pools. But for the moment the weather was pleasant, warm but not hot, the morning promising a long afternoon of lazy sunshine.

"Look, Kay," Andrew said, setting the plate of eggs down in front of her, then turning back to the stove to get his own. The muscles in his chest stood out in sharp definition against the morning's light. His smile was handsome and tinged with regret. "There's something I think we need to talk about."

The unexpected sincerity was enough to break Kay free of her musings on Sadler, at least for a few minutes. "What?"

"They're calling me back to D.C.," he said. "There's no point in having a CIA liaison for the Black Bear investigation when—"

"When Black Bear is over," she finished. "I expected as much." Although knowing it was coming didn't erase the trickle of disappointment that she felt upon hearing the news. "How long do you have?" she asked with an almost authentic nonchalance.

"A few weeks," Andrew said, as if he were apologizing. "Write some reports, brief some people . . ." He shrugged.

"What about your place?"

"It's month-to-month," he said. "And the furniture is all rented. Come July, it'll be like I was never here," he said, with more than a touch of melodrama.

Kay put her hand on his. "Not quite," she said.

"You know how much I care about you, Kay," Andrew said. "But I've been thinking about it, and with me in the capital and you up here . . ." He sighed. "It's not like either of us have so much free time anyway. They'll assign you to something else soon enough, and me also, and in a couple of weeks you won't even remember you knew me."

"I think you might be exaggerating the case just a bit," she said.

"Maybe just a bit," he admitted.

"But you're right," Kay said, biting down on any trace of sadness. "We're too busy for a long-distance relationship."

"Maybe they'll move you down to D.C.," Andrew said, perhaps only half kidding. "All the success you've been having? They'll be making you Director in no time."

Kay laughed. "That would be a hell of a jump," she said. "Besides, going to work in Washington, dealing with those suits all day? Not for me, thanks. I'd go mad if I wasn't operational."

It was only later, after Andrew had left, that Kay realized that that last statement hadn't been hyperbole. She had started the Black Bear investigation unsure if counterintelligence was the right spot for her to work in, and now she couldn't imagine doing anything else.

48

TORRES CALLED her the next Wednesday on her direct line, and beneath his usual friendly jawing there was something of an edge. "I got that thing you wanted," he said, and then he didn't say anything for a while.

Which Kay could only take to mean that he didn't want to discuss it over an open phone. "Thanks," she said noncommittally.

"I thought maybe I'd drop it off to you when I came into the city this weekend."

"You? In New York?" A Baltimore native, Torres had left the city only during his first years in the Bureau. He had a little cabin on the eastern shore of Maryland that he went to in the summers, and apart from that traveled little. In particular, he had very little positive to say about the Big Apple, a parochialism common to many of the denizens of the cities bordering New York.

"It's sort of a . . . package deal; my wife got it. One of those Internet sites. A room and a show, supercheap, that kind of thing."

"A show?" Kay said, trying to keep the mockery out of her voice and not quite succeeding.

"You married, Ivy?" Torres asked, somewhat irritably.

"I'd have mentioned it to you, probably."

"In the happy event that you one day wed, you'll shortly discover that you sometimes have to do things that you don't want to do to keep your spouse happy."

"Is it *Cats*? You can tell me if you're coming up here to see *Cats*, Torres. I won't make fun of you. Much."

"Do you want the thing or not?" he said testily, and Kay decided she'd better not ride him too much harder after all.

"All right, all right. Saturday evening it is. I'll make us dinner reservations."

"See you Saturday," Torres said.

"See you Saturday."

• • •

Kay met Torres and his wife, Eileen, at a sushi restaurant she knew in the Village. Torres looked skeptical but soon got into the swing of things, especially after Kay explained that it was perfectly acceptable to eat the rolls with his hands. It was only the second or third time that Kay had met Eileen, but she felt like she knew her better than that, having watched Torres call her from every stakeout and late-night investigation they'd ever been a part of. It was like that anytime two people loved each other long enough, it occurred to Kay. They start to wear into one another, acquire habits and phrases, shared idiosyncrasies. It was like that with Luis and Justyna. Kay supposed it had been like that between her own mother and father, although she couldn't remember well enough to be sure.

After dinner Eileen excused herself for a cigarette, laughing off Torres's judgmental scowl. Fried food, alcohol and the job were the only vices for which Torres had any affection: as far as he was concerned smoking tobacco was an abomination, although to Kay's mind it said something about their relationship that he had never managed to get his wife to stop.

Kay waited until Eileen was outside before speaking. "Are you going to pass over what you have," Kay asked, "or am I going to have to ask you questions about the musical you just sat through?"

Torres took an unnecessarily long look at his wife, making sure that her attention was taken up with other things, then swiveled his attention around at the restaurant, reached into his satchel and set a manila folder on the table.

Kay looked at it awhile but didn't touch it. It was a slender thing: there couldn't be more than a page or two inside. Whatever connection her father had had to the FBI, it apparently had been less than extensive.

"This is it?" Kay asked, knowing the answer but somehow not wanting to touch it.

"Yup."

"Did getting it . . . cause you any trouble?"

Torres shrugged, half shook his head. "People like me, Ivy. And I've been around long enough to earn a few favors here and there. Don't worry, it won't come back to bite me. It's you I'm worried about."

"Me? What do you mean?"

"What are you up to here, Ivy? What exactly do you think you're going to find in this folder?"

"The truth. Isn't that our job?"

"My job is to catch criminals. Yours is rather more complicated altogether, but last time I checked, it was as much about keeping secrets as it was unveiling them. Jeffries have any idea about these . . . extracurricular activities of yours?"

Not so long ago, Kay would have blushed at that. Working counterintelligence, however, had sharpened her capacity for obfuscation and dissimulation, and her face was solid and unreadable. "I'll make sure to inform Jeffries of my situation as soon as it becomes appropriate to do so," she informed Torres.

"When do you think that would be, exactly?"

Kay shrugged. "That would depend on what I find inside the folder," she said, running her fingers down the paper as if it were something secret and precious. "Did you look at it?"

"No," Torres said after a few moments. "And if you feel like taking my advice, you won't, either. What's in there won't change anything for you, Kay. Won't improve anything, at least."

"But I'll know the reason why they died."

"What good is that going to do you? It won't bring them back to life. It won't let you talk to them or hold them, won't make up for being the only girl in high school without parents. Won't save your brother or fix the mess he made of his life." Torres put his hands up as if to defend himself. "I'm not trying to be cruel here, Kay, I'm being honest. You need to get some perspective on this whole thing."

"I haven't looked at the folder yet. Maybe there's nothing to it." Although Kay didn't really believe that.

"I am your friend," Torres said, sitting up straight. "And I'm also a sworn Agent of the Federal Bureau of Investigation; have been that since you were still wearing your hair in pigtails. And I take both of those responsibilities very seriously, Kay, very seriously indeed. Remember the FBI's motto—*Fidelity, Bravery, Integrity*? It was one thing to bend a rule or two—I've never been known as a particular stickler for every little bit of protocol the Bureau decides to lay on us—but there's a difference between bending rules and breaking them. It looks to me like you've got it into your head to run your own parallel investigation: just you, all by your lonesome. What if you open up this folder and there is something in there, something secret, something important? Are you going to go to Jeffries with it? Or are you thinking about going off the reservation?"

"I won't know until I've seen it," she said. "And how about you? You planning on dropping a dime to my new supervisor?"

Torres looked hard at her. "I'd think you know me better than that, after everything."

Kay looked down at what was left of her drink, felt bitter and foolish, unsure how exactly she wound up midway through a fight with an old friend who had done her a serious favor. "I'm sorry," she said quietly. "There's been a lot of stress at work lately," she said. "I guess I'm a bit on edge."

Torres grunted, far from satisfied, but he didn't push the matter any further. Kay didn't suppose he'd enjoyed these last moments of unpleasantness any more than she had. "Just be careful, Kay," Torres said. "You're playing without a net."

Kay nodded and finished her coffee, entirely aware of that fact.

49

THE FOLDER was causing trouble all out of proportion to its size. The night before, after she had finished saying good-bye to Torres and his wife, Kay had taken it home, set it on her desk, drunk three cans of microbrewed beer while staring at it warily, then gone to sleep without opening it. She had woken up the next morning with the feeling that it was staring at her; had ignored that feeling, taken a shower, put on her weekend clothes, shoved the file into her satchel and gone to grab some brunch. It had sat beside her as she picked at her omelet, an unpleasant garnish that had ruined the meal. It hung heavy on her shoulder during what should have been a pleasant walk along the waterfront, like a rain cloud blotting out the sun.

And now it sat on the table at the coffee shop she had stepped into, mainly to escape from the summer heat, the air-conditioning on full blast. At the booth next to her a skinny boy wearing Coke-bottle glasses typed away at a MacBook. Most of the rest of the seats at the café were filled with virtually identical members of his species.

If Kay opened it, she was committing herself to a course of action. Torres was right: Kay was an FBI Agent, one closely bound by rule of law. Her badge meant—or should mean—that she followed the rules more closely, not that she was free of them. The

mission came first; wasn't that her credo? This wasn't the mission, and Kay's powers of self-delusion were insufficient to convince her otherwise. This was personal, this was about the Malloy family and what had been done to it. As long as she could remember, since the rest of her friends were chatting about the latest boy band and slapping stickers of ponies on their binders, Kay had wanted to belong to something—like her father. She had struggled, toiled, sacrificed. What was she if she wasn't an FBI Agent?

Reaching over to open the folder, the answer seemed clear. She was the daughter of Paul and Anne Malloy, and that carried with it responsibilities as well. Less obvious than those of the Bureau, perhaps, but no less strict. Inside the plain manila envelope was a single sheet of paper and a few short paragraphs inked onto it. The copy Torres's friend had made for her was fuzzy, but Kay could still recognize the outdated typewriter font. She forced herself to read it line by line, carefully, making sure not to miss anything. When she was done she read it a second time, then a third. Then she put it back in the folder and put the folder in her satchel.

In the days shortly before his death, Paul had reached out to a contact within the Bureau, trying to set up a meeting with someone in counterintelligence. He claimed to have information regarding a matter of national security but was unwilling to share it except at a face-to-face meeting. A short addendum explained that this meeting had never happened due to the untimely demise of Paul Malloy, killed on a third-world street corner. The timing was suspicious, certainly, but with nothing more to go on, the authorities had been forced to close his file. So far as the FBI had been concerned, the death of Dr. Malloy had brought the matter to an abrupt end.

Years ago, in one of the required classes that Kay had taken at Princeton, she had listened to a lecture on black holes. So

unimaginably dense that even light could not escape their pull, they were impossible to identify with a telescope. They could only be recognized by the effect that they had on other objects in their proximity, shifting the flights of asteroids and the paths of planets and the placement of the stars themselves. This idea had fascinated Kay—that some things can only be identified indirectly by the ways in which they distort the existence of what is around them. Kay began to think about that now, about the strange way that this new information was pulling on everything that she knew of her own life and history, of who she was, of the fundamental core of her character.

Her father had not been, so far as she could remember, a paranoid sort. He would not have reached out to the FBI for no reason. He must have known something. Was it something important enough to kill him over? Or had it been something else, something personal?

"Son of a bitch," Kay said, the expression of rage undirected, or more accurately, directed at whatever as yet unknown entity had murdered her parents, this faceless entity that had turned her into an orphan. The hipster next to her, deep in what he no doubt imagined would become the next great American novel, was about to say something, but then he saw the hard set line of Kay's mouth and decided against it.

50

T HEY HAD a good-bye party for Andrew on the roof of Kay's apartment on a late afternoon in July. A simple thing, a grill and a few haunches of meat, several coolers full of beer from the liquor store down the street, someone's iPod on shuffle. Technically it was against the terms of her lease to be grilling on the roof, but with roughly a dozen Agents in attendance, Kay did not think they would have any trouble with the super.

Apart from the Black Bear squad, Andrew had brought some of his own people, mostly neighbors and casual acquaintances that he had picked up in the time he had been stationed in New York. He had a gift for it, Andrew, some ineffable but indisputable quality to make strangers acquaintances and acquaintances friends. It had worked on the Black Bear team, at least, most of whom had come out to eat cheeseburgers and drink a bit and watch the sun set on a Manhattan skyline.

Not Jeffries, of course, although Andrew had been gallant enough to ask her. Their ASAC was good at many things, but frivolity was not one of them.

A bittersweet occasion, but Kay was enjoying it. They hadn't discussed the future of their relationship after that one day at breakfast a few weeks earlier; had done their best to enjoy what little time was left to them. In truth, with everything that had happened to her lately, the dissolution of her union with Andrew was not foremost in Kay's mind.

"Shame about Mike Anthony," Marshall said slyly, standing over the grill, watching Andrew work.

Andrew nodded seriously and flipped three beef patties in rapid succession, the sizzle of fat against heated metal. "No question. Anthony is a master, done more good for this country than anyone without a security clearance will ever know. But he'll be all right: they're moving him to Deputy at the National Counterintelligence and Security Center. It's real work for a counterintelligence professional."

"Who do you think will take over his position?"

Andrew bent down and took a long peek at one of the sausages, then righted himself. "Lots of good people down in D.C. Same as it is here: the mission is what matters. The mission is all that matters."

"But it'll be you," Kay said quietly, after Marshall went to grab another beer.

Andrew smiled his even, white smile, gave a shrug that was mostly confirmation. "We'll have to see. Nothing's been decided yet. The ADDO is pleased with my work, or seems to be. I'm a bit junior to be given a position of such authority, but . . . it's not unheard of."

"Counterespionage Group Chief," Kay said. "That's quite a coup."

He looked up at her abruptly, sharply, but then he laughed and went back to his work. "Hard work and some good fortune, nothing more. Besides, I'm not even sure if I'll get it."

Although he seemed pretty confident. Andrew never bragged or boasted, but he carried himself with a quiet and unflappable confidence, as if he were following some clearly marked line through the byways and vicissitudes of day-to-day life. Normally, it was one of the things Kay liked about him.

"You never liked Anthony, did you?" Kay asked.

"Mike Anthony is a very skilled case officer," Andrew said. "And I have great respect for him. But he and I were never what you'd call close," he admitted.

"Why?"

"I wouldn't want to presume."

"Because he knew you were angling for his job?"

"Everyone was angling for his job," Andrew said. "Everyone beneath him, at least. I don't have any sense of shame in admitting that, none at all. Ambition is not, in and of itself, a sin. Yes, I want to rise in the ranks. I want to be important; I want to have a big oak desk and a plaque with my name on it." Although his broad smile seemed to make a mockery of his words, his eyes were clean and clear and even.

"And all that about the mission?"

"That was true," Andrew said. "That was all true. The mission is the only thing that matters—but someone has to carry out the mission, Kay, and as far as I'm concerned I'm as good a person to do so as any. I would think—I would hope—that every member of the Bureau feels the same way and is hungry to make their own impression, to rise to the level of their own ability. Don't you?"

Kay considered the question for a moment. Three years now she'd been in the FBI, and she'd spent most of it just trying not to make any unforced errors and figuring out the nuances of violent crime and gang investigations, let alone the peculiarities of the Baltimore Field Office, and then assigned to counterintelligence with all of the concomitant difficulties that it entailed. All her life—most of her life, at least; all her life since that day twenty-odd years earlier when she had come home to learn that she would never see her parents again—she had wanted to work in law enforcement, to solve crimes, to—though she would not have said this out loud—right wrongs. But beyond that? The idea of rising through the ranks, of wielding power within the organization, power and all the benefits that came with it? "Not really," Kay said finally, honestly. "Not really."

"You should," Andrew said, judging the beef patties could sit a minute and setting down his spatula to put a hand on her shoulder. "The FBI, the CIA—these are organizations like any other at the end of the day, not much different than Ford or Bank of America."

"Ford doesn't arrest traitors," Kay said.

"No, of course it doesn't—but, like the FBI, it is made up of a very large group of people, all of them working at once towards a common goal and in the furtherance of their own individual ambitions."

"I don't feel that way," Kay admitted.

"Well, you should. Look, Kay, Anthony was a good guy and I don't wish him any ill. It's bullshit that he got moved; you know and I know that Sadler getting iced wasn't his fault, didn't have anything to do with him. But the suits, in their infinite wisdom, decided that his was the head to get chopped. If they decide that I'm the next in line on the chopping block, I could be pushing papers in Poughkeepsie this time next month. As of right now, I'm the golden boy, and they're overimpressed with anything I can do. I don't expect that to last forever or pretend that luck didn't have some hand in it. But neither am I going to ignore an opportunity to further my career. You might be wise to think about your own," Andrew said.

"What do you mean?"

"It means that you've gotten quite a reputation over the last year and a half: first with your . . . good work in Baltimore, and now as part of the Black Bear investigation."

"I thought you said the Black Bear investigation was a failure."

"I said it wasn't an unqualified success, but that's not quite the same thing. People, important people, people at your head-quarters, they know your name. You could be a blue-flamer. Jeffries won't be around forever. No one is around forever. If you want to spend your career as a brick Agent, working cases, that's fine, that's admirable, there's nothing wrong with that. But I think you have more ambition in you than you let on. And for good reason: you've got the most talent of anyone over there; I know it and so do you. And why shouldn't you rise to a position appropriate to your ability?"

After a long silence Kay said, "That's not how I think about it." Although she said it quietly, and without any great excess of confidence.

51

THERE WAS a banging on Kay's door very late one Saturday night—very early Sunday morning—and she was up like a shot. She grabbed her service weapon off the chair next to her bed, slipped it out of its holster almost without thinking, checked to make sure it was loaded even though she knew it was, switched the safety off and sidled stealthily towards the door, crouching low. Another loud knock. The practical side of her mind told Kay that it was nothing: some drunken buffoon visiting a lover who had gotten his doors mixed up, a neighbor locked out and looking to make a phone call. But the other half flashed images of SVR hit men or grim-eyed associates of Rashid Williams who'd come up from Baltimore looking for payback.

When she called out, she was crouched around the corner from the entrance hall. "Who is it?"

A muffled response through the door that she could not make out.

"Speak louder and slower."

She still couldn't make out what was being said, but she knew the voice, and Kay sighed and went to open the door for her brother.

As a rule, people banging on your door at three a.m. rarely come dressed in a suit and tie, with their shoes freshly shined and their hair combed back neatly. But even by his usual standards, Christopher looked bad. Christopher looked very bad indeed. He was drunk, first of all, or stoned—Kay couldn't tell with certainty—but his eyes were dark, frightened dots in a sea of red capillaries. He looked very thin, and he had an ugly bruise below his cheek. It was not at all the first time that he had awakened her this way, but she had a sneaking certainty that this would be the worst.

"How did you get in?" Kay asked.

"It's the weekend," Christopher said, a little trace of his usual devil-may-care attitude slipping out. "Not everyone goes to bed at eleven. I just waited around until someone came in."

"Why didn't you call?"

"I think I left my phone somewhere."

"Where?"

"Not in my jacket pocket," he said. "Are you gonna invite me in, or were you going to shoot me and bury my body?"

Kay looked down at the Glock in her hand as if she were seriously considering the question. Then she moved out from the doorway and waved him inside.

He half collapsed on the sofa in her small living room. Kay went into the kitchen and poured him a glass of water. When he was finished she poured him another. When that was finished she sat down on the chair across from him. "Well?"

"I'm in trouble," Christopher said.

"Really?" Kay asked. "You didn't just come by for a game of chess?"

"I'm serious, Kay. Something . . . I think I did something really bad."

Kay was still wearing her sleeping clothes: long flannel underwear and a well-aged T-shirt. A warm evening but she felt the chill all the same, and brought her legs up against her body to preserve some heat. "Is it bad enough that maybe you shouldn't be telling me the specifics? There's only so much I can look the other way on."

Christopher righted himself from his slouch, pulled a box of cigarettes out from his jacket. "I think it's pretty bad."

"Don't smoke in here," Kay said.

Christopher put the cigarette back into its box and the box back where it came from. "Sorry."

"I imagine that's not the last time you'll be saying that to-night."

"Probably not."

"Is this going to be long?" Kay asked.

"Yeah."

"I'll make some tea."

After she had made it, and put it in two cups, and brought one over to Christopher, Kay returned to her perch, took a sip and said, "Well?"

"Bartending doesn't pay all of my bills," Christopher said.

"No?"

"No."

"What does?"

"I . . . I moved a little bit of blow."

Kay put her head in her hands, held them there for a while, as if looking through an old-fashioned viewfinder. "I'll get you a lawyer. I've got some money. But if you're thinking I can just wave my magic FBI wand and make the NYPD disappear, you're in for a rude awakening. It doesn't work like that."

"It's not the law."

Kay brought her eyes back up. "Then what?"

But he didn't answer at first, just sat there listening to the loud hum of the air-conditioning, staring down into his tea as if it held some sort of answer. "I was just small-timing it, Kay. Really—

a gram or two behind the bar, just to people I knew, friends from the neighborhood. Hipster kids and slumming yuppies. No one ever would have found out. I'd never have gotten into any trouble."

"There are a lot of people in jail right now who thought something similar."

"You're probably right about that."

"You keep saying 'was.'"

"Sorry?"

"You've been talking in the past tense. What changed?"

"A couple of months ago these guys started coming into the bar. Not like our regular clientele: big guys, Russians or some such, tracksuits and open noses. Friendly, though. They seemed like good guys. I mean, not quite tax-paying citizens, but good guys."

"They sound absolutely charming. And what did these paragons of virtue want with you?"

"Nothing at first. Just came in to drink and to talk. Like I said, they were friendly."

"And then?"

"At some point they found out about my . . . side business. Told me they had a source for it, could hook me up whenever I wanted. For cheap, real cheap. Like, crazy cheap."

Kay could feel a lecture gathering steam on her tongue, was preparing to give it full vent, sighed and let it escape out into the air. "And you went through with it."

Christopher nodded. "They were friendly about it. Said I could pick something up on consignment, no cash up front."

"Jesus Christ, Christopher."

"That's not all of it," Christopher said begrudgingly.

"No? What exactly could you have done that is worse than felony distribution of narcotics?"

"Funny thing is, Kay, I never actually got to that stage. I was holding on to it for a day or two. The truth is . . ." A glimpse of that old smile came back, that foolish, shit-eating grin, that I-know-I-done-wrong-but-I-can't-help-myself look that Kay knew as well as she did the back of her own hand. "The truth is I didn't really even know who to sell it to. I'm not much of a drug dealer. I guess maybe I'm not much of anything."

"Don't do that," Kay said sharply. "Don't take shelter in self-pity. You made your decisions: Be man enough to own up to them."

But this little bit of meanness seemed to have no effect on him, like water poured over barren earth. "It doesn't matter anymore. I got robbed: four guys in masks broke in, grabbed the stash."

"When?"

"Kicked in the door late last night. Early this morning. Terrified my . . . bedmate, near scared her out of her wits. Didn't do much for me, either."

"That's where you got that shiner?"

Christopher brushed at the bruise above his eye. "Yeah. Butt of a shotgun. After that, I told them where I'd hid the coke, and they took it and disappeared."

"How did they know you were holding on to enough drugs to make robbing you worthwhile?"

"I guess word must have got out."

"From who? You just said you couldn't even figure out who to sell it to."

"I don't know, Kay. The men who robbed me weren't real forthcoming."

Kay went silent for a while, looking through the thing in her head, moving it about, checking the undercarriage. Two possibilities had begun to emerge in her mind. The first and most likely was that Christopher was just very high, higher than he had seemed, and most or much of what he was saying was false. The second possibility was strange and dark and somewhat terrifying.

Kay decided to start with the first. "What are you on right now?"

"I had about a half bottle of vodka after the conversation, but that was six hours ago."

"Nothing else?"

"Nothing. I swear."

Kay did not want to believe him but found somehow that she did. "You ever mention me in conversation to anyone? At work or with your . . . friends?"

"No," he said. "Christ, no."

"Like it would be the worst thing you've ever done," Kay mumbled.

"Believe it or not, Kay, the people I spend time with, they wouldn't be all that enthusiastic about discovering I have a relative in law enforcement. It's not something I make a point of mentioning when I'm passing out dime bags."

Kay sat for a long time with her legs folded up against her chest, staring off at the wall. Christopher reached for his cigarettes, then recalled their earlier conversation and settled his hands in his lap.

"These men who approached you," Kay asked, "what were they like?"

"Brighton Beach types, like I said. Big guys, Russian or Eastern European."

"Lots of them out Bushwick way?"

"No," Christopher said. "Now that you mention it, there aren't. I guess . . . I guess when you put it like that, it sounds a little strange."

"It sounds more than strange," Kay said, but quietly, almost to herself.

"Look, Kay, I know you're angry. I'm sorry." His tongue wagged out of his open mouth, back and forth as he shook his head. "I know I say that a lot, but it's always true and it's twice as true now. I'm sorry, but I don't have anyone to go to: these guys, they're no joke. They're going to kill me. I gotta get out of town. Portland, maybe Seattle. I know some people out there. But I don't have the money," he said. "Just let me hold on to a thousand or two, just enough to get out to the coast and set myself up for a few months. It's my only way out."

Kay went silent again, silent for a long time, the tea growing cold on the table beside her, Christopher yawning and wiping at his eyes and yawning again.

"No it isn't," Kay said finally.

52

K AY WAS late to brunch, which was rare verging on unheard of, at least in Justyna's experience. Her god-daughter did not show up tardy, never missed appointments or forgot engagements. She had always been that way, even as a child, stern and perhaps overserious, with a way of staring at you that eight-year-old girls generally did not possess, perhaps more severe than precocious. And of course after Paul and Anne had passed . . .

Justyna was sitting outside, finishing her mimosa, had a good view of the subway station and noticed Kay walk out of it finally. She looked haggard, worn, even from a distance. She had on loose jeans and a drab blouse, and she moved swiftly through the packed crowds of tourists and Sunday brunch–goers, waving once she got close.

"Kay!"

"Auntie." She leaned in for a kiss, holding herself there, lips against the thin skin of Justyna's cheek, then took the seat across from her.

"Coffee," Kay said to a passing waiter.

"And another mimosa," Justyna added.

When he was gone, Kay settled back into her chair, rubbed

at the skin between the bridge of her nose and her bleary, red eyes. "I'm so sorry to have kept you waiting."

"Think nothing of it, nothing of it. Late mornings in bed with the beau?" Justyna asked hopefully.

"Actually, Andrew had to go back to D.C."

"Oh," Justyna said, trying not to let disappointment show on her face. "What does that mean for the two of you?"

Kay didn't answer for a long time; seemed almost to have forgotten the question. When the server came back with her coffee, she brought it swiftly to her lips, then set a half-empty cup back down in the saucer. "I'm not sure," she said.

And of course Justyna knew better than to push her. Justyna prided herself on her decorum, an old-fashioned sense of etiquette that allowed for the uncomfortable to be swiftly forgotten. And anyway, Kay had never been the sort of person to answer a question she did not want to, or to be bullied into anything generally.

They ordered breakfast, a happy interruption, a useful segue from the awkward beginnings of their conversation. They made small talk for a while. Kay asked about Luis and about her charity work. Justyna avoided asking about Andrew or about Christopher, although they were the only two subjects in which she had much interest. The waitress came and Kay gave a desultory order after a casual glance at the menu, food apparently not on her mind.

"What's wrong, dear?" Justyna asked. "You seem like you've just been put through a wringer."

"It's been a stressful few weeks," Kay admitted, with what Justyna suspected was a palpable understatement.

"Work?"

Kay shrugged and stared at the dregs of her coffee. "It's a lot of things," she said. "I was thinking of taking a vacation," she offered awkwardly, as if she had been looking for an opportunity to say it.

"What a wonderful idea!" Justyna said, clapping her hands happily. "You've more than earned it; just the thing to get you out of the doldrums. Where were you thinking? Perhaps something coastal? We have friends on Cape Cod we could put you in touch with. Or perhaps intercontinental? A busy time of year, but then, there's never a bad time to go to Monaco. I'll have to think of who I can put you in touch with."

"I was considering making a visit farther east. I've never been to Eastern Europe, you know. I was giving some thought to Poland, in fact."

Justyna made a sound in the back of her throat: melodious, sweet-sounding, having no clear meaning of any sort.

"Do you still know anyone out there?" Kay asked.

"Not . . . so much these days," Justyna responded neatly. "Besides, the cities in summer are miserable. Much better off on a beach, burning yourself and drinking something slightly sweet and moderately alcoholic."

"I've heard Kraków is very beautiful."

"It was once. Then it wasn't. Perhaps it is again," Justyna said softly. "I'm not sure."

"You haven't been back? Not since . . . ?"

"No," Justyna said.

"Even after the Iron Curtain fell? You never wanted to see what had become of everyone?"

"There wasn't anyone left," Justyna said. "I was an only child, of course, and both my parents died when I was young."

"And your friends?"

Justyna imitated a person smiling. "I had many friends," she admitted. "The good ones are lost. The bad ones . . . The bad ones have their own sins to weigh them down and don't need an old woman reminding them."

"You never talk about it," Kay said.

Justyna nodded, forked a bit of watercress between red lips. "No, I never do."

"Was it so terrible?"

Justyna dabbed at her mouth with the corner of her napkin. "Yes," she said, as if it hadn't been.

Kay could see the wound clear, raw and red, although it had been decades since it was made. She steeled herself and poured more salt inside. "Why did they take you?"

"Why is this important to you, Kay?"

Kay could not say—or at least she did not say, swallowing an explanation. "It just is. Please?"

Justyna sighed and set the napkin down. For a long time it did not seem as if she was likely to speak, and when she did, it was in a flat and affectless monotone. "Because I was young, and foolish, and righteous, and thought that these alone would be enough to keep me safe from the hands of men. Alas"—she shrugged—"it was not. It never is. At the time I imagined I was fighting for something greater than myself, for my country, for the future. I think it was mostly just innocence. The young have so much energy—far more so than sense."

"You were a part of some sort of . . . dissident movement?"

"Looking back, it all seems very childish, our pretensions that we might change the system, that we were on the cusp of a new utopia, if only we could reach out to grasp it. Nothing violent, of course, though I suppose after a few glasses of red wine some of our members may have grown rather . . . animated. But it wasn't real: Luis used to call them paper tigers, and laugh at our dreams."

"And your friends? How did they feel about him?"

"Everyone loved your uncle," Justyna said, smiling at distant times. "He was charming beyond any measure; any room he walked into he walked out of to a chorus of happy voices. And for us, at the time, America was . . . something like a dream. Americans were an alien species, unmarked by war or struggle. And being in the diplomat corps, he could do small favors for us: a pack of Marlboros now and again, that sort of thing."

"But he couldn't stop them from taking you?" Kay asked, forcing the words out from her throat.

Justyna set one gloved hand on Kay's, the hand that was missing two digits, and said, "Isn't the answer to that obvious?"

"I suppose it is," Kay said. "Why did they take you?"

"Because they could, Kay. Because they could do whatever they wanted and no one could stop them. If you mean, was there some reason, some obvious proximate cause . . . ?" She shook her head. "None that I knew. None that I ever learned. I was walking out of my apartment one day—on the way to meet your uncle, in fact—and some men came up on either side of me and walked me to a car, and from that car to a box."

"You don't need to talk about it," Kay said suddenly, her face red and miserable.

But Justyna continued over her interruption, spewing forth like a punctured abscess. "They would ask me questions that they must have known I didn't have answers to, my relationship to spy rings, assassination plots which were, which they knew to be, entirely fictitious. It didn't matter. Their aim was only to break you. I think perhaps that might even be giving them too much credit: I think for most of them it was simply something that they had become, the way one begins to think of oneself as a doctor or a lawyer. Can you imagine kissing your children good-bye every morning, then going in to torture a stranger?" Justyna shrugged, shook her head.

Kay found that she could not imagine it. "How long were you inside?"

"A long time," Justyna said. "A long time."

"How did you get out?"

"I don't know why I was released," Justyna said, looking off down Fifth Avenue, at the towering edifices of American civilization and perhaps beyond that, to a past that was not as distant as she might have liked. "I do not know why I escaped those cells, that torment. At the time I was in no position to question the matter. Perhaps they knew they had frightened me enough to leave, that I would never again trouble them, that I was broken. When they took me out of my cell, I was sure it was . . . I was sure it was to kill me. That was the only reason you left: another body to be put in an unmarked grave—'killed attempting to escape,' they would tell your people, assuming they bothered to tell them anything at all. Anyway, I was too tired to fight then. I think . . . I think I had accepted it. They led me down a long hallway, then into a little holding area, and they removed my cuffs, and left, and the door opened . . ." Justyna smiled, for the first time since she had begun telling her story. "And he was there."

"Uncle Luis?"

"He saved me," she said with firm certainty. "He saved me," she repeated. "We were married shortly after, and moved here, and said good-bye to the whole . . . horrible, sordid business. And I've lived in peace and contentment ever since," she said with a half-mocking smile. "A happy end to an unhappy story."

Kay did not say anything for a long time, although Justyna could read the heavy thought in the crinkling up of her eyes. "I'm sorry to have brought this up with you, Auntie."

"It's fine, Kay," Justyna said, forcing a smile to her face, although Kay could see that it wasn't fine at all. "It was a long time ago. It doesn't matter anymore. It doesn't have anything to do with our lives any longer."

"I'm not sure that that's true," Kay said quietly, underneath her breath. But after saying it she switched the topic quickly, onto more salubrious grounds: casual chatter, movies she'd seen and restaurants she had been to. But even in the midst of it, and even walking to the subway and even while kissing her good-bye, Justyna noticed that Kay's smile did not quite reach her eyes.

53

TOM OPENED the door of a small side-street bar nosebleed-high up on the West Side, just about where million-dollar condos the size of shoe boxes gave way to the rapidly gentrifying grit of southern Harlem. It was dark and rather dismal. The bartender was making what Tom felt was a not particularly sincere effort to clean the bar with a dirty rag, or at least an effort that was not crowned with great success. A handful of patrons eyed him vaguely, went back to their own drinks, their own troubles, their own lives. All except one.

Pyotr had given him a picture, and Tom had spent a long time staring at it before holding it over the flame of his Bic lighter and scattering it into a sewer grate. Longer than he needed to, long enough to make sure. Wasted time, as it turned out, because Tom would have known Luis even without the picture, would have picked him out as soon as he walked into the bar. Not that he did anything particularly dramatic to give himself away—it was simply that, as many years as he had dedicated to his job, Tom had developed a nose for sin, or guilt, at least, and this last rolled off the man like a bum's stink on an August afternoon. No, he hadn't needed the picture: Pyotr could have told him, simply, to find a man who looked as if he had come to the edge of a very high precipice, and was seriously considering continuing onward.

Tom sat down on the bench beside him, a whiff of expensive but not overpowering cologne reaching his broad nostrils.

"You're late," Luis said.

"By a minute and a half," Tom said. "And you should not have picked a booth by the window."

"Shall we move?"

Tom shook his head, although Luis could barely see it, given their position. "It would draw more attention," he said sternly. Pyotr had warned him that Luis would be unhappy to be meeting with him, might buck a bit, might make a little trouble. They did sometimes, Tom had found. Angry at what had brought them to this moment, although what had brought them to this moment was their own decisions, their own sin and foolishness. Important to shut that kind of thing down as quick as you could.

The waiter came over, smiling and overfriendly, as they were in this country, trying to earn a tip as always, false good humor a faint covering for the cold, naked capitalist machine. Tom kept up his end for a few sentences, in part because rudeness gets remembered, while faint gregariousness does not, but mostly because he could see it made Luis uncomfortable.

"Did you need to sit next to me?" the contact said unhappily. "People will think we're lovers."

"This is Manhattan, my friend, in the twenty-first century. Two men sitting together will not get a second look. And this is the sort of business best discussed in hushed whispers. Or do you disagree?"

"No," Luis admitted. "No, I don't."

Tom waited for his drink to come, sipped at it, then began to speak. Outside, the summer light was fading, pedestrians walked home in the warm weather, cabs passed by with their signs shining bright, a beat-up sedan sat aimlessly across the way. "The brother has taken the bait," Tom said.

"Fine," Luis said irritably. "Then why are you talking to me?"

"Because Christopher is not the problem. The problem is that Christopher is not of any interest to us at all, obviously. Is only of any use insofar as his sister's sympathy is attached to him."

"It is."

"So you say."

"Pyotr was convinced," Luis said.

"And Pyotr is a very wise man," Tom said. "But it will not be Pyotr in the room with her, not Pyotr making the pitch."

"Kay loves her brother."

"No doubt she cares for him deeply. Does she care enough to endanger her career? Does she care enough to betray her principles? Would she put blood above country, above her own future?"

"She would."

"You're sure of this?"

Luis did not say anything for a while. He stared out the window, at the night and the darkness and the city. He stared at his hands, withered and bent with age. "I'm sure," he said.

"Why?"

"Family is . . . everything to Kay. After what happened to her parents . . ." Luis shrugged and fell silent. "She would not betray Christopher. She would not do anything which would endanger him. He is the chink in her armor," Luis said unhappily. "He is all that she has left. She will do whatever it takes to save him."

"That is very good," Tom said, putting a finger of gin through a crooked smile. "That is excellent. That is the best thing for everyone, absolutely," he said. "It should be easy for you to explain the situation to her, then."

Luis tore his eyes from the evening, brought them back to Tom. "What are you talking about?"

"It has been decided that the initial approach would best come from someone whom Kay is comfortable with. Someone whom she trusts." Tom made sure not to smile while enunciating this last word.

"I won't do it," Luis said firmly, or with what he thought was firmness. It was always strange to Tom, the sudden decision a man makes, too late, far too late, to grow a backbone. "There was never any discussion of that. Pyotr . . . Pyotr assured me that I would be kept out of it. That no one would ever know of my involvement."

"By 'no one,' you mean your family, your wife and adopted children? Do you imagine that your betrayal is less significant because they are unaware of it?"

Luis began to curse then, halfhearted and miserable, bits of vileness dribbling from his mouth. Tom let him go at it for a little while; knew, from long experience, that they had come to the last bit of rebelliousness, the pointless anger, the final stage before complete submission. Outside, a pair of lovers passed, tourists, to tell by their bright smiles and fat cameras, holding hands and taking in the city. The sedan sat unmoving. A homeless man pushed an overloaded grocery cart down the sidewalk. Tom fancied he could smell the stink through the window.

Luis fell silent finally. Tom smiled and waved to the bartender for two more drinks.

"I will not argue with you, Luis, because this is not an argument. This is not a dialogue, not even a conversation. I am relaying orders to you, orders which were given to me by men that are more important than either of us. This is the way this works: you are a part of an organization, Luis, as am I. A cog, nothing more. It is not up to a cog to dispute the workings of the whole. The end result is not his consideration. Do you understand, Luis? Do you understand?"

"Yes," Luis said, after a long pause.

"Excellent. The meeting needs to happen soon, within the next couple of days."

A long pause, Luis fighting through the liquor and his despair to try to focus on the plan. "I could set something up for the weekend. Sunday."

"Sunday will be fine. Sunday will be perfect. Invite her to your house. Make her feel comfortable. Explain what has happened with Christopher, the trouble he has gotten himself in, how serious, how very serious, how terribly serious, that trouble is, and that there is only one option for saving him. If she loves her brother as much as you believe, then she should come to her own conclusions about how to help him."

"I know how to make an approach," Luis said, hollow-eyed, and Tom had to admit that he probably did, having been on the receiving end of one, delivered by a master of the form.

"Excellent. Once you have . . . made the situation clear to your niece, you will call me to deal with the particulars."

"And then?"

"And then your part in this story ends. You may continue on to a happy retirement, sure that you have done nothing more than what you had to and your troubles all finished."

"And Kay's just beginning," Luis said quietly.

"Not your concern," Tom reminded him. "And when you begin the approach, Luis, I want you to understand something. It is important that you understand something," he repeated, holding one thick finger in the air. "You are doing her a favor. You are not her enemy, you are not her corrupter, you are not playing devil to her Christ. You are her friend. You are her friend and you are the friend of her brother. You are doing her a favor, though she may not feel it as such at that moment. But that is only because of Kay's own peculiar perspective; that is not the truth of the matter. Because if she is not convinced . . . If she is not convinced," Tom said, turning his sausage-length digit and butting the end against Luis's shoulder, "should she be unwilling to go along with the tide, the inevitable force of consequence, or should she, God forbid, decide to go to her people with what you have told her"—Tom shook his big head back and forth, sorrowfully, regretfully—"this would be a very bad thing, Luis. A very bad thing for your niece, a very bad thing for you and a terrible, terrible thing for your nephew."

"You don't need to threaten me," Luis said.

"Threaten?" Tom cocked his massive skull, as if this were a word with which he was uncertain or unfamiliar. "Who is threatening anything? I am simply clarifying the situation that you find yourself in. Either you will convince Kay to work for us, or you will be responsible for the loss of two generations of Malloys."

Luis had not touched his drink, but he did so then, downing three stiff fingers of vodka in one fierce, desperate gulp. "I understand," he said.

And Tom thought that he did.

"Is there anything else?" Luis said, a sliver of a man, made no larger by the liquor he had imbibed.

"I think we have about covered it," Tom said with a smile. "No, no," Tom said, holding up a hand as Luis reached for his wallet, "do not dream of it. The drinks are on me." He leaned in closer. "I will expense it to our organization."

Luis left quickly, stumbling as he got up from the chair and hurrying out, not looking back. Tom finished up his drink, not in any particular hurry. He chatted briefly with the server when he came back, about the weather and baseball, although only the former was really of any interest to him. He left a few dollars more on the bill than he needed, but not enough to get remembered.

He walked outside with a happy buzz from the alcohol and from the sensation of a plan running smoothly.

54

L UIS HAD asked her to come to the apartment on Sunday morning for brunch, one of Aunt Justyna's special meals: eggs and bacon and a pitcher of mimosas big enough to take a bath in. Luis had told her ten thirty, and ten thirty was when she arrived, with a box of donuts from one of the boutique bakeries on her side of the river. Walking inside, however, she did not smell anything frying, or baking, or grilling, and all of the lights were off, and Luis was sitting quietly in a chair at the kitchen table, and Justyna was nowhere to be found.

Luis was dressed, as always, perfectly, in a charcoal-gray suit with the jacket unbuttoned, a pink handkerchief in his breast pocket the only dash of color. "Kay," he said, "take a seat."

Kay looked at him but didn't answer. There were a number of broad windows facing the street outside, and Kay went past each, opening the blinds one by one. When she was finished, sunlight illuminated the room, and she dropped down opposite Luis.

"Hello, Uncle," Kay said. "Where's Aunt Justyna?"

"She's out with some friends, won't be back for a while. I'm afraid we're going to have to postpone brunch," he said.

Kay reacted to this unexpected development with her usual steady equilibrium. "All right."

"We need to have a talk, Kay," Luis said, and it was in the

same tone of voice in which he had once informed her she would not be receiving a pony for her twelfth birthday. Serious but not unkind.

Kay gestured for him to continue.

"Your brother has gotten into some very serious trouble, Kay," he said. "Very serious indeed."

"That doesn't sound like my Christopher."

"This isn't the time for levity," Luis said, the slightest hint of disapproval in his voice.

"No, I suppose it isn't."

"He's been selling narcotics."

If Luis had been expecting Kay to react with surprise, or shock, or horror, he was disappointed. Kay nodded, almost absently, as if this were a matter of passing importance or, at most, casual interest, and then she gestured again for him to continue.

"Cocaine, from what I understand. First, behind the counter at that bar he works at, but he's recently moved on to more serious infractions."

"Has he been arrested?" Kay asked, voice even and neutral. "Because there isn't very much I can do about that. That would be a matter for the NYPD, not the FBI, and I don't have any sort of pull there."

"Unfortunately, Kay, right now Christopher has more to worry about than the police."

"I'm afraid I don't understand."

"Our Christopher . . ." Luis said, staring off suddenly at the open windows, squinting against the sunlight, then shaking his head and turning back to the conversation, ". . . is, as it turns out, no better a drug dealer than he was a college student, or a guitar player, or . . . or . . ." He waved his hands, as if at that wide panoply of activities that his errant nephew had attempted and failed.

Kay narrowed her eyes. "He's actually not a bad guitar player," she said quietly. "But I suppose that's neither here nor there."

"No, it isn't. The point is, in his efforts to become this generation's Al Capone, your brother has made an enemy of some very powerful people."

"The mob?"

"Of a sort."

"Then I suppose the police will have to be involved," Kay said. "A terrible scandal for everyone, but better prison than a coffin."

Luis's heart seized up at this, but he fought his nerves back down and continued. "That would be premature," he said. "There are other aspects to be considered."

"I don't understand," Kay said. "Christopher came to you to talk about this? That doesn't sound very much like him at all. He must really be desperate. And why would he think you would be able to help him?"

"Christopher has not . . ." Here it was: the big moment, the reveal. Beneath the table Luis had clasped his hands tightly together, afraid if he let them go they would tremble uncontrollably. "Christopher did not reach out to me."

"Then how do you know all this?" Kay asked, confused, or seeming so.

"The people he's gotten involved with," Luis said. "We have . . . friends in common. Friends who would be willing to keep his criminality a secret, to forgive his debts. To keep him out of danger."

"Friends," Kay repeated.

"Friends," Luis said a second time.

"I'm surprised to hear that. I hadn't realized your social circle was so varied."

"I've had a long career, Kay," Luis said. "I've met a lot of

people in it. Thankfully, some of them might be in a position to help us."

Kay narrowed her eyes. "You'll have to forgive me, Uncle, I must be a bit slow today, but I'm still having trouble following. Are you trying to tell me that you have some sort of . . . criminal contacts? That your time as an ambassador, a respectable career but one long ended, has put you in touch with the sort of people who would help my brother sell cocaine?"

"Not criminals," Luis said after a while, but quietly, as if he weren't quite sure. "Not criminals."

"Then what?"

"Professionals."

"Professional what?" Kay asked.

"Members of . . . Members of a foreign intelligence service."

Luis had turned his gaze towards the wall, and so did not see the sudden gleam come to Kay's eyes, then retreat again quickly. "I see," Kay said finally. "And these professionals are friends with the people to whom Christopher is indebted?"

"Very seriously indebted," Luis said. "Tens of thousands of dollars, the sort of loss which cannot be taken casually even by wealthy people."

"And these friends of yours, they can get Christopher out of his trouble?"

"They can make it go away entirely. They can make your brother's problems disappear. As if they never existed," he said.

"And what would they want in return, exactly?"

"That would be a matter best discussed with them, I think. One of my . . . friends . . . is waiting nearby. He can explain the matter more clearly to you. What they can offer, and what will be required."

There: it was out, Luis was thinking, and it hadn't been as terrible as he thought it would be. It had been bad, certainly,

but it hadn't been terrible; it hadn't been nearly as bad as . . . as some of the other things he had done. He even felt a momentary sense of freedom, as if of a great burden being eased, and better perhaps to be damned than to have this weight hanging forever over his shoulders, although of course he had been damned long, long ago.

"That was very neatly done, Uncle Luis," Kay said quietly, turning her cool green eyes back to face him. "That was almost professional."

Luis cleared his throat and continued. "Kay, I'm doing my best to protect you here. But we don't have much time. There are certain things that you need to do. They may be difficult for you, but they are the only way out for your brother."

"That's good, Luis, that's very good. You're my lifeline. You're the only thing standing between the cold hard hand of the SVR along Christopher's throat. Along mine. Very neatly done, as I said. But then again, this isn't your first time making this pitch, is it? Not even your first time making this pitch to a member of my family."

Luis did not gasp, but his blue eyes went very wide, as if seeking to escape from his face.

"How did he react?" Kay asked.

"I . . . I don't know what you're talking about."

"Paul Malloy. You remember Paul, right? Your best friend for twenty years? Husband of Anne, father of Christopher and Kay?"

"Kay, you must listen to me. We're on a clock, and—"

Kay checked her watch. "We've got a few minutes," she said. "And it's a little late in the day for you to play coy, don't you think? You've already as much as told me you're a spy. What is there left to hide?"

"We all have things to hide," he said almost inaudibly.

Kay gestured to the bright light streaming in through the windows. "Today is a day for revelations. Today is a day for throwing off masks. Where were you when you made the approach to my father?"

"Central Park," Luis said softly. "Near the reservoir."

"What was the angle?"

"I would . . ." Luis licked his lips. "I'd rather not say."

Kay bit back a smile: to think, after everything, after all of it, he still wanted to protect the memory of Paul Malloy. "I'm afraid we're past the point of half truths. And there's nothing more you can do to hurt them."

Luis flinched, looked off towards the wall. "His work required him to be away from you for weeks, sometimes months at a time. He had committed . . . indiscretions."

Amidst the betrayals and perfidies that Kay had discovered over the course of the last weeks and months, that her father had once been unfaithful to her mother seemed rather insignificant. "Interesting," she said.

"Your father was a good man," Luis said suddenly, adamantly, as if it were very important to him that Kay believed it. "He was the best man I ever knew. But no one is perfect, Kay. We all . . . We all do things that are beneath us. We all find ourselves in situations sometimes that we would rather not be in, where our only escape is via a sewer."

"What a neat turn of phrase, Uncle. Tell me, would you include his murder in this category of lamentable misbehavior?"

Luis closed his eyes for a long time, pursed his lips as if undergoing some pain. "I didn't have anything to do with that."

"No?" Kay raised her eyebrows. "Nothing? Hands are clean and unmarked?"

Luis did not answer.

"I'll speak for you, then. My father was many things, as we

all are, and perhaps some of those things weren't perfect. But he wasn't a spy, and he refused to become one. And you began to get very nervous that he would tell someone that you couldn't say the same, didn't you? Perhaps the SVR heard that he had contacted the FBI; perhaps they simply decided that they couldn't afford to lose such an important and influential contact. And happily, conveniently, he was always sprinting out of the country on some mission of do-goodery. It would have been an easy thing to ensure an accident befell him. My mother, I can only assume, was a mistake. But then, these things happen sometimes, don't they? Collateral damage in this great game between two mighty nations: a few lives snuffed out, no worse than the loss of a pawn."

"I knew nothing of it," Luis said again. "I swear. It is true that I made the approach, and it is true that your father reacted . . . angrily. But I had nothing to do with what happened to him afterward. If they did it . . ."

"If? *If?*"

But Luis continued over her, his voice rising with intensity. "If they did it, they did not tell me," Luis said, again, growing animated. "I swear to you, I knew nothing of it. I swear on . . . on—"

But he did not finish. Kay cut him off, for the first time in the long conversation a spurt of rage coiling itself behind her eyes. "What would be left for you to swear on, Uncle? Country? Family? God? What haven't you betrayed?"

"On your aunt," he said finally.

The sudden flash of anger, uncharacteristic, eased off of Kay's face, and what was left might have been regret or sorrow or nothing at all. "She was the start of it, wasn't she? All those years ago in Poland. It wasn't money or prestige. You did it for her, didn't you?"

Luis nodded, swallowed hard.

"That was how she got free of the secret police?"

Luis did not answer for a while, and on his face Kay could see the scars left from a day long past in a country far distant. "We had a date," he said. "We were to meet for coffee at one of the small cafés in the city center. She was late. At first I did not worry: your aunt was always making me late. She would get caught up in a conversation, or something would catch her fancy, and she would forget all about her duties and pursue it wholeheartedly. But after an hour I began to worry, and after two I was terrified and certain. That was the way they did it, you see: there was no warning; you would leave your office or your home and a man would come up to you on the street and walk you into a car and then you would never be seen again, swallowed up in the bowels of some concrete government building or settled into an unmarked grave."

"What did you do?"

"Everything I could," he said, the memory making him miserable. "Which, in the end, was nothing. I rang every contact that I knew, I made the loudest ruckus that I could, called in every favor I had accumulated in years as a diplomat. To no end. They could do nothing, none of them. I found out she was taken, but that was as much as I could learn."

"And then?" Kay said, after her uncle had been long silent.

But he did not answer at first, not for a long time. "Two weeks she was gone," he said. "The most terrible time of my life. Nothing to match it, and I have had some bad days, Kay, you had best believe I have had some bad days. But nothing like that: I was going mad. Mad, truly. I was sure she was dead, and I was thinking—I had come to think very seriously—about joining her. A razor, a drop from a tall height, and then we would be together, or at least I would no longer be alone." Kay could read the memory of that despair on his face, even all these years later. "And then a man sat down next to me at a bar that I frequented, clean, neat-looking, very serious. And he told me that there was still time to save the woman that I loved. That her crimes had been very terrible, but that there was still a chance for her to be forgiven. That she could be released, that she could be set free. That arrangements could even be made for her to leave the country, to return with me to the U.S., if that was what we wished."

"The carrot," Kay said.

Luis smiled nastily. "Indeed it was. And this . . . very serious man, this polite and well-dressed man, he made it entirely clear to me what would happen to her if I did not go along. What . . . What would be done to her."

Kay thought for a moment of the two missing fingers on her aunt's hand, of the ghostly pallor that had dropped over her face while speaking of her time in prison. "And then?"

"I said yes, of course," Luis said. "In a heartbeat, without consideration. And do you know what?" he announced, wide-eyed, shaking his head slowly. "I would do it again. Despite everything, I would do it again. I would sell every secret I ever learned, I would betray my country and the service, I would betray your father, and your mother, and your brother, and you, to keep your aunt alive for a single day longer. It is a terrible thing, to discover your own weakness—to be broken in that spot."

"As you were hoping to break me, Uncle?"

He seemed to close down around himself then, head dropping down into his shoulders, shoulders weighing down into his chest, as if she had put something heavy on his back and it was bearing him down through his chair and into the floor and below it, to the very foundations themselves. "You have cause to hate me. I am worthy of your loathing. I have earned it. And I know how this must sound to you, Kay—believe me, I know. But the truth is that we, all of us, have less control over our lives than a gnat carried along in a storm. Random chance, the hand of fate or some . . . other engineer: these determine the course of our lives more than any of us would like to believe. Our pretensions of morality, the certainty we have about who and what we are, these are nothing but comforting illusions. We do what is required of us. When your aunt was captured and they offered to free her, I responded without hesitation: there was no alternative; that was what was required of me. Right now, what is required of us is that we do whatever we must to help your brother."

"Your friends," Kay said after a long time. "What would they want in exchange for their help?"

For a moment Luis seemed to regain his footing. "Not much," he said. "They're reasonable people. They're really very reasonable people. You wouldn't need to do anything . . . unsavory. Nothing that would jeopardize your career. Indeed, it may well prove to be the opposite: it is as much in their interests as yours to see you continue to ascend in the hierarchy."

"Has that been your experience, Uncle?" Kay asked. "Did it help your career, becoming a spy? Did they ever ask you to do anything unsavory?"

"That's not important right now," he said, trying to convince someone. "What matters right now is your brother and what we can do to save him. There aren't two options; there isn't any other way out. Your brother is in terrible danger, and you're the only one in a position to help him. You may feel any way you want about me—God knows I deserve it. But I'm only the middleman, the conduit; hating me or breaking me will do you no good. Kay," Luis began again, struggling into composure. "If you know all of this, then you know what sort of people we're dealing with. Nothing I said was false. Your brother is in terrible danger. Please," he said, and for the first time in the conversation his voice squeaked into a higher register. "Please, for the love of God, do not make me a murderer twice over. Your father left the two of you in my charge. Perhaps he was a fool to do so. I did my best," he said, dry-mouthed, sorrowful, licking his lips, eyes like some caged beast. "I did my best."

Kay looked at her uncle for a long time. Then she got up from her seat, walked over to the kitchen cabinets and removed a glass, filled it with water and set it in front of Luis. After a moment's pause he drank from it greedily, swallowed it in one gulp and set it back down on the table.

"That's almost true, Uncle. Everything you told me you believed to be true." Kay put her hands in her lap. "This is indeed a very desperate situation—not for me, however, and not for Christopher, either."

"Now's not the time for false courage, Kay."

"I can't promise you much," Kay said sadly. "Treason, that's what we're looking at, and no one could pretend otherwise. I won't lie to you: you'll probably be dying in prison. There's only so much that I can do for anyone, and even if I could do more, I'm not sure that I'd do it for you. I'm truly not sure." She shook her head as if clearing away confusion. "The FBI are waiting outside," Kay said simply. "And this conversation isn't about you making your pitch to me: I'm making the pitch to you. Christopher is fine—well, not fine: Christopher is broken, broken by the death of his parents, broken by the lies of the man who was to raise him, perhaps also by a sister who didn't believe in him the way she should have. But he's in no danger from the SVR. That much, at least, I can assure you."

"You . . . You knew?"

"For a while," Kay said. "For longer, maybe, than I realized. This man who made the approach to you—your handler these last years. What was his name?"

"I knew him only as Pyotr," Luis said. "But his true name I cannot say."

Kay swallowed a deep intake of breath, tried not to show her surprise or excitement. "And you were to hand over the rest of this conversation to him? He's to be your . . . relief, as it were?"

"No," Luis said. "There is another man—a man I only met recently, a week or so ago. His name is Tom. He's—"

"His name isn't Tom," Kay informed him. "And I know more about him than you do."

"Whatever his name, he was to serve as closer, after I made the initial pitch."

Kay nodded thoughtfully. "You've made the pitch," she said. "Now make the call."

55

TOM WAS nervous. Tom was often nervous, in truth. It was one of the things he had learned from Pyotr, from before, even, from his first rounds of training in that dim age before he had left Russia; what would be paranoia in a normal person, what would get you locked up in a padded room, well-meaning medical health professionals prescribing high doses of antipsychotics, was perfectly reasonable to a spy—was, indeed, entirely necessary. In the intelligence Agent's toolbox, a thousand times more useful than a pistol, was a roll of antacid tabs, one of which he was chewing while waiting for the phone call, chalky powder reduced to nothing on his tongue.

Although in point of fact he had a pistol also, a little holdout piece, five shots in a metal casing, held tight against his ribs in the little pocket. As a rule he did not go about armed, for the same reason that he did not walk around wearing a hard hat: the dim possibility of its being needed weighed less than the hassle of carrying it. But, waking up that morning, there had been something that had whispered to him that it might be required, some cautious instinct that he knew better than to ignore.

Tom sat in a chain coffee shop just across from Luis's apartment, watching yuppies roll in and out, the bourgeois tide ebbing and flowing, the cup of tea beside him long grown cold. He did not jump when the phone vibrated in his pocket, but he answered it very quickly.

"All is well?"

"Yes," Luis's voice said from the other end of the line. "You should come on up."

He had sounded terrible, Tom thought, exiting the coffee shop and crossing the street, but that was entirely appropriate. The doorman smiled at Tom as he entered Luis's apartment building, and Tom reminded himself, belatedly, to smile back. Easy amiability, friendly but not noticeable. It seemed to take a long time for the elevator to arrive, even longer for it to deposit him at his destination, some twenty stories above the street. He knocked twice on the door, heard a response from inside telling him to enter. A woman's voice, Kay's voice. He felt his heart in his chest, twisted the knob and stepped smoothly inside.

All seemed well at first glance. They were sitting across from each other at the small kitchen table off the main entrance. They both looked miserable, exhausted, uncertain. Tom would have been concerned if he had found them otherwise.

"Good morning, Kay," he said, taking an unoffered seat smoothly between the two of them. "My name is Tom."

"Is it?" Kay asked quietly.

"For our purposes," Tom said, still smiling. "Your uncle has made clear the situation for you, then?"

"As best as he was able," Kay said, even-faced, giving away nothing. "Perhaps you'd like to run through it as well."

Tom shrugged, undid the buttons of his coat. "It is one of the upsides of dealing with a fellow professional that we can normally skip the preliminaries."

"Indulge me," Kay said. "I'm quite a catch: Don't you think I deserve the full press?"

A creeping sense of uncertainty, but Tom stepped on it, broke its neck like he would a scurrying mouse. Complete composure, as Pyotr had taught him; no hint of worry. "Absolutely you do. Absolutely. To summarize, then: your brother is ten thousand dollars in debt to some acquaintances of mine, unfriendly people, people you would be better off not knowing, never having met, people whom you would very much not want to owe money. He, moreover, owes this money as part of an illicit drug transaction. In short, your brother's life hangs by a string. I could snip it, quite literally, allowing my associates free rein to resolve Christopher's debt in any way they feel. Or, if I was feeling gentle— or perhaps cruel—I could drop a hint of his activities to any number of different law enforcement agencies along with a note suggesting that perhaps they investigate how it is that Christopher walked out of lockup last fall, if perhaps his beloved sister has not been using her influence unduly. That was how he got himself out of that little bit of trouble, wasn't it? You slipping a finger on the scales?"

Kay smiled but didn't answer.

"But of course, it doesn't need to be like that. We don't need to be enemies. This is not a trap laid for you; at least, it does not need to be, Kay, truly, it does not. We are very good at this, we have long practice. You would pass us what information came your way—nothing so terrible, nothing which would harm any member of your organization. You've been doing this long enough to understand that it's a game more than anything else. The stakes are not so high as any of us like to pretend. The United States of America will muddle on as it has this last half century, and if our people are occasionally further ahead than your superiors would like, it hardly presages the apocalypse."

"And who are your people, exactly?"

"Are we not beyond that point? Surely you can guess."

"I'm a little bit slow," Kay said. "That should be obvious

to you: Luis has been playing me for twenty years, and I never picked up on it."

Beside him, Luis flinched. Tom smiled a bit at his discomfort. "Let us just say that your payment, which will be ample, will come in rubles."

"And who is in charge of this operation? Who would I be reporting to?"

"For the moment, you would be answering to me."

"And when the moment ends? Tomorrow, and the day after?"

"These are not questions requiring an immediate answer," Tom said, smiling sternly, like a grade school teacher bringing his class to heel. "For that matter, you are not really in a position to be asking questions. I can appreciate this must be an . . . uncomfortable situation for you, Kay, but it is where we find ourselves. You will come work for us or you will see your life destroyed. There is no third choice."

For a woman who had just discovered that her surrogate father was a Russian spy, that her brother's life was in serious danger, that everything she had worked and struggled towards was about to be torn away, Kay seemed distinctly unperturbed. And again now, despite the chalky-white antacid still heavy in the corners of his mouth, Tom could feel the rising tide in his stomach: not paranoia but a clear, oncoming sense of doom.

"This is a very interesting offer, Tom," Kay said, leaning forward in her chair. "Let me counter with my own: Come work for us."

"I have to say, Kay, in all the time I've been . . . familiarizing myself with your background, personal habits, behavior, you never struck me as the sort given to frivolous jokes."

"Your initial impressions were accurate. My sense of humor is, sad to say, underdeveloped. I'm a much better investigator than I am a comedian. I've been following you for two weeks,"

Kay said. "Well, my associates. You were lying a moment ago, lying twice over, and so perhaps inadvertently telling the truth. This is not a trap you are laying for me. It is the end of one pitched towards you."

Tom shot a quick look over to Luis, sallow as a starveling, unable to look at either of them, and he remembered that gray sedan he had seen more often than he ought, and he knew that Kay was not lying. How strange, after all these years, to finally taste what he had distributed so much of! The numbing sense of horror, the sudden discovery that the structure you were standing atop was built upon sand, that it was collapsing even at that very moment, a rumbling from far beneath, feet shaking and unsteady . . .

"You're bluffing," he said, the classic refrain, one he had heard countless times, and being on the other end it sounded no less foolish, no less childlike and juvenile.

"The whole thing became clear enough once I started looking at it from the other end. The surveillance, the elaborate plotting—it didn't make sense: Christopher didn't have anything worth that sort of trouble. The only thing Christopher had is a perhaps too-loyal sister, one who might, potentially, be convinced by that loyalty to betray another. I spent a day or two watching you watching him, trying to run your plates, coming up with false names and dead ends. By then I was sure enough to call in the Bureau. The last two weeks you've been running around frantically, thinking yourself one step ahead, and you didn't even know what game you were playing. You're in the net, Tom: you're already caught. I understand you might need a moment to accept the reality of the situation. Feel free to take it."

"You knew about this?" Tom asked, directing the question towards Luis.

But his onetime contact and current betrayer did not look

at him or at Kay, indeed had not spoken since Tom had come through the door.

"Don't worry, Tom," Kay said, and for the first time Tom could hear a hint of victory in her voice. "We don't need to be enemies. You would pass us what information comes your way— nothing so terrible, nothing which would harm any member of your organization." His own words thrown back at him, sharp as the edge of a razor. "I have my own friends waiting to speak to you; they won't be more than a moment."

And, as if standing on a hill and overlooking a desolate and miserable countryside beneath, Tom could see his future laid out before him. His overseers denying all knowledge of his existence, no diplomatic immunity for poor Tom, twenty years an Illegal, and that meant prison. Tom did not suppose there was a way to pin Sadler's murder on him, but even so, he would be spending the rest of his life in a very small room, seeing the sun once a day in the company of a few hundred other hardened felons. Or turn traitor, and Tom knew well what sort of a life that was, what sort of misery that foretold, the constant worry and the strain, the endless and ongoing deceit, hypocrisy rising to your throat till it choked you.

Tom lost himself for a moment in a miserable future, and then there was the cold feel of metal in the palm of his hand and Tom realized that he was holding his gun, holding his gun and looking at the object of his long chase, the prey who had become the hunter. The sun was very bright coming in through the very clean windows; it seemed brighter than it had been when he was walking here, bright to the point of blinding.

"Do not do anything foolish," Kay said sternly, still just as cold as ice water. "You're a professional: there is no chance of shooting your way out of this, and you hardly need another murder charge added to your sheet."

And something about Kay's damnable reserve, that steadiness that she had displayed these long months he had been following her, pushed him further over the edge. Tom raised his gun, even in that last moment unsure if he would use it, and if so where, whether the muzzle might not be pointed at the underside of his own chin rather than the chest of the woman who sat in front of him, seeming calm, seeming altogether unfazed by the threat against her life.

He had forgotten about Luis, the old man relegated to the sidelines, his part played out; and so when Tom suddenly felt an arm reach around his, the gun pulled downward, he reacted with shock if not fright. The pistol jerked in his hand: it was not deliberate, not really, only the stress of the movement and his index finger reacting involuntarily, and then a sliding wetness running down his shirt and his pants, a strange, not unhappy look on Luis's face, and then the body striking the ground.

Kay moved quickly, up and off the chair, rolling sideways and drawing her weapon as she had been trained to do from reflex years ago at Quantico. Neatly done but pointless, because before she could aim or fire her own weapon, it was over. Tom did not hear the very clean windows breaking, the pane of glass shattering from the incoming bullet and then entering his head, oblivion brought so quickly that he was not even aware of dying.

Two bodies on the kitchen floor then, blood leaking onto her aunt's floor. Kay lowered her weapon and moved to her uncle as swiftly as she was able. "Don't talk," she said, pressing her hand against the wound in his side, trying unsuccessfully to stanch the blood, her voice rising and fearful. "Don't talk. Just lie back: help is coming. Help will be here in a moment."

A show of strength that she would not have credited him with, and he pushed her away from his wound, the river of red coming faster. And after a long moment's consideration, Kay let her hand fall to her side, her uncle's lifeblood soaking into her dark pants and the bottom of her blouse.

"Sorry," Luis said, red spilling onto the floor and the light leaving his eyes. "Sorry."

His blue eyes staring up at her, fever-bright and then dimming and then entirely dark.

The rest of the team had been waiting next door, and they were not slow in entering, not at all slow but still much too late. When they came in, Kay had her uncle's head in her lap. Her eyes were mournful but her mouth was stern.

56

O N A sunny day in late summer, they put Luis into the ground. Justyna wore a black dress and did not cry. Kay and Christopher stood just slightly behind her, and she did not turn back to look at them during the length of the service. The sermon was flat, given by a clergyman who had never met the deceased. It mentioned his state service, his taking in of Kay and Christopher after the tragic deaths of their parents. The family and friends whom he left behind, bettered by his existence, lamenting his absence, hoping for some future reunion. Kay found herself agreeing with more of it than she would have anticipated. When it was over, they lowered the coffin slowly into its hole, and Kay threw a handful of dirt onto the box, and moved aside for the rest of the mourners to do the same.

Christopher was red-eyed but sober, fingers wearing away at the twenty-four-hour chip he had earned earlier that week at his first Narcotics Anonymous meeting. If Kay had had more energy, she would have been worried about him, even more than usual. He had quit his job as a bartender, moved into a halfway house. There would be no legal repercussions for his brief foray into serious distribution of narcotics, the slate wiped clean by his assistance in bringing to heel a dangerous foreign Illegal, and the man who had come near to ruining his life.

He gave Kay a weak smile when he saw she was watching him, raised two fingers in greeting and then lost himself in the crowd.

And there was a crowd, a throng, a pack, a thick swarm of mourners, old associates and business acquaintances, friends from the building and the neighborhood and the city, and Justyna's own people, bridge-and-tunnel folk mostly, down from their expensive exurbs. If you had been watching over it from a distance, you would have supposed the man's life a happy one, Kay thought. And perhaps it had been, although thinking of him in those last moments, the weight of guilt on his face, Kay was not sure she would have agreed.

"Ms. Malloy?" a voice asked.

"Agent Malloy," Kay answered before she had turned to see him, a dark-eyed man in a neat suit.

"Forgive me. Of course," he said, sweeping his hat off his head in an old-fashioned but not unbecoming gesture of apology. "I just wanted to express my condolences for your loss." He had the faintest trace of a foreign accent, like that of someone who had lived in exile for so long as to have forgotten their native tongue. "Your uncle was a man of . . . great depths."

"Thank you," Kay said flatly. It was the tenth or the fiftieth or the hundredth such conversation she had had that day, the butt end of a wave of compliments towards the man who had raised and perhaps loved her and whom she had never really known. Kay snapped herself back into the moment: there would be time enough for consideration, sleepless nights, recriminations if need be. For now there was etiquette, as much defense as obligation, rote words allowing for conversation to continue without conscious thought. "How did you know my uncle, exactly?"

The man's teeth were gray and uneven, but his smile seemed sincere and made up for it. "We were old acquaintances," he said. "Back in Europe, many years ago."

Not for the first time, not at all for the first time, it occurred to Kay how much more there had been to her uncle than she had ever known. "He was a man of many parts," Kay said.

"All of us are—vices and virtues intertwined, inexorably, un-knowable even to ourselves." The man bowed and swept his hat back upon his head. "I hope the Almighty judges him kindly."

It was only as Kay watched him walk off that she realized she had never learned his name.

There were other concerns that day. Kay had been expecting the funeral to be busy with friends of Luis and her aunt, but she had been surprised to see the Black Bear team show in full strength, dark-suited, looking serious and sad. Jeffries she had half expected, but not Wilson or Marshall or the rest. And Kay had never been the easiest colleague, she could see that now. But they were polite and more so, they were the only people present who knew the entire truth of the situation besides Christopher and Kay. Andrew had sent his condolences, a long e-mail and a short phone call relaying his sympathy, although events in D.C. had kept him from attending in person. Which was just as well, so far as Kay was concerned. There was too much to think about right now to be adding the gray area that was their relationship to the mix.

Jeffries appeared, as she often did, unexpectedly, standing beside Kay's shoulder—a few inches below it, in fact, gray eyes waiting for Kay to notice her.

"Ma'am."

"Kay," she said, extending her hand. It was, to the best of her memory, the first time Jeffries had ever used her first name. "Condolences on your loss."

"Thank you," Kay said. "And thanks for coming."

"This was neatly done," Jeffries said after a long moment. "Even if the ending wasn't quite what we had hoped for."

"Not quite," Kay agreed.

"My instincts about people are rarely wrong."

"I don't doubt it."

"At least they weren't in your case," Jeffries said flatly. It was the least emotive compliment that Kay had ever received, and probably the best. "If you need some time off, however long, we can put you on administrative leave. It won't be held against you, I can promise that. And there'll be a spot waiting for you in my program whenever you're ready."

"Thank you," Kay said, "but that won't be necessary. I'll be in the office on Monday."

"That's just as well," Jeffries said. "I was hoping to have your assistance on something."

And, despite the emotion of the moment, Kay found her investigative instincts breaking through. "What, exactly?"

Jeffries shrugged, her walls back up as swiftly as they'd come down. "Let's call it Black Bear 2.0," she said, then nodded and walked off.

Torres proved more talkative, looking awkward in his black suit, the coat ill fitting, his biceps and gut bulging against them.

"How you holding up, Ivy?" he asked.

"All right," Kay said, realizing to her surprise that it wasn't even a lie.

"I guess it's been hell over the past eighteen months," he said. "First Williams and then—"

"I remember it," Kay said, cutting him off.

Torres realized midway through his laugh that he was at a funeral, then managed to swallow most of it. "How's your brother?"

"I'm not sure."

"How are *you*?"

"I have no idea," Kay admitted.

"You did the right thing here, Kay," Torres said, and suddenly he was no longer smiling; he was covering her upper arm between his thick, worn hands and looking down at her with adamant seriousness. "You did the right thing. You ought to be proud of yourself. I'm proud of you. For whatever it's worth, I'm proud of you."

"It's worth something," Kay said, leaning into Torres for a moment. Just a moment—Kay did not need it for very long, but all of us need it now and again.

The funeral was starting to break up: there would be no reception afterward—Justyna's decision, although Kay was happy she had made it. This had been enough—more than enough. Kay saw her brother slip away from the crowd and walk slowly east, up the manicured greenery and away from the funeral. She knew where he was going and decided to give him a few minutes before she went to find him. Justyna had returned to the graveside, staring at the coffin as if it might tell her something.

"How are you holding up, Auntie?"

"All right," she said, eyes still on the box that held her husband of forty years.

Kay wanted to say something but wasn't sure what.

"Luis was better than the worst thing he did." Justyna pulled away as soon as she said it, as if she couldn't bear to look at Kay any longer, the shame or despair too great.

Kay watched her aunt walk off towards the parking lot. Justyna was right, of course—as close as she had come to the edge these last few weeks, she knew her aunt was right. What if Christopher hadn't come to her? What if her instincts had not been sharpened by working counterintelligence? What if she had not been able to sniff out the SVR plot behind it? What if she had walked into the meeting with her uncle innocent as a lamb, without the understanding and weight of the FBI behind her? Would she have turned traitor, if the alternative had been the death or imprisonment of her brother? Would she have been strong enough to hold to the code and the mission against everything?

Paul and Anne Malloy were buried at the other end of the cemetery, a fifteen-minute walk and not an unpleasant one, the evening beginning its certain if temporary victory over the day. When she came in sight, she saw that Christopher had carried two roses from the shrine of flowers that had been left for their uncle, and when she arrived he had just finished placing them over their parents' graves.

"I suppose I wasn't very decent to Luis," Christopher said finally.

In spite of herself, unexpectedly, Kay found herself chuckling. "I suppose you weren't, exactly. Though I'm surprised to find you only realizing it at this belated moment."

"He did his best with us," Christopher said. "Raising us, I mean. Do you remember when I stole his car and drove it up to Cape Cod for the weekend?"

"You were all of seventeen."

"Still sixteen," Christopher informed her. "How many parents would put up with that kind of thing? You know, he never once hit me," Christopher said with unexpected seriousness. "Never even raised a hand."

"I know."

"He did his best with us," Christopher said again. "That still means something, I think."

Kay pursed her lips but didn't say anything. "I'm not sure what it means."

"I spent twenty years being angry at him without much reason," Christopher said absently. "And now that I have one I feel . . . empty."

"He made his choices," Kay said.

Christopher shrugged. "It's not that simple," he said. "I think maybe I understand him better than you do. Better than you can, maybe."

"Maybe."

"What would you have done to get Justyna free? What would you have sacrificed? What is right and wrong, measured against the life of someone you love?"

"I don't know," Kay admitted. "But afterward, once it was through, he could have gone to the authorities. He could have come clean."

"It takes a lot to throw your life away on a point of principle," Christopher said. "Easier to keep your head down and hope things improve. It wasn't like it was an everyday thing. Probably there were weeks, months, maybe even years when he forgot that he had done what he did, forgot that his life was in hock, forgot that he was living on borrowed time . . ." Christopher shrugged.

"Forgot that he'd murdered our parents?" Kay asked, waving a hand at the gravestones and what lay beneath them.

"No," Christopher admitted. "I don't suppose he ever forgot that."

They stayed like that for a long time, the two of them, the last of the Malloy clan, standing over the corpses of their parents, silence hanging over them, the sunlight beginning to dim. "Sin is sin, Christopher," Kay said finally. "Even if we regret it, even if we were forced into it, even if it's understandable, it marks us. It stains us, corrodes and corrupts. Innocence is a precious thing and needs to be guarded."

"Then I suppose it's a good thing that you're around to protect it," Christopher said, taking her hand in his, staring east towards the river, and the skyline of Manhattan, and the vast world beyond it. Kay smiled and squeezed herself against him, and they stayed like that for a time.

ACKNOWLEDGMENTS

THIS BOOK exists because of the support and guidance of two people, Jonathan Karp and Marysue Rucci, who gave me the opportunity to tell a story. You're both amazing. I still marvel at the serendipitous way in which my path intersected with Jonathan's, and from that intersection, the concept for this book was born. His enthusiasm has been inspiring. I owe Marysue a debt of gratitude for her patient and insightful editorial guidance throughout the process. I consider myself extraordinarily lucky that she took this project on personally.

Thanks to all the wonderful people at Simon & Schuster who fielded my many questions and made the publishing process look so easy when it seemed so overwhelming.

I would like to express my deepest gratitude and sincere appreciation to Daniel Polansky. Your expert guidance and willingness to listen were very special to me. I learned much from you and can only hope I was a good student of the art. Till we meet again, good writing and good fortune.

And finally, to the men and women of the Federal Bureau of Investigation, who keep our nation safe.

ABOUT THE AUTHOR

Jan Fedarcyk retired from the FBI after twenty-five years, rising through the ranks to serve as the first woman assigned as the Assistant Director in Charge of the New York Office, the FBI's largest and most prestigious field office. A Maryland native, she resides in the Annapolis area and runs her own consulting business. *Fidelity* is her first novel.